The End of All Things Beautiful

Nikki Young

Copyright © 2015 by Nikki Young

All rights reserved. This book may not be reproduced, scanned, or distributed in any printed or electronic form without permission from the author. Please do not participate in or encourage the piracy of copyrighted materials in violation of the author's rights. All characters and storylines are the property of the author and your support and respect is appreciated. The characters and events portrayed in this book are fictitious. Any similarities to real persons, living or dead, is coincidental and not intended by the author.

Cover Design by Sarah Hansen of Okay Creations
www.okaycreations.com

ISBN 13: 978-1508468011
ISBN 10: 150846801X

"Forgiveness is the fragrance that the violet sheds on the heel that has crushed it."
-Mark Twain

Prologue

It wasn't supposed to be this way. We grew up together. There were five of us; they were my first everything—each one of them. Until they weren't anymore.

We were supposed to be together forever. But sometimes forever is a lie and things fall apart before you even realize what is happening. An ugly interruption of perfection, an uprooting of everything you've ever known and everything you've ever come to count on. But at the time I was too young and naïve to believe what would happen.

Invincible.

It couldn't happen to us.

It would never happen to us.

We were happy and loved, and when you grow up believing the world is at your fingertips, nothing bad can ever happen.

But with the good always comes the bad. And it's with the bad that you find the ugly side of life. You find people aren't who you think they are, and that situations can separate bonds that were never meant to be broken.

I never believed one day, one single day, could change my life, change our lives, so drastically, cause such upheaval and make me run from the only people I ever loved; but that's exactly what happens when secrets rip apart your world.

One day changed us.

It ruined everything.

Chapter One
Nine Years Ago

"Come with me," Benji says, and I laugh at his words. He's said this to me before, but the context and the scenario were different. "Get in the car, baby," he pleads, standing with his hands on his hips, his voice firm, but still somehow playful. He'd never demand anything from me and today is no different.

He loves me.

He needs to be near me. I understand. Completely.

I look down at my watch knowing I have an early class tomorrow morning, but something in his eyes won't let me say no. He has an inexplicable hold on me, yet I know I have the same affect on him.

"What the fuck, Cam?" Sam shouts from inside the car. He's called me Cam from the day we met. I hate nicknames, but for some reason, I've taken a liking to him calling me Cam, even if I won't tolerate it from anyone else.

As I'm debating what I know is right and what I really want to do, Kelly jogs up behind me and climbs in the passenger seat, kissing Sam with far too much fervor than necessary.

"See, Campbell?" Benji states, again with a humorous quality to his voice, as he reaches for me. His arms slip around my waist pulling me tightly against his chest as my heart begins to flutter. It's moments like this that it's a wonder I ever say no to him. He knows what makes me weak. "Baby," he whispers, his breath tickling my neck as he presses his lips against my skin. "I just lost my spot in the front seat. Who's going to keep me company now?"

"Cam! Get in the fucking car!" Sam screams this time, and it makes me laugh. I bury my face in Benji's chest and nod my head only to hear a riotous cheer leave the car as Benji lifts me off the ground swinging me around.

"Where are we even going?" I ask, as Sam whips out of the parking lot, the radio blaring while Kelly giggles at something inappropriate that has just come out of Sam's mouth. It's at this that moment that I feel my body shudder, a small chill rushing through me, making me question exactly what I'm doing, as if something about this moment feels off.

"The beach, Cam," Sam says casually, like it's obvious to everyone but me and in a second he lights a joint and passes it to Kelly, who in turn takes a hit and passes it to Benji.

I know everything about this scenario is wrong. It's been wrong since the moment we started doing it years ago. And although I'm feeling uneasy, I glance around the car and know this is exactly how it should be.

This is our normal.

We've been together now for, well, forever, honestly. All of us growing up together; the same suburban Chicago town, upper-middle class families, kindergarten through high school, living the dream.

We never intended to go away to college together, but somehow the pieces fell into place and we found ourselves attending the same school. Looking back on it now, our connection has always been intense and I'm not sure we could've survived apart. Each one of us needing the other for balance, support, normalcy and love. We complete each other in ways that only we understand.

Before I know it, I've taken a hit off the joint and passed it back to Benji who can't seem to keep his hands off me. Groping at my thigh as his hand slides farther up my leg and under my skirt. His fingertips brush the edge of my underwear and I know where he's headed and my body is already responding.

My breathing is growing heavy, my heart racing in my chest as Benji's fingers slip into the side of my underwear and when his fingers find what they're seeking, he lets out a low groan in appreciation.

My head falls back and my eyes close, knowing this is the last thing we should be doing with our friends sitting in the front seat, but I don't stop him. I can hear his labored breathing as he begins to grow desperate for me and my hand slides across the bulge in his jeans.

"Fuck!" Benji yells out and my eyes spring open, wide and questioning as I'm hit with a moment of panic. "I dropped the fucking joint," he adds as he scrambles to the floorboard searching.

"Maybe if you'd kept your hands off Cam's pussy we wouldn't be having this problem now," Sam says from the front seat.

I lean forward and slap him on the shoulder glaring at him as he looks at me in the rearview mirror. "Do you have to be so graphic?" I ask, disgusted with him even though this is nothing new and the only response I get is a wink. I shake my head at him, a shy smile on my face as I watch Benji find the joint and flick it out the window.

And again a strange feeling takes over, my body growing cold as my palms begin to sweat. I mentally begin to list all the things I should be doing instead of spending the afternoon, and more than likely the evening getting drunk and high at the beach with my friends.

I suddenly want to tell Sam to turn around, that I have a bad feeling about today, but even in my own mind it sounds idiotic and strange. There's no explanation for why I'm feeling this way and I chalk it up to guilt about not being at home studying or working on the million other things I have due over the next week.

The car slows to a stop and the door is immediately flung open, startling me. Tommy climbs in, forcing me over with his body until I'm practically sitting on Benji's lap.

"Move over, Campbell," Tommy says, his hand squeezing my thigh, making me giggle. I remember a time when this car held all of us comfortably, before Tommy was six foot three and had a body like a pro-football player, when Benji and I could make out in the backseat without feeling like I was going to smother him, and when Sam could drive without the seat being set back as far as it could go.

We've all grown up, yet for some reason, it still feels exactly the same as it always has. Like we're still just kids. An incestuous grouping of five people who have a connection that no one understands.

For a while, I was one of those people.

You see, Kelly, Sam and Tommy have one of those relationships that somehow thrives despite the fact that she won't choose. She loves them both, she says, and there was a time when it bothered me. I watched Tommy get hurt and I hated it, because he will always love her more. It never really bothered Sam, or at least he never let on that it did. But now, like everything else in our lives, it has become our normal.

Tommy pushes up on his feet, his head bumping the ceiling as he leans forward and plants a quick kiss on Kelly's shoulder. I see her smile grow, reaching behind her, she runs her fingers along Tommy's cheek. I don't doubt she loves them both, but I've always doubted the equality. Can she really love them both with the same amount of effort?

Kelly and I have talked openly about her relationship with both guys and she has always explained to me that she does in fact love them both, but for different reasons. Without the two of them, she feels lost. Tommy is her constant, her calm and her understanding. Sam is her no excuses, her harsh and her unforgiving. Both guys opposite yet somehow whole when together.

Maybe I just don't understand it because I've never loved anyone but Benji. I fell in love with him before I even knew what it meant to fall in love, to be in love with someone. It was before we knew the world was full of disappointment and flawed people and liars. I found him somewhere between a dream and a nightmare. We found each other, and there was a trust there that existed only within our small bubble of a world. I remember holding his hand at age five and thinking I never wanted to be away from him. And from that day on, the connection only grew. It turned from companionship and friendship to an overwhelming need to be together. Without him, I would have crumbled to pieces.

Maybe this is how Kelly feels about both of them. I've grown to understand that.

I rest my head against Tommy's shoulder and he presses a kiss to the top of my head. I just want him to be happy. I hope he's happy.

"How was your day?" he asks as he gazes out the window, his voice quiet.

"It was okay. Long, but better now that I'm avoiding any responsibility with you assholes."

"There's no better group to avoid life with than us," Tommy says, leaning forward and flicking Sam in the ear.

"Benji threw our joint out the window, but not before fingering Cam and trying to start my car on fire," Sam quips,s and again I smack him.

"Fuck off," I answer back as I give Tommy a look that says *feel sorry for me.*

"Glad I didn't miss anything new," Tommy says before pulling another joint from the pocket of his jeans.

"Light it up, baby," Kelly says with a huge smile on her face.

A few hours later we find ourselves on the beach, the shores of Lake Erie, quiet and desolate. The season is already over, but that's the reason we're here. It's empty and it allows us to do as we please without repercussions.

We're only nineteen and we understand the ramifications of what we're doing, but like everyone else our age, we still do it. We live recklessly, as though we're invincible.

I'm on my third beer, falling behind the rest of them as I lay with my head on Benji's leg listening to Sam drag on about god knows what since I tuned him out at least twenty minutes ago. Kelly and Tommy have disappeared and I often wonder if Sam rambles on, all nonsensical and bullshit-like to keep his mind off what's going on with Kelly.

I watch him grab another beer and down it quickly while Benji follows, giving my side a pinch to tell me to get moving. He knows me well enough by now to know that by the fourth beer I'll be buzzed, by the sixth I'll be drunk and he'll more than likely get laid. And right now, the more I drink, the less anxious I feel, so I keep drinking. While everything looks normal on the surface, I can't help but feel like I'm watching the slow sinking of everything we've ever known go down with the ship.

I'm being stupid.

It's nothing.

The music from the car is playing in the distance as Benji strums along on his guitar. I close my eyes; listening to the sound of his voice as he sings with the music. Sam has grown quiet now and the only noise is coming from the comfort of Benji's guitar. A few seconds pass and the music blends with the noise of the water. I feel Benji press his lips lightly to my forehead, and then his hand weaves with mine as he pulls me up off the sand and into his arms. His arms wrapped around my waist, he tugs me close and begins to slow dance in the darkness, singing softly into my ear. His voice is melodic and deep, and each word makes me press into him even more. But something about this moment feels different, like it's the beginning of the end. It's like the dying breath of our relationship, and I whisper, "I love you."

"I love you more than you'll ever know, Campbell," he says back and I know now that something awful is going to happen. I feel his lips brush lightly against my cheek and what he says next nearly kills me, "You'll always be the only light I'll ever see."

By the time night falls, we're all drunk and attempting to sober up so one of us can drive back to campus. It's a forty-five minute drive and while we've stopped drinking, none of us will be legally sober to get behind the wheel. Yet we've done it hundreds of times before and tonight will be no different.

"You ready?" Benji asks, slipping his arm around my waist and pulling me against his side. I nod and make my way back to the car. Feeling exhausted and still drunk, I stumble into the backseat, taking my place in the middle between Benji and Tommy.

Before Sam has even started the car, Kelly is passed out and Benji has his face pressed into the curve of my neck. I'm giggling as he nips at my neck, I feel his breath hot against my already flushed skin.

I remember very little from the night and after the car starts; it's all a haze. I fall in and out of consciousness as I feel Benji's hands run up my thighs, his lips on mine, needy and pleading as his tongue parts my lips.

I catch bits and pieces of a conversation Tommy and Sam are having, punctuated with long pauses. Either that, or I'm blacking out. Something about deer and tans, or is it beer and cans?

Before I know it, I'm straddling Benji's hips, his hands are moving up my shirt until he's pushed it up over my head and it hasn't occurred to me to be concerned about the other people in the car. I'm lost in him and what he's doing to me. Lost in the drunkenness and the darkness, and wanting only one thing.

Benji.

I'm sliding my hand into the front of his pants, completely prepared to forego my inhibitions and do god knows what with him in this car, when the sound of squealing brakes cuts through the quiet of the night and the next thing I hear is the sound of metal scraping on metal.

I feel a jarring, violent shaking of the car and it feels like we're spinning. We collide ruthlessly with something equally as heavy and the car finally gives way, crumbling under the pressure. I vomit spectacularly, my stomach emptying all over Benji and me as he screams out loud.

But something about this moment is strange, like I'm watching it from a distance, like it's a dream and I'll wake up and find myself in bed or still on the beach. Passed out from too much alcohol and pot. In slow motion almost, the car fills with the cold air from the night, I realize the windows are gone; tiny circular glass particles raining down on us and covering the floor.

Then everything around me goes black, yet my nose stings with the smell of burnt rubber and gunpowder. My eyes are watering and a searing pain radiates through my head as if I've been hit with a baseball bat.

I call out, but no sound escapes my mouth. My eyes feel heavy and every time I attempt to open them, they fall shut again. Over and over, everything is weighed down, like I'm swimming through mud.

I hear my name, but the voice sounds distant and when I finally place it, I smile.

Benji.

I can hear him calling my name and I see his face. His beautiful blue eyes are staring at me, making me feel safe and I want him to take me in his arms and tell me this is all a dream. I love him and he loves me. Everything will be just fine. But the panic I hear in his voice startles me and he begins tugging at my arm, screaming at me to get up.

I turn my head to catch the time on the clock. I blink and when I open my eyes, it's gone, but not forgotten. I crawl out of the car, my knees hitting the gravel on the road, cutting into my flesh as I gain purchase and stand up. My legs are weak and Benji catches me before I fall, but when I look up at his face, it's covered in blood.

I back away from him in horror.

"What happened to your face?" I ask, my voice shaky.

"Fuck, Campbell!" he screams, his hand tugging at his hair as I start to cry. He's never yelled at me in all the time we've known each other.

"Why are you screaming at me?" I ask, still completely unsure of what has just happened. I know there was an accident, but it all feels surreal.

"We have to get out of here!" he yells again, this time grabbing for me and pulling me away from the wreckage.

I take it all in, the headlights of two cars shining on the empty road, illuminating and accentuating just exactly what has occurred over the last few minutes. Both cars are completely devastated, destroyed, and to be honest, I can't believe anyone survived.

I brace myself, pulling back against Benji's incessant tugging.

"No!" I scream back at him. "We have to call the police!"

He stops immediately and his face takes on a terrifying look I've never seen before; his eyes wide and his lips set in a firm line. He shakes his head slowly before tightening his grip on my wrist and yanking me in the direction of two shadows I see standing a few feet away. As I'm being pulled away from the crash, my body too weak to fight anymore, I see Sam's lifeless body covered in blood and slumped over the steering wheel of the car. The white of the airbag swallowing his head until he just looks like a lumpy bloody pillow.

My head turns back, watching as I'm pulled past him and my brain finally catches up. Crumbling to the ground, I realize what is happening all around me.

We're running away from what we caused.

The other car unrecognizable.

Sam is dead.

And somehow, as this is all going on, the first thought that crosses my mind is, *Tommy can finally be happy*. It's a disgusting thought and it makes me vomit again.

"Fuck, Campbell," Benji screams again. I hate the sound of his voice. I hate what we're doing and right now I hate him. "Stop crying and stop fucking barfing!" His hold on my wrist is so tight that I begin to feel it cut off the circulation, my hand throbbing and tingling under his grasp.

I struggle to get away from him, twisting against his hold, but I can't break free. By this point I'm sobbing uncontrollably, deep, heaving sobs as Benji lets go of my wrist and takes me in his arms.

"Campbell, baby, please," he whispers in my ear and suddenly the Benji I know and love is back. His hands stroke up and down my back, soothing me. "We have to go. We can't stay here. Do you know what will happen to us if the police find out we were here?"

"We can't leave him," I plead with Benji.

"He's dead, Campbell. Sam is dead." I know this already; it's obvious, but hearing him say it out loud makes this all far more real than I'm ready to cope with. When he starts speaking again I want to stick my fingers in my ears and sing "Mary Had a Little Lamb" loudly like I did as a kid to drown out what I didn't want to hear. "They're all dead," he says, his voice cold and emotionless.

"Who's dead?" I ask, knowing full well he's talking about the people in the other car.

"The family in the other car."

"Oh fuck, it was a family? Oh my god, Benji, no. We can't run away from this." I'm begging by this point as the distant sound of sirens ring out in the night. My tears are still falling uncontrollably, but I don't know what else to do, so I follow him.

I leave.

Chapter Two
Present Day

I'd like to say everything went back to normal and we all existed as if none of this ever happened, but that would be a lie, of course. You don't recover from this. Ever.

Physically we were bruised and battered, but surprisingly, we came out of it without any serious injuries. Actually most were barely noticeable, and since we were in college and spent many weekends drinking, explaining away a black eye or bloody lip wasn't too difficult. We had no broken bones or any lasting scars. Everything was internal; a deep wound that won't ever heal. But emotionally and mentally, we were a mess.

Each one of us fell apart at some point or another, but nothing as devastating as what happened to Kelly. Unable to live without Sam, she killed herself on the one-week anniversary of the accident. I was the one who found her and by that time I had become desensitized to the thought of death. To say I hadn't considered doing what she did would be a lie. The thought entered my mind as often as most people think about eating. I watched her lifeless body hanging from the doorway of our dorm room as her feet dangled just above the floor. The rope strung from the rafters in a shabbily tied knot that looked as if it could've given way before she actually died. But it didn't.

Unfortunately the repercussions from that were equally devastating, and the guilt that Tommy carried with him nearly broke my heart. He couldn't save her; he would never be enough for her, and watching her take her own life drove this point home harder than a knife through his chest. I tried to help him, but my own problems took control and I bailed before I could fall any deeper.

We were just kids and these problems were far greater than our friendship could handle. I loved all of them, but not enough to save us.

I wanted to love Benji forever. I wanted to get married and live happily ever after, but after the accident, I saw a side of him I never knew existed and I couldn't be a part of his life anymore. A constant reminder of what we did, somehow we ruined each other being together, yet each day I wake, it destroys me that we're apart.

But I let him convince me that walking away from the scene of the accident was what was best. I watched him lie to the police, lie to himself and to me until it was more than I could handle. But it's not like I ever came clean. I carry it with me to this day. All the secrets and the lies, they live hidden behind the fake smile I wear.

It wasn't long before we all fell apart; the bond that at one time seemed irrefutable, severed in one tragically flawed night. What was left of five was only three, an incomplete set of broken lives that couldn't be pieced back together.

I left school mid-semester, walked away from Benji and Tommy and to this day I have no idea where they are. Yet not a day goes by that they don't cross my mind, that I don't ache for what we once had. But more than anything, I miss Benji.

I've never stopped loving him.

I roll over and take in his peaceful face, a look of calm that only a restful night's sleep can bring. His name is Carson and he loves me. He loves the fake me.

"Campbell and Carson, it's so cute," people say. "Two C's, it's adorable. You're perfect together." Every time it's said, I get nauseous, but this is who I've become: a shell of my former self. As time goes by, I'm starting to falter. The depression, the sleepless nights, the tears and the guilt all eating at me. I'm growing cold and disinterested in life. Pretending to be someone I'm not is exhausting.

Carson has no idea the person I was, the person I still am or what I've done. Or worse, that I'm in love with another man. I've learned that in order to survive this bullshit that has become my life, I have to pretend it didn't happen.

And that's why I'm sharing a bed with a man I don't love.

My eyes fill with tears and squeezing them shut, I will myself not to cry. I wake every day before Carson just so I can have this time to myself, time to remember who I am and what I've done.

He stirs next to me and I run my fingers under my eyes brushing away any stray tears that may have escaped. I can't give him any indication that something is wrong. Two years I've lived like this and he's still oblivious.

He's a good man. Wonderful, actually. And it's why I stay. He makes me want to forget what I've done, what I've left, and what I've lost. Yet it's still never enough.

"Good morning," Carson says, his voice raspy with sleep, a loose smile on his lips.

"Good morning," I answer back, my eyes closing and not from exhaustion. I can't bear to look at him this morning, knowing I've spent the last hour wishing it were Benji in my bed.

"What do you have going on today?" he asks, moving closer to me until I feel his hand connect with my hip. A small shudder rolls through my body.

It's not that I don't like Carson, I do, I honestly do. But at times, just living my life is a struggle. There are times when he makes it easier and there are times when he doesn't. Right now is one of those times.

"I have a few meetings at work, but nothing really going on," I respond as I roll away from him and climb out of bed.

"Okay," he says with an annoyance to his tone and the guilt pools heavy in my stomach.

I take a deep breath and close my eyes in an attempt to purge my thoughts and start over again. "How about you?" I ask, trying to engage him.

"Busy at work, but I was thinking we could hit up that new Thai place by your office for dinner tonight? Meet me there around six?"

"That sounds amazing," I answer, as I try on a smile before climbing back into bed and snuggling against Carson's warm body. And when I take a deep breath I think, *He's perfection to my failure.*

My day goes by without complications. Two out of the three meetings I had scheduled were canceled and about an hour ago my assistant ordered in sushi, which I'm now eating quietly at my desk.

My computer alerts me of my next meeting and when the calendar pops up on the screen, I realize it's been exactly nine years since the accident. I don't know how it slipped my mind this year and maybe it didn't. There's no way it could have. Eventually I would've remembered, because at least once a day something reminds me of it. Whether it's a song or the sound of someone's voice, a name, a comment or a phrase, it's always with me.

A few seconds later my assistant notifies me that my one o'clock meeting has arrived and she escorts the man into my office. He's in his late thirties, possibly even early forties, impeccably dressed, not that I'm surprised. I'm dealing with presidents of large corporations. And the look on his face is the same one I get from everyone who steps through my office door.

"Hello, Ms. Forester," he says, but I can hear the astonishment in his voice and when he raises one eyebrow, a questioning look on his face, I know he's wondering just how the hell I ended up in this position. But he doesn't ask...at least not yet anyway. As if his face has given him away, he quickly adds, "Wonderful to finally meet you."

"Mr. Walters," I greet him with a nod of my head, my hand extended out. When he takes my hand, I tighten my grip. "You can call me Campbell," I request, a firm smile on my lips.

"And you can call me William."

Again I nod in response before taking a seat around the large conference table in the corner of my office. I would've liked my office to be smaller, more personal, but I was told that wasn't an option.

"So tell me," William says, opening the conversation. "How does someone like you find yourself in this job?"

I chuckle a bit at his words, *someone like you* and I wonder just what he's referring to. The fact that I'm a woman or that I'm only twenty-eight or that I'm attractive and thin and I couldn't possibly have the brains or ability to go head to head with him or any of the other men that have graced my office.

"I give amazing blow jobs," I deadpan and his jaw nearly hits the floor.

Unprofessional? Absolutely. But I couldn't give a fuck to be treated this way anymore. I've grown weary of this response at my ability to hold down this desk.

Before he has time to respond I cut in. "But today I've worn a skirt and I really don't feel like being on my knees for the next ten minutes, so I'll just have you sign this and we'll call it done."

"What makes you think I'm signing that?" he questions, indignantly.

"Well, I see it one of two ways, William. You can sign your company over to me and avoid filing for bankruptcy, having your name tarnished and everyone in your company finding out you've mismanaged funds or you can watch it be plastered all over the papers tomorrow morning." I lean back in my chair and shrug my shoulders. "Your call."

"You're blackmailing me?"

"Oh no, not even close. I want to buy your failing company, get you out of debt and let you live the life you always wanted: Wealthy on a beach somewhere."

"You just said it yourself. My company is failing. It's no good to you," he says as if he's trying to convince me not to buy him out. I shake my head and give my eyes a quick roll. He's missing my point and I'm growing annoyed.

"You called this meeting, William because you're drowning. Do you want my help or not?"

"How will this benefit me?" he asks, and again I chuckle. It's always about them. Self-absorbed pricks that can't hack it financially, but decide to question my ability.

"The profit margin is small and of course there is risk, but you wouldn't be sitting across from me if you hadn't done your research." I lean forward, my hands folded in front of me. "I buy your company, get you out of debt and you walk away. And once a year, I send you a check, that if you manage correctly, will allow you to live comfortably for the rest of your life."

"It's too good to be true."

I'm beginning to feel smug and I'm about to tell this asshole to leave. Too many questions and this is taking far longer than it usually does. I'm wondering if I'm losing my touch, but then I notice a change in his posture and I know I have him.

"I'll restructure and the company will begin to turn a profit in less than a year. You'll receive royalties for the rest of your life, a small amount, honestly. But two percent of a million is a lot of money, William and that's what I intend to make within the first year. Plenty more after that."

"How can you be sure?" he asks. Again with the questioning and I let out an exasperated sigh.

"I do my research and I'm good at my job. I'm an investor, William. This is an investment firm. It's my job to turn a profit. I wouldn't be sitting here right now if I were incompetent, uneducated, and ill-informed, would I?"

What I would love to tell him is that I've thrown myself into this ruthless career to distract myself from the shit show that has become my life. It keeps me even and it never allows me to get close enough to anyone to feel. I have no friends in this business and I like it that way. No friends, means no one knows who I really am.

This time he's left speechless, only a slight nod of his head to indicate he finally grasps what I'm saying. And before I slide the contract across the table, my lawyer enters and I give him a quick wink to let him know he can begin his proceedings.

"It's been wonderful doing business with you, William. I do hope you manage your money a little better this time around." I extend my hand once again, but this time there's some hesitance on his part to take it. "You'll be leaving now. This is my attorney; he'll handle everything from here on out. Take care."

I escort him to the door and as he's leaving he turns back to face me.

"Campbell," he says, and I cut him off.

"Ms. Forester," I respond, giving him a cold look. There's a reason I do things the way I do. You want that comfort factor in place, to give them a sense of power over the situation, but in the end, it's business and I own them.

"Yes," he says, swallowing hard. "Thank you."

"My pleasure," I say before adding, "you fuckwit" after the door to my office closes and my fake smile instantly disappears.

I hate my job.

Chapter Three

The day finally comes to an end well after seven and I've now left Carson sitting at the restaurant alone for far too long. I run a hand through my hair and let out an exhausted sigh. It will piss him off, but there's not much I can do at this point.

I didn't intend to work past six, but circumstances beyond my control arose and I had to deal with a financial issue before leaving. I've explained to Carson that I didn't get where I am by working nine to five or by cutting out early. Most of this is a lie. This job comes easy to me and like I said, it leaves me emotionless.

I step into the restaurant and scan the room for Carson and find him almost immediately. He has a presence about him, he can captivate a room and it's not just because he looks like he was made for movies. Chiseled jaw, perfect nose, beautiful brown eyes and a body that could make any woman weak. But combine all these things with his infectious laugh, brilliant sense of humor and charming personality, and he's hard to say no to. I obviously couldn't.

While I know he loves me, I don't love him. It's not that I despise him or anything even close to that; I just can't bring myself to love him. Eventually he'll leave. We can't possibly carry on the way we have been. I give him nothing in return. Cold and unfeeling most days. It's been two years and while we have our moments where the sun peeks through, those are few and far between. Recently, we've been happy, but it's a cycle and we're reaching a peak. It's downhill from here.

The accident has made me a wholly negative person. I find it hard to see the good that life can offer; especially when the perfection I once loved and knew, was ripped out from under me without warning. I've felt empty ever since.

I've considered therapists and medication and all the recommended cures for what controls my life, but in order to do that, I have to admit what happened. I can't do that. This doesn't just affect me. It's not my story to tell alone.

Carson signals to me from across the room, his hand in the air, a smile on his beautiful face. And when I make eye contact with him, all I can think is, *He's the opposite of Benji.* Maybe that's why I chose him. There are no similarities, nothing to remind me.

As I make my way through the crowded restaurant, I notice the table where Carson is sitting is occupied by more than just him and I let out a loud huff along with a quick closing of my eyes.

His sister, her boyfriend,q and her best friend are all with him and he's smiling and laughing as they sit and talk.

Michelle is Carson's sister and well, she hates me as does her best friend, Allison. Carson should've ended up with Allison or at least that's what Michelle thinks. I watch Allison lean a little too closely to Carson for my liking; her hand subtly brushing his arm and the jealous side of me wants to claw her eyes out. The only saving grace of this situation is Michelle's adorable boyfriend, Quinn: a bike messenger without a care in the world. How the hell he ended up with Michelle is beyond me.

I plaster a smile on my face and take a seat next to Carson.

"Hi, baby," he says, beaming. He kisses me and because I know it pisses Michelle off I kiss him back for just a little longer than necessary. I don't want to be a bitch, but she makes it far too easy.

I greet everyone at the table after we separate and Michelle's response is cold as usual. A few seconds later Michelle looks over at Quinn and then at Carson, a self-satisfied look on her face and simply states, "Well, dinner was great, thanks again, Carson."

I roll my eyes at her blatant attempt to piss me off.

She turns her attention to me as she's standing at the end of the table. "We ate without you, Campbell, seeing as you were so late."

"Funny thing, Michelle," I respond back, accentuating her name and shooting her a filthy look. "I didn't even know you were going to be here."

"Must have slipped Carson's mind," she says, intentionally impolitely.

"Yeah, something like that."

As much as I enjoy Quinn's company, I'm happy to see Michelle and her overly friendly bestie be on their way. But as soon as I look back over at Carson, I kind of wish they would've hung around.

"Can't you be just a little nicer to her?" he asks as he shakes his head like he's chastising a child.

"She's really unpleasant."

"She's my sister."

"I know that," I say, raising my eyebrows, wondering if he'll ever side with me. But he drops the conversation there and signals for the waitress.

"You hungry?" Carson asks, never making eye contact with me.

"Not really, considering you ate without me." My feelings are hurt and I don't know why. I run so hot and cold with him that I should expect that sometimes he's not going to wait around for me.

"Then I'm going home," he says, emotionlessly.

I watch him walk away before I order a drink and wonder how I'm going to fix this. Maybe if he knew why I was cold with him he'd understand. But I wouldn't dare share it with him.

The waitress brings my drink and immediately my mind begins to wander to that day. How normal everything seemed, but how it also felt completely foreign. It was one of those moments you can't explain, but it just wasn't right.

I thought by now the effects would have lessened, that I'd be able to go on living a normal life, but each day, each month, each year that passes, it gets even more difficult. The guilt is haunting.

Nine years is a long time, but not long enough.

I pay my bill and head home to try and correct my massive fuck up with Carson. Being late, being a bitch to his sister, shutting him out; it's going to take a hell of an apology and with the exact time of the accident growing closer, I'm not sure I have it in me.

I walk into the house a few hours later to find Michelle sitting on my couch with Carson and all I can think is, *What the fuck?*

"Are you kidding me?" I ask out loud, probably too loudly.

"Don't give me that shit," Michelle responds rudely.

I can't even acknowledge her because I'm certain what will come out of my mouth will be anything but kind. "Did you seriously call her over here?" I ask Carson and his lack of response says more than enough.

"He's tired of being treated like shit," Michelle says, the insinuation in her tone is completely unnecessary.

"Oh my fucking god, Carson, did you bring your sister here to break up with me?" I'm appalled at his behavior as he just stands there staring at me. "Grow the fuck up, Carson, and Michelle, get the fuck out of my house."

Michelle widens her eyes at me, but says nothing.

"I'm serious, Michelle, get out. You're not welcome here. This is between me and your brother, who by the way is a grown ass man."

The seconds tick by as both of them stand looking at me but not speaking. And I, in turn, say nothing more.

Carson is the first to speak and I'm not at all shocked by what comes out of his mouth.

"I'm going to stay with John for a few days. I think you need some time to yourself and I don't think I should be here right now."

"Good choice," I answer back, leaving both of them in the living room as I storm out of the room.

The hours tick past and I'm lying in bed staring up at the ceiling wishing I'd have drugged myself so I could sleep through all of this. I look at the clock; each minute that disappears bringing me closer.

It wasn't late when the accident happened; it felt late to me back then, but when all was said and done, it was only a little after eleven. If I'm being exact, not like I could ever forget, it was 11:17 p.m. The time is seared into my brain as if it were branded there; it was the last thing I saw when I climbed out of the car. Disoriented and confused, but certain about that one thing, that one detail, it was so minute but so huge at the same time. The clock on the dash was flickering a dull red and I paused for just a second as I watched it fade away, eventually turning black.

11:17 p.m.

The road that led back to campus was deserted, or so Benji told me when we tried to rehash what exactly went wrong. He said that we hadn't passed a car for miles and considering the tourist season was long over, I wasn't surprised. But then out of nowhere, a Volvo station wagon came around a curve and since Sam was drunk, he took the curve too quickly, crossing over into the other lane, striking the oncoming vehicle.

The four of us knew very little about what actually occurred. Kelly was passed out and I was on top of Benji. Tommy was the only one aware of what happened and he claimed not to see any of it. I always felt like this was a lie. How could he have missed it? It literally crashed right into us.

I never pushed or pried him for information. I eventually assumed he knew exactly what he saw, but the tragedy was far too extreme to talk about. And I don't blame him.

When Kelly killed herself, the university wasn't nearly as sympathetic as I would've thought. They told me that I would have to stay in my dorm room despite the fact that my roommate's dead body hung from the rafters just hours before, because they didn't have any open rooms. They asked me if I had any place else to stay until they could make other arrangements. I simply nodded and packed a bag for Benji's place, but that proved just as difficult.

Benji and Sam shared an apartment and while I was lying in bed next to Benji that night, I asked, "How can you stay here?"

His response was completely devoid of emotion, and it was only after his words that I knew I couldn't stay any longer. "How come you can't just get over it?"

I left the next morning without saying goodbye to him or Tommy.

I can't believe it's gone on this long. They say time heals all wounds and with the passage of time, memories fade. I know this to be untrue. No matter how much time passes or what has happened since that day, my memories hold firm. There are some things that can never be erased.

When I roll over and look at the clock for the millionth time, it stares back at me bold and illuminated.

11:17

It's then that I feel the first tear fall, and all the others that come after it are the reason I finally fall asleep.

Chapter Four

The next morning I wake with a pounding headache and swollen eyes, and when I sit up, I'm met with a wave of nausea that has me scrambling from my bed. Clutching the sides of the toilet, I heave, but nothing leaves my stomach. This is the way I've woken up on the day after for the last nine years and you'd think I'd have gotten used to it, but it still hurts just as bad.

Wiping my mouth, I pull myself up off the floor and into the shower. The water is scalding as if I can burn the horribleness out of my body. It's strange though, life that is, you think the world stops when something awful happens or at least you think your life should stop. But for the last nine years my body and myself became two different things. My body began to go along doing what I normally would while I followed unwillingly. Sleeping and waking, eating and drinking, bathing and using the bathroom, as my life fell apart; my body betraying me every single day and it still does.

I go through the motions and arrive at work without remembering how I even got here. I'm sitting behind my desk, hazy and confused as I attempt to navigate my way through a conference call. I'm certain my name is said a total of eight times and I probably only heard it said once. I end the call by faking an illness and then I have my assistant cancel any other meetings I have scheduled for the day. I'm utterly useless.

This is the worst it has been since the accident happened. I can usually carry on once I'm at work, but there's something different about today. I begin to wonder if it has something to do with my fight with Carson coupled with the anniversary.

I've scheduled an appointment to get a massage and as I'm packing my things up, my assistant comes into my office.

"Hi, Claire," I say greeting her, yet still wondering why she's here.

"Campbell, there's a woman here to see you."

"You canceled my meetings today, right?" I ask her and she nods.

"I did, but she isn't a client. She says she's a friend of yours from college."

"I don't have any friends from college," I blurt out and Claire gives me a strange questioning look.

"What would you like me to do?" she asks.

"Um," I stutter out as I try to process who could possibly be looking for me. I left Michigan my sophomore year and finished school back in Chicago where I made no friends. *There is no one from college*, I think, before eventually saying, "Send her in." I can't help but be fearful with what I'm about to be confronted with. This person apparently has a connection to my past, to everything that has happened and it scares the shit out of me.

A woman about my age with blonde hair and a slight tan enters my office a few seconds later. She's well put together, wearing a black trench coat and a pair of black patent heels. She removes her sunglasses exposing her swollen and red-rimmed eyes. Wetting her lips, she's the first to speak. "Are you Campbell Forester?" she asks, as she looks me up and down.

"I am and you are?"

"You don't know me, but my name is Samantha Allington…" she trails off when she watches me stumble backward, my hand instinctively covering my mouth in shock as I collapse into my chair. "You know who I am?" she asks.

I nod and swallow hard as I try to process what is happening.

"You have something to do with Tommy," I say, the words leaving my mouth on a long exhale, and this time it's her who nods.

She pulls an envelope from the pocket of her coat and hands it to me. My name is written on the front and when I turn it over the back says, *Please do whatever you can to find her.*

"It wasn't very hard," she says as she watches me read the back of the envelope. She waits a moment, pausing as if she's trying to think of what to say next. "I'm Tommy's wife."

I don't know what to say and I don't have to think about it anymore because in the next breath Samantha lays into me.

"I don't know what happened between the two of you, but it ruined him. He never told me and now he won't ever be able to. Because thanks to you, he's dead."

I gasp out loud and the nausea that consumed my morning has taken over again. I shake my head over and over again. This can't be happening.

"He died yesterday," she says, spitting out her words and I want to tell her I'm sorry, but nothing comes out. "He loved you and I couldn't compete with that. I tried to save him, but every day was a struggle. He never recovered from whatever happened between the two of you, but clearly you have."

I can't continue to let her berate me; she's misinformed, but how can I tell her this without confessing.

"He did love me, but it wasn't like that," I explain, but it falls on deaf ears. She's hurt and angry and grieving, nothing I say will matter.

"It's over. You've got your letter," she says hatefully as she begins to leave my office.

"Wait," I call out and she stops just short of my door. "I loved him too," I whisper and after that my voice fails me and suddenly I can't speak.

"But it never occurred to you to find out if he was okay?" She doesn't give me the opportunity to answer, not that I deserve it. I can only imagine what she thinks has happened between the two of us. With her hand on the doorknob, she turns away from me and hisses, "Obviously it didn't, and you seem to be doing just fine."

She leaves me standing stunned and speechless clutching the envelope in my hand, but I can't let it end this way. I chase her out into the lobby, my assistant watching me the entire time.

"I'm not okay!" I shout, startling everyone within an earshot. Samantha turns and looks at me, the tears have already begun to fall, my voice shaky and weak. "I'm not okay," I say again and her only response is, "Neither was he," as she steps into the elevator and leaves.

I scramble back to my office hoping that no one has noticed that I've come completely undone. Falling into my desk chair, I bury my face in my hands and sob, my eyes burning and hot with a mass of tears that won't seem to stop. The dull ache in my chest that has never faded has now ripped wide open, painful and hopeless. The guilt I feel is unreal, and while I know his death isn't my fault, I can't help but feel somewhat responsible.

My heart breaks for his wife and what she had to deal with; I can't even imagine how difficult it was to be married to him if the life I live every day is any indication. Tommy, Benji and I each coped in our own way, but all equally distraught and self-destructive. And while we haven't been together in years, I know that we will never be alright.

The letter is lying on my desk, Tommy's handwriting on the front a reminder of what we once had. He loved to leave me notes; he'd been doing it since we learned to write. Small things, really, just simple words to make me smile or laugh or cry sometimes. He was one of the most thoughtful and selfless people I know, always concerned about everyone but himself.

There are times I often wonder why Tommy or Benji never reached out to me, but I never did either and when I left, I made it clear that I wanted nothing to do with them. Now that Tommy is dead, I wish I would have. I wish I wouldn't have spent so much time trying to forget and more time trying to save us.

I turn the letter over, reading the back once again. *Please do whatever you can to find her.* It wasn't like I hid from him or anyone else; I just became personally invisible after walking away from them. No social media, email address, listed phone numbers or things to link me back to Michigan, the accident or my past. Though I knew once my career began to flourish I would be easily reachable and in a way I guess I hoped I'd hear from one of them. That they would be the one to take the first step in repairing what we once had. I never expected the first step to come in the form of what I can only assume is a suicide letter.

I can't bring myself to open it, the pain far too great at the moment and I know the letter will only intensify what I'm feeling. I stuff it into my laptop bag just as a knock comes on the door to my office. I quickly wipe at my eyes like that's suddenly going to make me look like I haven't spent the last ten minutes crying. I need to pull myself together.

When the door opens it's the last person I expect to see.

"You okay?" he asks, but his tone is formal like always. "Claire said you were upset."

My boss, who also happens to be my brother, rarely mixes our personal lives with our professional and the fact that he's standing here nearly knocks me on my ass.

"I'm fine, Jack," I respond just as formally.

While we grew up together, we were never close, but when he began his company he saw something in me that he knew would contribute to his success. I've been working for him since I graduated from college with degrees in business and finance and we've been nothing but professional. I never wanted anyone within the company to think I achieved my position because of my connection to Jack. It has been easy to remain professional, partially due to the fact that Jack and I have very little in common and because I've kept everyone at arms length since the accident, including my family.

"I don't know what's going on, Campbell but things have been off for the last few days."

I let out an annoyed sigh. Things have been off? Ugh, I want to tell him to fuck off, because I'm still bringing in revenue better than anyone else at this company and that should be all that matters. My personal life is none of his concern.

"And I was just informed that you closed the deal with William Walters, but not before telling him you give amazing blow jobs." Jack glares at me with a look that screams disappointment.

"That guy's a prick," I shoot back.

"They're all pricks in this business, Campbell, yet I still expect you to treat them with the utmost respect."

"Got it," I say, but never looking up from my desk; my eyes focused on the calendar sitting in the center. If I look up he'll know I've been crying, not that he doesn't know already.

"Why don't you call it a day and come back tomorrow rested and back to normal?" He states it like a question, but I know it's more of a request than anything. It takes everything in me not to ask him what normal is. I haven't been normal in nine years and after my encounter today, I'm certain I won't know normal ever again.

"Sure," I answer sharply, packing up my laptop bag and slipping on my coat. I walk past him, but Jack reaches out and takes hold of my elbow, stopping me before I can leave.

I look up into his eyes and what I see is sympathy, pity for what he knows I'm feeling but can't fully grasp.

"You know you can talk to me, Campbell."

"No I can't," I say not trying to be ambiguous, but speaking the truth. I don't know what more to say so I leave. I feel like that's all I've been able to do when it comes to my life.

Leave.

Walk away.

I arrive home to an empty house with the letter burning a hole in my laptop bag, but I still can't bring myself to read it. Fearful of what it might say, what it might do to my already unstable life, so I leave it in the bag.

I reach for my laptop and type Tommy's name into Google. I have no way of contacting his wife and while I know it's far too late for any salvation or apologies, I feel compelled to find out if funeral arrangements have been made.

In my short search I find out that Tommy's wake and funeral will be held only forty minutes from where I live, just west of the city in a suburb just like the one we grew up in.

The wake is tomorrow, but I won't attend. I know I'm not welcome and I wouldn't dare show up and have his wife and family upset by my presence. Before everything happened, Tommy's mother and father adored me, but I'm certain their sentiment has changed. I just disappeared, never saying goodbye and now after his death, I'm certain his wife has filled them in on her assumptions.

Growing up next door to each other, we became fast friends at a young age and our friendship, for some reason, lasted long after most girl and boy friendships would've faded. While I fell in love with Benji, I loved Tommy in a way that was completely unconditional, like family. I remember walking out of school on my first day of third grade, the first year that I didn't have Kelly, Sam, Benji, or Tommy in my class and he was waiting for me. I started crying. At the time I didn't know what that feeling was or why it upset me, but looking back on it now, it was that feeling of empathy he had for my situation. It was a selflessness that came completely natural to Tommy. He knew I would be upset and made sure his was the first face I saw at the end of the day.

I locate the address of the church and the cemetery knowing I can easily attend and remain unnoticed this way.

During my research, I was unable to find an obituary, but I did find the address to his house and am now feeling an overwhelming need to see where he lived.

Before going to bed, I decide to take the next two days off, despite knowing this will send up a red flag at the office. In the six years I have worked for my brother, I have only taken off five days. Not even one day a year.

I'm not prepared to return to work right now and I know eventually I'll have to read the letter.

And it's going to be brutal.

Chapter Five

The letter is now on my nightstand, staring at me when I roll over the next morning. I pick it up and slide my finger along the sealed end but immediately toss it back to where it was.

I can't read it. I'm not ready.

Every single fucking time I look at that letter my mind becomes overcrowded with what ifs and all the horrible things that could be said. But I think what scares me more is the fact that I know Tommy well enough to know that what's in that letter isn't horrible. He could never hate me, just like I could never hate him. What's in that letter will bring me to my knees, will devastate me and remind me of why I've held onto his memory for this long.

And even though I won't open it, I know it contains absolution, a conclusion to an end, a way to finally move on.

I drag myself out of bed, not bothering with a shower; I pull on a pair of leggings and a sweatshirt. My hair still in a messy ponytail from the night before, I grab my keys, the letter and my purse and head out to my car.

I punch Tommy's address into the GPS, prepared to do god knows what when I get there. I guess just drive past his house. I'm sure it puts me in the category of a stalker or some shit. At this point what do I have to lose? His wife already hates me and thinks I was in a relationship with him where I broke his heart so badly that he never recovered. If she only knew that the truth is so much worse.

Forty minutes later I'm driving by a two story in an upper middle class neighborhood; a nice house on a quiet street. It's the kind of house that doesn't appear to be out of the ordinary. It's not the kind you look at and think, *The people who live there have issues.* There's a welcome flag hanging on a pole on the front porch, a few fall mums in pots, a pumpkin sitting next to them, along with a well-manicured lawn and a BMW SUV in the driveway.

I'm not sure what I expected. I guess I hoped that he led a terrible life and his passing wouldn't be in vain. I wanted him to be a cruel and disgusting drug addict or a wife-beater or something that would relieve me from the guilt I feel over him dying. But I know deep down he was none of those things; he could never be. And I hate myself for even thinking it.

I drive by three more times before eventually telling myself if I don't plan on ringing the doorbell or at least getting out of my car, I need to move on. In a neighborhood like this, my presence could possibly be misconstrued and I could find myself on the receiving end of a visit from the local police. That's the last thing I need.

During the ride to Tommy's house and back, my phone has been ringing incessantly making my anxiety shoot through the roof. I remember why I rarely take days off. The fact that my office can't seem to get by without me for one day is proof of that.

I take my phone from my purse and see that I've missed fifteen phone calls, under the assumption that most are from work, I scroll through quickly only to find that ten are from my brother and the other five are from Carson. I'm not sure how to handle this, but I do know I need to give Claire a raise because I haven't received a single work-related call.

I know they're worried about me. I get it, but right now I need to be left alone. And that's exactly how I spend the rest of the day.

Alone.

The next morning I wake up early, ahead of my alarm, knowing I need to be in the suburbs for Tommy's funeral. Dressed in all black with my hair down, I take my sunglasses even though the sky is dark. It almost seems too fitting given where I am heading. A darkness hanging in the air, the clouds low and gray as if they know the mourning of someone is occurring today.

I still haven't called Jack or Carson and today I woke up to find a voicemail from my mother. She isn't one of those parents that worries about her kids, while she loves us both dearly, once we left her home, she figured we were old enough to take care of ourselves. She and my father now live in Florida, visiting only when necessary and calling only when she has news to share, which has never really bothered me.

I know Jack called her; otherwise she wouldn't be calling me. And as the message plays, my thoughts are confirmed.

"Hi, Campbell, it's your mother." Her voice makes me smile along with her introduction. It's an inside joke. When I first left for college she'd call to check up on me once a week; leaving a message identifying herself like I didn't know who she was. She still does it and it makes me laugh every time. "Jack called. He's worried about you. So if you could do me a favor and call him so he stops bothering me, I'd love it. Hope you're well. Love you."

She's casual, not at all concerned about me or about Jack's need to get ahold of me. If anything she probably finds it odd that he's searching for me knowing we spend little time together outside of work.

I won't call her back either, the difference is, she won't care. And I'm sure that should bother me, but it doesn't. At least not right now.

I stuff the letter into my purse as I'm leaving my house. The edges of the envelope are starting to show signs of wear and the spot where I began to open it, is starting to curl. I've pretty much carried it with me everywhere I've gone since Tommy's wife handed it to me.

At this point it's the only connection to him I have left and by leaving it behind, by not having it with me, I feel like I've lost him completely.

The ride to the church is incredibly long, the traffic unyielding and when the rain begins to fall, relentless and pounding, it makes it almost impossible to see. The clouds are an ominous deep gray color and when the first bolt of lightning streaks across the sky, I'm suddenly hit with the memory of something I once read. *Rain on a funeral means the dead are on their way to heaven.* If I believed in that shit I might have felt better, but it's all bullshit. A fucking joke. Do religious people really find comfort in these thoughts?

My mind wanders to the accident. I want to chastise myself for even thinking it, but there is no way Tommy is on his way to heaven, whether I believe in it or not, not after what we did.

I pull into the overcrowded parking lot of the church, and I can already feel my chest closing in on me. *This was a mistake*, my mind is screaming at me as my heart beats painfully and rapidly against my ribs.

I shouldn't be here. This isn't a part of my life, he wasn't a part of my life anymore and I know if I'm seen by his parents or his wife that I'm fucked. Yet I'm compelled by something greater than me, something that is forcing me to enter this church. Salvation, redemption, guilt or a morbid need to know that he's really dead; I don't know what it is, but I know I can't leave.

I look at the clock and then watch the last few people exit their cars and enter the church. I'm holding back, waiting for a moment when I feel like I won't be noticed. The service has already begun and I'm hoping to slip in and take a spot in the back.

The rain has let up, but everything is shrouded in a deep gray, a light mist falling, ceaseless and depressing. But despite the rain, I don't hurry, my legs heavy and my body aching as I finally trudge up the steps of the church. With my hand on the door, I pull, the large wooden door creaking and I close my eyes and swallow hard. I can picture the entire congregation of people turning around to stare at me, interrupted by the noise of the door in what I expect to be an utterly silent room.

Eternally grateful, I find the door opens to a vestibule and I let out a long exhale in relief, but it's not over yet.

I turn and come face to face with a small child who looks to be about four years old. He looks up and me and I know in an instant who he is. Practically identical; it's Tommy's son. I'm crying before I even have the chance to turn around and run. He smiles up at me and then I feel his tiny hand slip into mine.

He's standing next to me, his eyes never leaving mine, his hand warm and soft against my skin. And when he whispers, "This is for my daddy," I nearly fall to the floor. Not only does he look exactly like Tommy, his voice is the same melodic voice I remember from when we were kids.

I nod my head, wanting to take this small child in my arms, to hug him and hold onto him as if it were Tommy standing here. I want to tell him that his father was an amazing man. The most kind and selfless person I have ever known, and that if he remembers one thing about his father, it was that he loved with all his heart.

I'm clutching his hand, my fingers tightening because letting go feels like I'm letting go of everything Tommy and I once had. I find a strange feeling of solace take over as the boy squeezes my hand in return.

The door leading into the church opens slowly, but just barely and an older woman pokes her head out. Her eyes flick from the boy to me and back to the boy again before she speaks.

"Thomas," she quips sternly, "What are you doing?" She reaches out and snatches his other hand and yanks him out of my hold. My hand grows cold instantly and I immediately miss the feeling of comfort I found with him.

Thomas pulls back against her hand and he looks back at me with that same reassuring smile on his face.

"Bye," he whispers like he knows he's supposed to be quiet and I give him a small smile back.

The woman's face is harsh and she glares at me with a look that says, *you should know better than to stand so close to a child you don't know.*

I watch Thomas being pulled back into the church, his child-like innocence lost forever and as the thought hits me so do the emotions that come along with it.

The vestibule suddenly feels hot and stuffy. I pull at the collar of my coat, unbuttoning it as I begin to sweat and grow nauseous. I'm crying again, but this time it seems loud and booming in the echoing silence of this small room.

I suck in a hard breath and before I know it I realize I'm going to be sick, all of this is too much to handle. Knowing Tommy's dead, seeing his son, the church and the thought of this child growing up fatherless, it's all too much to bear.

I step outside, the cold, damp air crashing into me but doing nothing to subside this feeling. Finding a small garbage can, I vomit into it as the tears continue to fall. I'm not sure I can go inside; I'm not sure I'm capable of handling any of this.

I reach into my purse searching for something to wipe my mouth on when a woman hands me a tissue and a piece of gum.

I give her a weak but grateful smile and she returns it as she asks, "Are you okay?" I almost laugh out loud at her question and I want to respond with, "I haven't been okay in nine fucking years." But I think twice and just nod my head.

"Are you sure?" she asks, an almost over exaggerated sympathy dripping from her voice and it annoys me. I hate people who pry, especially strangers. I responded to her, so why is she still here?

She waits for me to answer and I say the first thing that comes to my mind, what I know will get her to back off and what is also a complete lie.

"I'm pregnant," I retort with irritation.

I immediately walk away and go back through the doors of the church, this time not attempting to silence my arrival. With my eyes on my feet, I trail along the back pew before taking a seat on the outside edge of the last row.

The service has already started and I can hear the muffled cries of the people coming from within the pews, the vaulted emptiness above us unforgiving to the sounds.

As the priest speaks I try to focus on his words, I try to listen, but my focus is shit and everything I've taken in from this point sounds garbled as if I'm underwater. But what comes through loud and clear is the conversation that is being had next to me by two women.

Each one more perfect than the next, with their expensive blowouts and manicured nails, a stepford version of a wife and mother that I imagine live in the neighborhood where Tommy lived. I only met Samantha for a brief moment when she showed up at my office to deliver my letter, but even in her state of grief, I could tell she led the life of perfection on the outside. But what people couldn't see, what she hid from everyone was that her life was falling apart.

"It's so tragic," the woman with brown hair whispers, the compassion in her voice laced with falseness.

"Tragic?" the woman sitting next to her scoffs, a blonde with a bad fake tan. "It's anything but tragic. Tommy was a drug addict and a horrible person. All of this is so contrived and fake." Her hand flits from her lap, gesturing around the church.

"Seriously?" the brunette questions as she slides closer to the woman next to her, curiosity written all over her face.

"Oh my god," she says, her eyes rolling. "You really think he traveled for work *that* much? Please, he spent more time in rehab than he did at home." She pauses momentarily and looks reproachfully at the front of the church like she's trying to find someone. "And poor Samantha. She never would've married him if she hadn't gotten pregnant with Thomas."

"But I thought they had been together since college?" the other woman asks, her curiosity spiking even more.

"They were, but he was always so damaged. I think Samantha thought she could save him. Obviously not," she adds, again rolling her eyes as if to say Samantha was stupid to even think it. "Samantha once told me he was still hung up on some girl or at least that's what she thought. Their marriage was a mess and so was Tommy."

The brunette's eyes widen like this is the first time she's hearing this. "Wow, I always thought they had the perfect marriage. She hid it well."

"Would you want everyone in the neighborhood to know your husband was blowing your life savings on drugs on a regular basis?" the blonde asks with rude emphasis. "She's better off without him," she adds and that's about all I can take.

I turn my body so I'm facing them, my lips pursed as I stare at them, waiting for them to notice. It doesn't take long and their conversation ceases immediately. With perturbed looks on their faces, they wait for me to turn away, but they have no idea who they're dealing with here.

"Listen, you gossipy bitches, we're at a fucking funeral," I mutter through gritted teeth, trying to control my need to raise my voice. "And how dare you fucking judge him. You have no idea what he's been through; why he did what he did to cope with his life. Remember that when you decide to pass judgment on someone or something you know nothing about."

I push up from the pew and leave just as quickly and quietly as when I arrived. I've had enough and as I'm walking to my car I find my hand clutched around the letter in my purse. I didn't even realize I'd put my hand in my purse. But now it's holding onto the one thing I have left. The one thing I have left of him.

Chapter Six

I still haven't said goodbye; it's not like I believe it will bring me any peace, but I'm finding it harder to say goodbye than being left behind. But I also don't think I even know how to say goodbye to him in a way that won't be painless. I'm afraid of the pain and the rush of feelings and emotions I can't seem to control. Yet I find myself driving to the cemetery.

I can see the tent from where I park my car. A blue plastic tarp draped over a metal frame that is swaying precariously as the wind from the storm blows once again. I wonder what would happen if the tented frame blew away? Would the people stay and grieve for the one who died or would they flee from the rain, more concerned about their hair and makeup, wool suits and designer dresses? I like to believe that people are innately good, but it's a lie.

Ever since the accident my thoughts have become disjointed and strange. No real link to anything of purpose and maybe that's so I never think too deeply about anything.

I watch the tarp flap and the metal frame move with the wind, again wondering if it's anchored to the ground and wondering just what it would look like if it took flight.

What the fuck is wrong with me?

Opening my glove box, I find a tiny umbrella. I slip off the cover, open my car door, and pointing the umbrella out, I open it.

Part of me is grateful to have the umbrella and another part thinks I should sit in the rain, like it will wash away all this ugliness. That if I just wait long enough, that if I let it cover me, I'll finally be clean of what I can't rid myself of.

I find a bench far enough from the gravesite that I won't be noticed but close enough that I can watch. Even that thought is morbid and strange. Do I really want to watch his dead body be lowered into the ground and covered with dirt, only to know that eventually he'll decompose and there will be nothing left?

I watch the funeral procession arrive, black as the sky, a line of cars driving slowly like the passage of time doesn't matter and in a way it doesn't. He's already dead.

I pull my umbrella down, shielding my face, but I still watch. I watch Samantha and Thomas climb out of the hearse and he raises his face to the rain, opening his mouth and dancing a little. He doesn't understand. This hasn't affected him, lost in that invincible child's mind where people don't die and happiness is everywhere and finding fun is only a few steps away. Tommy and I were him once.

And it was beautiful.

As the mourners leave their cars, a sea of colored umbrellas moving as one, as they make their way to the tent. The women's faces are scrunched and they teeter on the tips of their toes, their heels sinking into the soft ground. This is what they're concerned about, but I'm not surprised.

To be happy, we must not be too concerned with others.

A quote that to me is bullshit at its best. It's a way to defend self-righteous behaviors, to not feel guilty when you realize you're an egomaniac. It's the way the world works, but it was never the way our world worked.

Sam used to pick all the marshmallows out of the Lucky Charms for me, presenting me with the bowl and a huge grin on his face. I watched Benji, when he thought I wasn't looking, hug Kelly after she failed her driver's ed. test for the second time; his hand stroking her hair as she sobbed into his t-shirt. It was all the little things, but it was all the big things too. Those moments, that without each other we would have never endured. After Benji's parent's divorced, the five of us spent a week sleeping in a tent in my backyard because he just couldn't handle being home. Or when Sam's dog died and we buried him in the backyard despite the protests from his mother. And when I fell ice skating and broke my ankle, Tommy was the one who carried me home. It was always us.

Each one of us more concerned with each other than we ever were with ourselves. And maybe that's what made us different, what allowed our friendship to remain solid despite all the disappointment that existed. But the accident was the one thing that tore us apart, the one thing that broke our bond. The moment we left Sam, dead and bleeding, we left our concern for each other. When push came to shove, we chose selfishness. We chose ourselves instead of each other.

It was the beginning of the end.

The last breath of our dying friendship.

I felt it that night and I still feel it today. It never fades.

Before I even realize it, the ceremony is over. The crowd has dissipated and all that remains is the priest and the cemetery caretakers. I take it all in, this is the part that no one sees and it's rather anticlimactic, yet harrowingly disturbing.

The crank is being turned as the casket is lowered into the ground, and I guess I always thought it lowered it the full six feet. But I was wrong, because I hear a muffled thud as it drops below the surface. The priest bends down, scooping up a handful of dirt, he tosses it into the darkness of the hole. A few seconds later there's a small bulldozer dumping dirt over the top. And like that it's over.

The priest walks away, wiping the dirt from his hands and instantly the lyrics to the Beatles *Eleanor Rigby* pop into my head.

No one was saved.

I stay longer than necessary, the bench wet and my pants now soaked to the point where they are heavy against my body. And when I stand it actually feels more difficult to walk than before.

The reason I'm still here an hour after it all ended is because saying goodbye means letting go. It means forgetting.

I find myself standing in front of his grave, no marker or headstone yet, but I know it's his. I watched them bury him. And then without warning, I'm on my knees, the wet ground sinking around me, my pants clinging to my skin.

"You're laughing at me," I say out loud, speaking to no one, because he's dead. "Watching me on my knees, crying into the dirt of your fresh grave." I swallow as I choke back the sob that has formed in my throat. "You know I don't believe in this shit, but here I am." I feel stupid talking to nothing. I always thought people who did this had to be crazy. The person is gone. And then I realize that maybe I've been crazy for the last nine years.

I fall silent, staring down at the ground, as my thoughts become a mass of confusion, of feelings I can't sort out or that I don't want to sort out.

"Why?" I ask, like he can hear me, like I'll get an answer from the wind, some epiphany or a sign from a god I don't believe in. I find the letter in my purse and watch my name bleed into the envelope as a drop of rain hits it.

"This," I say, angry, holding the letter out over the grave. "This was never supposed to be your goodbye. You weren't supposed to leave me. We lost so much, all of us and right now I hate you. I hate you so much." The last line comes out as a strangled scream. I'm sobbing, deep, heaving sobs until my body aches and I can't catch my breath.

And in this moment of weakness, I rip open the envelope, shielding it from the rain under my umbrella.

The letter is folded in my hand, I want to crumple it up and throw it as far as I can. I want to burn it and watch it turn to ashes, but it's all I have anymore. This and memories.

It's folded in thirds and I lift the first part, exposing only the first few lines of his letter, taking in his handwriting, seeing my name written by him. But after I read that first line, I'm broken. I scan the next few and that's enough for me.

And then there were two.
Campbell,
This letter will end the same way it began.
I love you.

Chapter Seven

I want to say I read the letter, but I didn't. I still haven't as I sit on the couch in my house; the TV on, but I'm not watching. A bottle of wine sits on my coffee table, the glass in my hand because classy girls get drunk off wine and wallow in their own self-pity. Crazy girls drink several bottles and cry alone in their house. That's me.

I don't have to be alone. I choose to be. Carson has sent me multiple text messages that I've left unanswered. The most recent coming in just seconds ago.

Carson: Campbell, will you please answer me. Just because we're fighting doesn't mean I'm not worried about you.

Fuck him and his attempts at self-preservation. He doesn't care about me; he doesn't even know me. But the last thing I need is for him to show up here and see me clinging to this letter like it's my only savior, drunk and crying. The explanation needs to remain hidden, because I can't even begin to process any of it. Returning to that day, even if it is just through memories, is far too disturbing.

I text him back, vague and formal.

Me: I'm fine. I'll call you tomorrow.

But I won't. Ideally, at this point, I'd like it if he just disappeared without me having to deal with the repercussions of being in a relationship with him for the last two years.

I knew it was wrong at the time when I accepted a date with him. It was one of those chance meetings, a fluke, something I thought would never amount to much, yet I still said yes. Looking back on it now, I think I was just looking to feel normal again. I thought if I fell in love, gave my heart away to someone else, what I had lost would return. But my heart was never mine to give away; it belonged to someone else. It always has and it always will.

I put back the last of the bottle, leaving everything where it is; I head to bed, only to be plagued with insomnia. Before finding out about Tommy's death, I had been sleeping fairly well. Averaging about six hours a night, which for me was stellar. I struggled to sleep for years after the accident, all of it replaying in various forms coming as nightmares that made sleeping almost impossible. Sometimes everyone died but me. Other times Sam survived but we didn't know that until after we left him there bleeding and near death. There was also a reoccurring one where I relived the accident in full detail, yet my mind filled in the missing pieces. Graphic. Horrible. Traumatizing. It was far too realistic, and the fear of nightmares haunted me every time I laid down.

So far the nightmares haven't returned, but sleep has eluded me and it's beginning to grow old. I'm exhausted and beyond drunk, yet I still toss and turn. My body finally gives up somewhere around two a.m. and while I'm grateful, my sleep is restless and unfulfilling.

I wake before my alarm, my head pounding and my eyes stinging. The whole thing only intensifies when I sit up, and then I realize I have to go to work today. If I ditch another day, Jack will be even further up my ass than he already is.

I haven't even looked at my emails or my calendar since Jack sent me home and I can only imagine what I'm going to walk into today.

Despite waking up far earlier than normal, I'm running late. I missed my train and then I flagged down a taxi that manages to get stuck in a slew of traffic. It all brings on a bought of morning rage that coupled with my epic hangover, has me swearing and telling the driver to pull over. I stuff ten bucks through the opening in the window and hop out, still at least three blocks from my office but not giving a single fuck. Maybe the cool fall air will clear my mind and help subside this hangover before I make it to the office.

As I'm navigating the crowded streets, some asshole slams right into me, his coffee dumping all over the front of my coat and spilling down into my shoes.

"Motherfucker!" I shout out loud and a few people stop and take me in.

"Hey, sorry," he mumbles, before leaving his cup rolling on the ground as he walks away.

By the time I arrive at work, I'm not in the mood for small talk. I buzz by Claire's desk greeting her tersely, "Claire," I say and then I close my office door with more force than necessary.

I toss everything onto my desk and in doing so, my purse turns over, scattering everything all over my desk and onto the floor. I fall back into my chair, a deep groan leaving my mouth on an exhale as I lean forward to begin cleaning it up. But as I do, there it is: the fucking letter.

I pick it up and I'm immediately hit with a million emotions and the first few lines replay in my head on a continuous loop. I know I need to read it and while my office isn't the place for it, I can't help but pull it from the envelope. My day has been shit already and it's only eight a.m. I might as well push it right over the edge. So that's exactly what I start to do when my office door is flung open and Jack is standing in the doorway, his hands on his hips.

"Jesus, fuck," he says as he looks me up and down. "You look like shit and we have a meeting in ten minutes."

"Get out," I respond not caring at all that he's my boss as my tone drips with disrespect. I push back from my desk, pointing a finger at the door, but Jack doesn't move. "I'll be at the meeting," I tell him hoping it appeases him.

"Campbell," he says softly and I want to punch him in the face. The pity I hear is sickening. "If you need more time off to deal with…" he trails off and shakes his head before continuing. "Whatever it is you're dealing with, you just have to say it."

"I'm fine, Jack."

"Yeah, you've told me that already."

"Well I am."

"Fine," he simply states, and then adds, "Be in the conference room in ten." His posture and tone returns to the formality I'm used to and for some reason I find it comforting; far more so than his ill-fated attempts at soothing me with pity.

I step into the conference room not a second sooner than Jack requested. Normally I'm not like this, but I'm suddenly consumed with an insane amount of bitterness over everything in my life. I guess I never realized it, but while I have not forgotten the accident and I never will, my efforts to keep the memories at bay were clearly somewhat successful. I was able to function on a pretty even keel, but with the letter and Tommy's death and the funeral, meeting his wife and seeing his kid, it has forced everything to the surface and it's ugly.

I greet everyone in the room and Jack begins the meeting while I zone out in the chair across from him. I'm not thinking about anything in particular; I don't really think in complete thoughts anymore. I hear a few bits and pieces of the conversation, but I have yet to interject, which is highly unlike me in this type of environment. This is the kind of thing I think about. Work. It's the one thing that blocks my mind and I can usually focus on it without too much effort. But today is different.

I hear Jack, but I don't comprehend. I catch the tail end of his sentence... "beginning to bring in temps and have started the process to outsource, but it looks like this might be a loss on our part. Campbell, what do you think?" he asks and I quickly look over at him. He widens his eyes at me, awaiting an answer. And while I haven't heard the majority of what he's just said, I can dig myself out of this without a problem.

"The Wright Group was purchased at a loss. I've been saying we should look into selling it off piece by piece in order to recoup some of what has been invested. At this point in the proceedings, we are too far gone to turn it around and need to look at possibly unloading it within the next year." I take a breath and lean back in my chair, as Jack seems to settle down. "While it was a poor investment in the first place, it's not a total loss on our part. There is a marketable solution to this, liquidate what is not in the red and what is, sell at wholesale and then work the numbers to find out where we can make up for the loss."

"Thanks, Campbell," Jack says and I immediately go back to half listening to the conversation.

The day finally ends and I'm exhausted. Secrets and lies take commitment and I'm finding it harder to be around people, afraid I'll slip up. But there's hypocrisy in it all. I ran because of what we had done, attempting to hide the truth and thinking that if I wasn't surrounded by it, I could forget it. Yet now, the only thing I want is to be immersed in it, to find peace in Tommy's death and stop running, but I can't even figure out where to begin. I'm scared and unsure, the reality of it too much, but at the same time possibly exactly what I need.

As I leave my office, I find myself wondering what I'm so afraid of. I lived through this whole thing once already, experiencing the accident, Sam's death, Kelly's suicide, and now Tommy. When looking at from a distance, it all hits me and I begin to wonder just why it happened to them.

What makes me different? Why am I still here and will I be the next to lose everything because of this accident and what we did?

It's what drives me to read the letter. I arrive home with my heart racing in my chest, my palms sweaty. Nothing weighs as heavily on you as a secret—crushing, an impossible burden that can only be carried for so long. It eventually wrecks you, shards of your former life crumbling all around you, loud and clear.

A glass of wine in hand, because fuck knows I'm going to need it, I sit down on the couch with the letter burning in my hand. Hot and sticky, the envelope is stiff and my name written in ink on the front is feathered from the rain.

I take in one long, deep breath and open the envelope once again. This time more prepared for what I might find, less angry, but the hurt is still thick in my chest. The longer I wait the more my uncertainty grows.

I chew the inside of my cheek hoping the tears will be kept at bay. But of course I'm wrong. All it takes is seeing his handwriting again, my name, and the words, *And then there were two.*

I know I need to finish this and although, my eyes are blurred with the tears that continue to pool, I move forward, re-reading what I already read and forcing myself to continue.

And then there were two.

Campbell,

This letter will end the same way it began.

I love you.

I'm sorry I failed you. No matter what I did I couldn't overcome the demons that plagued my life. What happened to us is something I will never forget. But this letter isn't about me; it's about you.

Campbell, please don't lose what we once had. At the heart of it all, life is good and we were good people, who made a poor choice. I need you to do something for me. I'm not asking you to solve what we created; it's too late for that now. I'm asking you to repair what's broken, to pick up the pieces of our shattered lives and end this cycle of death and depression we've all found ourselves in.

Find him and make us whole again.

I love you.

Tommy

While I thought reading this letter would be the key to finding out what exactly happened to him, it isn't. I can only speculate and that's the last thing I need to be doing. My life since the accident has been a fucked up series of speculations, each one worse than the next.

He never wrote the letter to find closure or to confess his sins or to admit his guilt in anything. No details about the accident and what he saw. It wasn't about him and even in death he's selfless. The letter makes me sick and pissed off; it's given me nothing I was seeking from it.

Angry tears sting my eyes and run down my cheeks. I step out onto the patio of my house, the cold air hitting me as I feel my tears dry. With the letter clutched in my hand, I sit down and re-read it for a second time, but it only stirs the disappointment and hatred for the whole thing all over again. Not just the letter, but what I've lived through for the last nine years, the accident, all the death. This was supposed to be the catalyst that would correct my world. I hate him even more. I hate this letter. And I hate my life and what it's become.

I step back into my house, the letter still in my hand. I grab my wine glass from the coffee table and stand motionless, unable to process how I'm feeling.

My emotions going through a series of highs and lows and when I walk into my kitchen, I've turned furious. I launch the wine glass into the sink. It explodes as soon as it hits the stainless steel basin. Shattering into a million pieces that scatter and fly all over my kitchen, the small amount of red wine left in the glass splattering the white cabinets and the tile floor.

I take it all in, the image far too similar to the accident and it breaks me. I fall to the floor, sobbing. Each sob comes out a strangled cry, unable to breathe and my chest closing in on me as I feel like my heart is literally breaking inside me. The letter lays next to me, I pick it up and in a fit of anger, I tear it in half and then again, tossing the pieces in front of me. I leave them lying among the shards of glass and wine.

Then I do the only thing I think will make me feel better. I drink myself to sleep.

Chapter Eight

I wake the next morning feeling worse than ever. My head is throbbing, my body aches, and when I look in the mirror it's apparent that I've spent the last night drunk and sobbing. Red-rimmed bloodshot eyes, my nose is stuffy and the tip is a light shade of pink. I look like hell. And I feel like it too.

I can't possibly go on like this and still function normally, especially since I have to be at work in less than an hour. I think I passed out sometime around two in the morning, but I can't be sure. All I remember is reading the letter, finding it left me feeling worse than before; all my questions about Tommy's death left unanswered and then I woke up in my bed feeling like I'd been hit in the head with a blunt object.

I shake my head and look at myself in the mirror one more time before getting into the shower hoping to wash away all this horribleness that won't seem to stop. But when I emerge thirty minutes later, nothing has changed.

I dress quickly, despite knowing I'm already going to be late for work. I've missed my usual train and the bus is long gone too. I hate to drive, but at this point I have no other options.

Shockingly, I've gotten myself together in just under ten minutes, makeup, hair and all, and I surprisingly look presentable. I might actually make it to work at a reasonable time, that is, until I see my kitchen.

"Fuck," I mutter, running my hand through my hair as I take in the shattered wine glass, the red speckled cabinets along with the tile and the torn up letter. Guess this little fit of rage slipped my mind. How could I forget; it's the reason I feel like shit this morning.

I take the broom from the hall closet and begin sweeping up the mess of glass knowing if I don't I'll come home to it and the remembrance of it all will return. Just as I'm about to sweep the torn pieces of the letter into the dustpan, I have second thoughts. I pick it up, setting it on the counter;

choking back the tears that threaten. Swallowing the lump that has formed in my throat, I will not cry over this anymore. It's over.

After vacuuming up what I couldn't sweep up, I begin wiping down the cabinets and washing the floor. So much for only being mildly late for work, but I only have myself to blame for this mess. As much as I'd love to blame someone else... Carson, Jack, Tommy, anyone but myself, I can't. I like to think I hate Tommy for leaving me like this, but it's far from it. We all harbored these issues and they are slowly destroying our lives. This is my burden, my life and my secret that I have to carry. And after reading Tommy's letter, it's clear that I'll continue to go this alone. The only connection left to all of this is Benji, and even though Tommy wants me to find him, I'm not sure I can do it. I'm not sure I can let him see that I've failed, that I've struggled all these years without him—without all of them.

As I'm packing up my things to leave for the office, I catch a glimpse of the torn up letter and although I'm still angry and hurting, I can't bring myself to throw it away. I gather up the pieces, putting them into a Ziploc bag, and I take it with me when I leave.

As I step out of the elevator, I plaster a fake smile on my face, determined to return to what these people think is normal. I'm tired of having to explain myself or claim to be fine every time they ask.

"Good morning, Claire," I say, a cheerful disposition to my voice.

"Good morning, Campbell," she says back just as cheerful and I almost tell her to fuck off. She isn't a bad person quite honestly. She's really a great assistant, a sweet young girl, who hopefully never becomes jaded and hurt by the cruelty that exists. I hope one day she doesn't make a decision she regrets and carries a secret with her that eventually kills her friends and disrupts her life. It's disgusting that I even think this way.

Before I can think anymore about it, I close my office door and when I remove my laptop from my bag, the ripped up letter comes with it. I look at it for a long second and decide right away that I can't leave it like this. I grab the tape from my desk drawer and begin piecing the letter back together, smoothing the pieces and making sure each piece fits together as best as possible. I read each line again as I put it back together and I can finally read it without totally breaking down. To say, I didn't shed a tear would be a lie, but at least now each word doesn't make me sob like a baby.

As I read it again, with all my questions about Tommy's death unanswered, I make a decision that's probably going to come back to bite me in the ass. But I'm certain it's the only chance I have to find out what might have led him to write this letter, and what I can only assume, led him to kill himself.

I find myself in Jack's office, my posture already defensive. I've never been intimidated by him, unlike everyone else in the office and with what I'm going to ask him for, I know he's not going to happy, especially since I can't give him an explanation.

I blew past his assistant, who at this point in my career, knows better than to stop me. I think she's even more terrified of me than she is of Jack.

"What do you need, Campbell?" he asks without looking up from his computer. I actually let out a sigh of relief. This is the Jack I know and it makes this all so much easier. The formality to his tone, all business-like and ready to handle things as my boss and not my brother.

"I need to leave today," I say and he still hasn't looked up. "Like now," I add and he finally stops what he's doing to hit me with a stern look.

"No," he shoots back and returns to his computer.

"What the fuck, Jack?"

"Campbell, you're the one who wanted a professional working relationship with me. And my answer is no. It would be no if anyone who works for the company came in here without an explanation as to why. So, no."

"Ugh..." I breathe out not wanting to do this, but it's probably my only chance to get out of here without telling him what the hell I'm doing.

"Jack, I need you to be my brother and not my boss for just a second and not question me on this. Hopefully someday I'll be able to fill you in on what the fuck is going on, but until I can sort that out myself, it's better that I don't say anything."

He stands up, and if I were anyone else it probably would've had me holding my hands up in defeat and running away. Jack's tall, around six-three, muscular and in a suit with a harsh look on his face, can be seriously unapproachable, scary even. He's known for being a hard ass, which is probably where I get it from too. Our mother is pretty much the same. But in this instance, and after growing up with him, it doesn't work on me.

And even when he raises his voice, it booming through the expanse of his office, I'm not shaken.

"What kind of fucking explanation is that?" he demands.

"It's not. It's all I can give." I shrug my shoulders as if we're just having a casual conversation.

"Campbell," he starts to say and then stops. He runs his hand through his hair and lets out a long sigh. "You took two days off without an explanation and I let it go. You showed up to work yesterday, detached and looking like shit, and I brushed it off. And now you storm in here and inform me that you're leaving for the day when your work day began less than an hour ago."

I interrupt him before he can say any more, blurting out, "Tommy killed himself," but my voice lacks the sympathy it should have when discussing the death of a friend. This is what I've created with Jack, a formal, emotionless relationship that is built around our mutual drive to make his company better. It has never had anything to do with our personal lives, our family or our sibling connection. Except right now, with what I've just told him, I'm certain I've crossed that line.

He's speechless and a whole series of thoughts are running through my head. I wonder if he's questioning my callous delivery of the news or if he's wondering why I care since I haven't spoken to Tommy in nine years. Or worse than all of these, is he thinking about everything that occurred with my group of friends that he's always been in the dark about?

Obviously, my parents and Jack know that Sam died in a car accident and that Kelly killed herself, but they have no idea my involvement in any of it. My mother, never being one to pry and my father just following her lead, never asked why I left school or what happened to my relationship with Benji and Tommy. I think my family just assumed Benji and I broke up, and since I shut down after the accident, no one bothered to ask. The same with my friendship with Tommy. After leaving Ann Arbor, it wouldn't be all that strange to lose touch with someone considering we were several hours away from each other. I just let them believe all of this. The truth was far too vile to share. Just the thought of telling Jack now makes me sick to my stomach.

"Holy shit, Campbell," he eventually says, his eyes wide, as he steps toward me. In a moment of panic, I step back. I don't want him to touch me, not that he's tried to hug me in at least ten years. "Why didn't you tell me?"

"I just did," I respond, coldly. "Please don't ask me any questions and for the love of fuck, don't try to hug me."

I watch him swallow hard and nod his head.

"So can I go?" I ask, my arms now folded across my chest, my eyes focused on his.

"Yeah, of course. Take as much time as you need," he tells me, his voice taking on that quiet quality you find when people talk about death. Yet in my case, a person dying seems to be a regular occurrence.

"Thanks," I say, forcing myself to be appreciative. Not that I'm not, it's just I've been emotionally detached for so long, it's hard to make it realistic.

As I'm walking out of his office, Jack calls my name and I turn around to face him. "Campbell, I know I told you before, but you can talk to me."

"And I told you before, I can't." The way it comes out is harsh and I immediately regret it. He's trying to help, yet I know there's nothing he can do or say to make this any easier. "Sorry, Jack," I apologize. "Maybe one day I'll be able to, but right now, I just can't."

An hour later, I'm parked a few houses away from Tommy's house wondering just what the fuck I think I'm doing. I know exactly how this is going to play out, but letting this whole thing go without a possible reason isn't something I'm comfortable with.

I exit my car; the walk to the front door of the house is long and my heart begins to race before I have even pressed the doorbell. I wipe my hands down the front of my pants and prepare myself for what's to come. Shit's about to get real.

As soon as Samantha opens the door her demeanor shifts and she looks like she's about ready to punch me in the face or call the police.

"You're not welcome here," she growls as she attempts to close the door. Against my better judgment, I shove my hand against the door and force it open.

"No!" Samantha shouts and while it should affect me, it doesn't. I'm used to people yelling at me in my line of work. It's rare for me to startle anymore. "You can't come here! You don't get to come to my home and upset me and my family." She's crying now and I feel so horrible for what I'm doing. She doesn't understand why I'm here or have any idea who I am. She knows what she's created in her mind, and it's not even close to the truth.

"Whatever you know, it's not the truth," I tell her, my voice almost pleading.

"I know nothing," she spits out as she wipes at the tears on her cheeks. "He told me nothing. You were a secret I found out about by accident and the more I asked the more distraught he became."

It's becoming difficult for me to hold back the tears as I watch Samantha sob in the doorway to her house, confused and grieving, and all the while believing that it's somehow my fault. And maybe it is.

I'm starting to believe it myself. Three people dead, all with a connection to me.

"He wasn't in love with me. He told you that, I'm certain he would have," I respond.

"He did. Many times, but why else would he dream about you, call your name in his sleep, write you a letter and insist I deliver it?" Her tone is filled with hatred and hurt. I want to be able to explain it all to her, but it's not my story to tell alone.

"Then please believe him, because it's all I can give you too. I can only tell you he wasn't in love with me. There's so much more to it than that, but it's complicated."

"I'm not going to do this with you anymore. You're vague and you're upsetting me. My son is inside and the last thing I need is him seeing his father's mistress or girlfriend or whatever the fuck you are arguing with his mother."

"I'm none of those things!" I shout and I instantly cover my mouth with my hand. I didn't intend for it to come out that loudly. My voice drops to a near whisper, "I'm a childhood friend. We grew up together."

She shakes her head; her tears now dry, but her pain still visible on her face. "Please go," she begs. "And don't come back."

"Wait," I call out, my hand on the door once again. "Can you tell me one thing?"

She rolls her eyes, a hand on her hip now, the door propped open with her foot. "What?" she utters clearly annoyed.

"How did he die?"

"He killed himself," she states very simply, and it confirms what I always suspected. "At first I thought it was a drug overdose," she pauses as if she's thinking about what happened. "He hadn't used in years. Five years to be exact. He stopped when he found out I was pregnant. And I really thought things were changing, that the baby would be what he needed to get well." She stops again and shoots me a filthy look. "Why the fuck am I telling you this? I don't owe you anything."

"You're right, you don't," I say attempting to appease her, but desperately needing her to keep talking. "Why did you think it was a drug overdose?" I ask even though I know it might be the question that causes her to slam the door in my face this time.

"Tommy was a heroin addict, but like I said he'd been sober for five years," she says as she closes her eyes and takes a deep breath. "I found him with a needle in his arm on our bathroom floor. He was already dead." She covers her face with her hands and I see the tears spill out from underneath. "But then I found the note he left. It wasn't about the drugs, it was about ending his life." She again wipes her hands under her eyes, the tears streaking through her makeup.

My heart breaks for her and their son. A tragedy that could have so easily been avoided and right now I can't do anything but blame myself. What if I had come back into his life? Would he be dead right now? Would we have been able to salvage what was lost, correct each other's wrongs and be there for each other? A secret so great, so debilitating that it's ruining lives.

"You need to go, Campbell," she asserts, my name falling from her lips like a swear word, cruel and unforgiving. Her arms are now crossed over her chest and she's ready to close the door.

"I'm sorry," I admit, not entirely sure what I'm apologizing for; the amount of things too large to even list, but they still run through my head. "I hope one day I can find you the closure you need."

She just shakes her head and closes the door.

I never expected her to even speak to me, but to know how things ended for him doesn't make it any easier to cope with. But it makes his letter scream at me loud and clear. What I didn't think I could do, is exactly what I need to. This cycle of death and avoidance can't continue.

I need to find Benji.

Chapter Nine

Despite leaving the office several hours ago, I'm on my way back. This whole situation has spiraled faster than I could have imagined and I'm now going to need more than just today to sort it all out.

I know I have a million things on my calendar over the next week, so I'm returning to take care of handing off clients and making sure meetings that are scheduled have someone present.

As soon as I step off the elevator, Claire greets me with a series of missed calls and all the information I asked her to pull regarding my clients and closings I have over the next three days. I can't put these off and I know, without my presence, there's a possibility things won't go the way I planned.

Jack put me in charge of these clients because they are some of the most difficult. But as much as this has consumed my life, I can't let it deter me from taking time off to find Benji.

A few minutes after I arrive Jack is in my office and I'm handing off all the information to him. The conversation is completely professional and Jack has yet to bring up our little stray from the norm and my admission of Tommy's suicide.

"How long do you think you'll be gone?" he asks as he's leaving my office.

I don't answer him right away because I have no idea. It could be a day or two or it could be a week. I haven't been in contact with Benji since I left school so I have no idea where he's living or how he'll respond to any of this once I find him.

"I guess as of right now, just a few days, but it could be longer." I pause and look up at Jack. I can tell he's struggling to not ask me any more questions and for that I'm thankful. I've told him more than I planned already.

"Just keep me posted," he says as an uneasy look forms on his face. "And Campbell?" he adds.

"Yeah, Jack?"

"Be safe. Call me if you need anything."

I raise my eyebrows at him and give him a small smile. "No worries, Jack. I'll be just fine." I try to reassure him, although I know my life isn't in danger, I'm still not certain what lies ahead.

He's now standing in the doorway to my office, his eyes focused on mine. "You haven't been fine in a really long time."

What am I supposed to say to that? It's the truth, but again, acknowledging it is somehow admitting too much.

When I don't respond, he gives me a quick nod and leaves my office. I breathe a sigh of relief and get down to the other reason I came back to my office.

It's about time I find Benji. Nine years apart and while I now realize it's something I should've done a long time ago, I just wasn't ready to confront that part of my life. I'm still not sure I am now.

I start simple by typing his name into Google, but I come up short almost immediately. Finding only a few old news articles from high school when he played hockey and some information on his enrollment at Ann Arbor. I try several different searches, but still come up with nothing. No information on him since basically after the accident. This shouldn't surprise me. I did the same thing. I disappeared for at least four years and it wasn't until I started working for Jack that my name began to appear in internet searches.

As ridiculous as it sounds, I ran searches on myself fairly regularly, because of the fear that all of this would at some point come back to haunt my life and not just through nightmares.

We left the scene of an accident, lied to the police and then all but disappeared. I was waiting for that moment when they showed up looking for me. It has yet to happen and there are times that I find relief in the fact that it's been nine years, but then again, I worry. I wonder why we were never questioned more than on just the day that the police showed up to tell us Sam was found dead. It never extended beyond that day.

After an hour of searching and finding nothing, I open up a program we use to research companies and clients before we decide to start the process of purchasing a business. If Benji works for a large corporation his name will instantly ping back to me. At the time I left, Benji was majoring in computer science and instructional technology, so if he graduated, it wouldn't be all that unrealistic to think he'd be working for a large business.

But again, nothing is returned and I'm beginning to grow frustrated. So I use the one last resource I have and I call in a favor.

"Working late?" Max says in the way of a greeting when he answers his phone.

"Hey Max," I respond. "Sorta. I need a favor."

"Oh course, Campbell. What do you need?"

Max is the private investigator the company contracts out to do all the research we're unable to do using the software Jack purchased to do background checks. The trouble is, he'll bill Jack for this little search I'm about to have him conduct and I don't want him to start questioning me again. It's just another lie I'll have to spin in order to keep everything quiet. Although I'm used to lies at this point; it's not like telling the truth now will suddenly right everything I've done wrong.

"Well, I need you to find someone for me, but I need you to bill me. Not Jack," I add at the end rather quickly.

"Okay, so this is something personal then, huh?"

"Yeah," I answer, but don't elaborate.

"Campbell," he states as if he can sense my hesitation. "I'm a private investigator. My job is to investigate people privately." He says this last part with a little humor to his tone, but turns serious again rather quickly. "And that's not just for the people I'm investigating, but also for the people I'm working for. Whatever you need is between you and me."

I exhale hard and realize I had been holding my breath. This whole thing makes me uneasy. Asking someone for help is not something I'm used to doing especially given what I'm asking him to investigate. I have no idea what he will come up with or if any of it will link back to the accident or to me or to all of us.

"Thank you. If you wouldn't mind, just bill me at my home address. I'll text it to you when we get off the phone."

"No problem. Let me just get some information from you and I'll get started right away," Max says and I can hear him shuffling through some papers before he tells me what he needs. "So, I'll need a first and last name, a date of birth and if possible a last known address."

I give Max all the information he's requested including the last known address. Sam and Benji's address for their apartment in Ann Arbor is still fresh in my memory like it was just yesterday that they lived there. And when I said his name, Benjamin Kennedy, a small chill ran through my body, nervousness mixed with uncertainty and sadness. It's been years since I've said his full name, but every year when his birthday comes around I feel myself grow desperate for all those days I've missed with him.

"Thanks, Campbell," Max says, but it's me who should be thanking him, given he's the one keeping this whole thing a secret. "When do you need this information by?"

"As soon as possible," I tell Max before adding, "And really, all I need is an address or a phone number of where I can find him."

"That's easy," he brags and it makes me laugh a little.

"Oh, Max, it's a good thing I like you or your conceitedness would be a real turn off."

"Funny, Campbell," he jokes. "If I didn't have a girlfriend I'd find your sarcasm and bitchiness a turn on." I giggle a little at Max's lame attempt at a joke and I hear him chuckle along with me. It's been a while since I've laughed and it feels good. I almost forget why I called Max in the first place. But the reason is back almost immediately and I lose that feeling of happiness, my smile fading. I hate what this whole thing has done to my life.

"Later, Max, and thanks again for your help."

I spend the next few hours answering emails and preparing to take a few days off; leaving everything in order for Claire and Jack. As much as I like to believe I'm organizing all of this to make things easier on them, it's a distraction of sorts to keep me from thinking about what Max is currently doing. I doubt he'll get back to me today, but I'm holding out hope that he will. Something in me needs this information, even if I do nothing with it. There's a need that is driving me to find out if Benji is safe, if he's still alive and if he has moved on with his life. Even though I know I won't get this information from Max, just knowing I have a contact number or an address for him might help me relax. After Tommy's death and knowing there are only two of us left, I can't lose him too.

The hours pass slowly and I run out of things to do at work and leave around seven-thirty. Again, wasting time and trying to distract myself, I stop off at a deli near my house and pick up dinner. The guy behind the counter eyes me suspiciously as I order enough food for five people.

"And I'll have a piece of that cheesecake," I say and he gives me a curt nod, adding it to my exorbitant amount of food. I've spent the last few evenings drunk and the subsequent morning hungover. I'm hoping this ridiculous amount of food keeps me from drinking myself to sleep.

I take the bag and leave with the judgmental eyes of the clerk watching me and it takes everything in me not to tell him to mind his own fucking business.

But by the time I arrive home, I've lost my appetite. It's been six hours since I first spoke to Max, and while I've told myself not to expect anything from him, I'm desperate for him to get back to me.

As the time passes, I begin to worry and my mind begins to wander to really horrible scenarios. I worry that Benji is dead and I've missed my opportunity. My chance to mend the way things ended and now I will find myself alone with this secret and the guilt of what we've done.

But then I think about the letter. Would Tommy have asked me to find Benji if he didn't already know he was alive and well? I hope that he wouldn't have led me to find him, only to be upset by his death too. I really need to stop focusing on this because all these made up situations make things so much worse.

So instead of worrying about Benji, I begin to worry about what Max might find about him, about us. Is there anything that will show up that will link us back to the accident? Is there something only the authorities are privy to that will implicate us in a crime, a crime we committed but won't admit to? Was what we did even a crime?

Just as my thoughts begin to get out of hand, my phone vibrates on the coffee table and it almost makes me scream out loud.

I see Max's name lighting up the screen and in a near panic I grab for it. My breath already coming hard and fast as the nervousness takes control of my body and although my stomach is empty, I've grown nauseous. The phone feels heavy in my slick hands as my palms sweat and I worry I might drop it.

"Hello," I answer, but my voice doesn't sound like my own and apparently Max feels the same way.

"I'm looking for Campbell Forester," he says, a small amount of confusion lingering in his voice.

"Hi, Max. It's me," I say, trying to gain some composure. "I'm guessing you have some information for me. At least I hope you do," I add.

"Yeah, I do and sorry it took me so long to get back to you. This was a tough one."

And now the nausea has settled as a tight knot in my stomach, heavy and painful. Why the fuck would finding Benji be hard?

I've grown silent and I realize it when I hear Max call my name. "Campbell?" he questions.

"Yeah, sorry. Thanks, I didn't think I would hear back from you tonight," I say, swallowing hard as I pray my hands stop shaking and I don't vomit on the spot.

"No problem. So like I was saying, there's very little information about this Benjamin Kennedy after 2006," he says and again I stop listening to him. That was the year of the accident and from the little bit of information Max has told me, evidently I wasn't the only one to disappear. I know he didn't come back to Chicago to live with his mom; our paths would've crossed at some point.

"Were you able to find anything?"

"Have a little faith, Cam," Max says and my heart sinks to the ground. He couldn't possibly know I hate to be called Cam, but that doesn't mean it doesn't sting. I feel the first tear roll down my cheek and I suck in a ragged breath. I can't start crying while I'm on the phone with Max. "So, I wasn't able to find a home address for him or a listed phone number and in today's age, that's really odd. But what I did find is that he owns a custom carpentry and furniture store in Hessel, Michigan. It's in the UP, the upper peninsula, about eight hours from here; a small tourist and fishing town on the lake."

I let out a sigh of relief, grateful that he's not dead and while I don't have an address, the business information will do. If it's in fact his company, I should be able to find him there.

"Thanks, Max. You got a name and an address for this place?"

"Yep. It's CB Custom Carpentry and Furniture and it's a rural route, which means it's pretty much in the middle of nowhere." He lists off the address and I quickly jot it down along with the name of the company. "And Campbell," Max adds, "I don't know what you need this info for, but be careful if you're heading up there alone. It's a long drive and it's pretty desolate, especially since tourist season is over."

"Thanks for your concern, Max, but I'll be okay," I respond knowing I'm going to be anything but okay when I finally find Benji. "And don't forget to bill me and not the company," I remind him.

"Got it."

"Thanks again, Max. I really appreciate you getting back to me tonight."

After I hang up, I stare down at the name and the address, it finally hitting me that I have a choice to make. Up until my phone rang, I had been torn on what I should do, but seeing it in front of me, side by side with Tommy's letter, I know I'll be heading up to Hessel, Michigan.

Wherever the fuck that is.

Although it's late, I start packing. If it's as far as Max said, then I'm going to need to get an early start and I definitely won't be back in the same day. I toss a few pairs of jeans and a couple of sweaters into my suitcase knowing the weather will be far colder than it is here. And as I open my underwear drawer, I find myself choosing some of my nicest lingerie because I'm totally going to strip off my clothes the moment I see him. *What the fuck am I thinking?*

He's never going to see me in my underwear and the last thing I need him to know is that I'm still in love with him. All of this makes this idea to find him seem completely insane. I'm insane.

But, despite all my crazy thoughts; the fear, the hurt, the anger and the guilt, all returning, I'm also met with an overwhelming desire to remember what it feels like to fall in love with him, to be in love with him.

It's been so long since I've slept well, but tonight I drift off to sleep almost instantly.

Chapter Ten

For the first time in weeks, I wake up with my alarm, a quiet peaceful feeling as the music plays softly. I slept straight through the night. No nightmares, no tossing and turning, no insomnia. And even though I know I have more that lies ahead in this fucked up mess that has been created, I find a calm in knowing that Benji is okay.

I guess the term 'okay' is relative because of what we've been through, neither of us could ever be classified as okay compared to normal standards. But in my eyes, him being alive is as okay as I need right now.

As I'm dragging my suitcase into the living room, the front door opens and in steps Carson. His face is completely unreadable and this is definitely something I wasn't prepared for.

"Hey, you going somewhere?" he asks, and I can tell by his tone that he's not here to have a casual chat with me.

"Yeah," I respond, even though I know he's going to push for more.

"You going to give me anymore than that?" he questions, his hands on his hips, as he shoots me an angry glare.

"No, probably not," I retort, knowing this relationship is long over, and it's all about to come to a head.

"Campbell, if you walk out of here without telling me where you're going we're done!" he shouts at me as if I'm a small child being scolded.

"We've been done for a while now, Carson; don't tell me you're just noticing that now?" I ask condescendingly, and I can tell it pisses him off.

Slamming the door shut behind him, he storms past me and into the bedroom. Following him, I find him pulling his clothes from the drawers and closet in an angry rage.

"I don't know what the fuck I ever did to you for you to treat me like this," he seethes, muttering as he continues grabbing his things from the closet. He turns and shoots me a dirty look, like everything that has ever gone wrong in our relationship is my fault. "You've been emotionally unavailable from the day we met. Like a fucking ice queen," he spits out, and it pisses me off.

While I know I've been all of these things and more, I don't deserve to have it thrown back in my face, to have him chastise me for a situation he chose to stay in.

"Why'd you stay?" I ask, my tone harsh.

"Beats the fuck out of me!" he screams as he pushes past me to get a garbage bag from the kitchen. When he returns, he begins stuffing his clothes in and I roll my eyes at the whole situation. He's being overly dramatic.

"You don't have to pack all your stuff now," I tell him. He whips around to look at me, his eyes wide and his face red. "I'm leaving and you can stay and pack your things."

"How fucking sweet of you," he hisses. "Now that it's over, you've decided to think about me for once, you self-absorbed bitch."

"Okay, Carson," I say, raising my voice. "That's enough. I get it, you're pissed, but you're not going to come into my home and call me a bitch. Get your shit and leave."

I'd be lying if I said his words didn't hurt. No one likes to be hated by someone and the fact that I've just been confronted by Carson and knowing I'm about to confront Benji, both people who I left hurt and confused, this day hasn't started off really well.

He laughs and it's condescending and rude. "See, that's where this all went wrong. I moved in with you. This was our house, but it's always been about you."

"Fine, whatever," I say detaching myself from this conversation. "Just get your stuff and leave."

I watch him haul the garbage bag full of clothes toward the front door, dropping it, before he heads back into the kitchen for another.

"And by the way," he says, his eyes glaring at me. "I didn't stay with John. I stayed with Allison, and I fucked her too."

My mouth falls open involuntarily and I cover it with my hand as I step away from him. While I was never in love with Carson, I never expected him to cheat on me. I'm sure there are people out there who would say I got what I deserved and maybe that's true, but it hurts just the same.

He laughs again and I look away from him not wanting him to see the hurt that is written all over my face.

"Finally, you show some emotion, but you'll always be a heartless bitch."

"Get out!" I scream so loudly my throat aches. "Get out now!"

Carson turns around, leaving the empty garbage bag on the floor; he grabs the other one by the door and starts to leave.

"Wait," I call after him and when he turns around, I swear I see a small amount of desperation in his eyes, like he hopes I'm going to ask him to stay. He's fucked up if he thinks that would ever happen. "Leave your key. I'll ship the rest of your stuff to your sister's."

"Fuck you," he spits out as he throws his key at me.

As the door slams shut, I stand staring at it shocked and silent. That's the last thing I expected to happen and to know he cheated on me is like a punch to the stomach. This world is full of lies, my life is a lie and everything I've created up until this point is a lie. I stand caught somewhere between reality and a living nightmare that I need to end.

So I do what I do best, I shake it off and act like this isn't happening, that this isn't my life and things aren't falling apart around me. It's all coming undone and I know it, but I don't even know how to fix it.

I grab Tommy's letter and shove it into the pocket of my coat before gathering my things and heading out to my car.

I guess I'm really going to do this… and I'm terrified.

Just before the nine-hour mark, I pull into the deserted town of Hessel, Michigan. A quaint little place, but as I drive through the town, I notice nothing is open; everything is completely shut down.

"Awesome," I mumble, as my suspicions from earlier are confirmed. As I approached the town, I had the GPS run a search for hotels in the area and the closest it came up with was about thirty miles from here. I figured it couldn't possibly be right, but I was so wrong.

If you want to disappear, this is the place.

I look at the GPS as it continues to navigate me to the address where Benji's company is located; I find the map, nearly blank. An endless sea of green and blue and one single road leading out of town. Wonderful, even the GPS has no idea where I'm going.

But as I follow the road, which eventually turns to gravel, I see a large sign stating "CB Custom Carpentry and Furniture next right." I take the first turn and there it is; a huge pole barn set back off the road along with a small shop out in front. I pull in, but find it as deserted as the town. Not a light on, not that there's any light out here at all. It's pitch black and without my headlights, I wouldn't be able to see my hand in front of my face.

I climb out of the car and approach the building, looking through the large glass window in front, I see no one inside, but the shop is filled with some of the most beautiful furniture I've ever seen.

But suddenly scared of the dark and the unknown of this little town, I scamper back to my car wondering just how the hell I'm going to find him. I could drive another thirty miles, find a hotel, head back here tomorrow and hope he happens to be working. Not that I have any other options.

Going back the way I came, my stomach growls and I realize I haven't eaten anything but a package of Zingers I picked up at a gas station. I'm starving and this isn't the kind of town where a McDonald's is going to pop up. I swear out loud, cursing the stupidity of small towns and their lack of all the things I'm used to.

While the town is empty, I do find a bar that is open and I pull into the parking lot. When I walk in the response is exactly what I expected. The five guys who are sitting at the bar all turn and look at me and then look at each other. The bartender stops what he's doing, his eyes immediately gravitating to where I'm standing.

He's much younger than I expected and quite cute, actually. I guess I assumed that with a small deserted bar in the middle of nowhere came a grumpy old man working behind it. This whole finding Benji thing possibly just got a little easier. He flashes me a smile and as if he suddenly realizes he's forgotten his manners, he greets me.

"Hey, can I help you?" he asks, and I give him a weak smile. But then it hits me: if I've learned anything from my job, it's that flirting with men can get you whatever you want. And I want to find Benji, preferably tonight.

I pull out a chair and sit down at the bar giving the bartender a sweet but totally fake smile.

"Oh my god," I trill. "I've just spent the last nine hours in my car and I'm starving."

"Sorry, but the kitchen's closed," he replies callously.

"Seriously?" I ask, pouting, and when he looks over at me he begins to soften. I shoot him a flirty look and ask, "You sure?"

"I'll see what I can do," he says as he gives me a little smile.

A few minutes later he sets a bowl of chips and salsa down in front of me and tells me he has some potato skins warming up. Bar food, but I guess I can't complain when there's no other choice.

"Thanks, I really appreciate it."

He gives me a quick nod before asking if I'd like anything to drink and I order a cider as he walks away to serve the few guys at the end of the bar.

I'm trying to figure out how to make small talk with this guy when he returns with my cider and opens the conversation perfectly.

"So what are you doing here? You know tourist season is over?"

I giggle a little and nod my head. "Of course I know tourist season is over. I'm looking for Benjamin Kennedy." And when I say his name the bartender stops and looks at me with a cross between curiosity and defensiveness on his face.

"What are you doing looking for Ben?"

Ben? Since when has he gone by Ben? I guess I wouldn't know and I don't dare question it. Instead I start another lie, hoping it's vague enough, yet accurate enough to pull this off. "I ordered some furniture from him and I'm on my way up to Ontario and thought I would stop by and thank him in person." I shrug my shoulders as I take a drink of my cider.

"Nice of you," he says, but gives me nothing else.

"Yeah, so his store is closed already and I'd really like to thank him today, seeing as I'm staying a few towns away. I'd have to back-track and everything tomorrow to get back here."

He waits, not responding, and just when I think this isn't going to work, he says, "He lives about a mile from his shop. It's the only house on the road. You can't miss it."

"Thanks," I say, putting back what's left of my cider in three long drinks. Leaving the chips and salsa, I slip my coat back on with a self-satisfied smile on my face.

"Guess you don't want those potato skins then," he says and it's not a question, but when I look back to answer him, he has a smile on his face. I give him a small wave of my hand as I leave.

It doesn't take nearly as long to find his house as it felt like it did when I was looking for his shop. Being slightly more familiar with the area makes navigating it easier and the fact that his house is lit up like it has a spotlight shining on it helps too.

I pull into his driveway, the gravel scraping noisily under my tires and echoing within the wide expanse of nothing. It couldn't be more obvious that I'm here and probably shouldn't be.

I take one last deep breath and pray that this doesn't go horribly wrong immediately. Suddenly I'm unsure of everything in my life and I'm debating backing out of his driveway and acting like I was never here. But I owe it to Tommy and I couldn't live with myself if I found out something happened to Benji.

Getting out of my car, I stop in front of it and look at his house. It's absolutely beautiful. A massive log cabin with a huge wrap around front porch surrounded by towering pine trees and a star lit sky. Before I have a chance to make my way to his front door, I see him.

He steps out onto the front porch a shotgun in his hand and I laugh a little to myself. He looks completely different: his hair is longer, one side tucked behind his ear; a beard on his face that looks like he's had it since I left him, and his clothes are worn, but for some reason he's still the boy I fell in love with. He's taller and more muscular and I'm sure most people would take one look at him, especially considering he's holding a gun, and leave.

I'm not afraid of him, I never have been.

"What are you going to do? Shoot me, Benji?" I ask, as I approach him.

"Don't call me that," he retorts.

I immediately regret my decision to come here. I'm not sure what I thought would happen; that he would welcome me with open arms and we'd have a heart-felt reunion. Not a fucking chance after the way things ended.

"I shouldn't have come here," I say, turning around as I start to walk back to my car.

"Why did you?" Benji asks, a harshness to his tone. "It's been nine fucking years."

I turn around and face him once again. My hands on my hips ready to have this conversation; one we should've had years ago. "You could've found me."

"You're the one who left."

"You changed," I say back, but my voice comes out as a shout and I feel myself growing defensive.

"So did you," he shouts back, his posture growing stiff as I watch the anger build inside him. Although the gun is resting at his side, he clenches his hand around it tightly, his knuckles turning white.

"It was stupid of me to come here."

"Then leave. Fucking leave, Campbell. Just like you did before." I step back as he yells this time, loudly, so loudly that it echoes in the vast emptiness.

His voice is a growl that startles me; I've never heard him sound so hateful and cruel before, not that I have any idea who he has become. But I like to believe that somewhere behind this man in front of me is the boy I fell in love with.

"Fuck you," I spit out, seething with anger. I slam the car door so hard it shakes everything inside. I tear out of his driveway bound and determined to drive off in a serious fit of rage and show him exactly how pissed off I am, and then I remember I'm almost nine hours from home, it's after eight p.m. and I have no idea where I am.

And there isn't a single fucking hotel in this tiny ass town.

Chapter Eleven

I'm swearing up a storm, as my GPS won't let me search for anything while the car is moving. Stupid fucking computer! I just need to get the hell away from here and everything looks the same in the dark.

I finally come across the bar I was at just a little while ago, and knowing there isn't anything else open, I pull in. I find my location on the GPS and begin to search for hotels, a part of me hoping that maybe it was wrong the two other times I ran this search and suddenly a hotel will appear out of nowhere.

Fat fucking chance.

Same as last time, thirty miles north of here there are a few, so I grab my phone and begin calling, but I'm shot down by all four that are available, which is unbelievable. The first one is hosting a wedding and is completely booked, the second one is filled with construction workers who were placed far from home to work on an oil pipeline that extends from Alaska all the way to the UP, the third no longer exists, and while the fourth had a few rooms, the pictures I found online look like the Bates Motel. No, thank you. As stubborn as I'm being though, it might be my only option.

My stomach growls loudly reminding me that I still haven't eaten. I look at the bar, the lights are still on, but the parking lot is now empty. Letting out a desperate sigh, I exit the car.

When I walk in the bartender is wiping down the counter and he smiles at me, but his eyes are twinkling with mischief. I take a seat on the stool I occupied just a little while ago. He reaches under the bar and pulls out the potato skins, setting them down in front of me.

"For you," he says, and chuckles a little. "I kept them warm." I give him a confused, but grateful look and he adds, "You think you're the first girl to come in here looking for Ben?"

"Guess not," I say, my tone dripping with aggravation. "I'm not other girls," I add, feeling the need to defend myself.

"You came back here looking like all the others. Guessing he pulled the shotgun on you?" He laughs, and shakes his head.

"And then he yelled at me," I say, as the bartender sets another cider down in front of me.

"He yelled at you?" he asks, his tone almost shocked. "That's not like Ben."

"That's because I'm not like other girls. I'm *the* girl."

As if he understands exactly what I'm saying, he slides my cider over and sets a tumbler of scotch down. "I think you're gonna need this instead."

"Thanks. I'm Campbell," I tell him, and something in his expression tells me I didn't need to introduce myself, like he already knows who I am. There's something in the way he looks at me that causes me to grow uneasy, but I still extend my hand across the bar.

"Alex," he says as he takes my hand. "Don't drink too much, there's no place to stay in this town."

"Yeah, I know." I roll my eyes, letting out an annoyed huff, and I begin to eat the lukewarm potato skins.

I put back the scotch rather quickly and immediately down the cider. Fuck Benji and his holier than thou attitude. At least I made the effort to find him. He did fuck all in nine years, but now he wants to put all the blame on me? I don't even know why I came here. I knew this was how it would turn out.

"So tell me, Alex, how'd you end up in this small town?" I ask, trying make small talk and take my mind off the fact that I have no place to go and that I know with certainty that Benji hates me. I'm zero for two when it comes to men, first Carson and now Benji.

"My dad bought this place when he retired from the military. We had a cabin up here for years; used to come for the fishing, and he decided to retire up here. Died a couple of years ago and I took over." He's casual in the way he speaks, like his life is easy, as if he has nothing but time. It makes me think that maybe this small town life isn't so bad. I feel like I never have enough time, my job demanding, and the city always loud and bustling.

"Have a drink with me, Alex," I propose, holding up my empty bottle of cider and he smiles at me.

"Why not?" he says, reaching back and grabbing a bottle of whiskey from behind him. Pouring us both a glass, he smiles at me again and says, "I think you could use some company and just so you know, I don't make a habit of drinking with my customers."

"Awww, I'm flattered, but see, Alex, I'm not a customer. We're friends now and I'm about to drink for free." I take a long swallow and he follows along, both of us putting back our whiskey far sooner than necessary.

"You think so?" he jokes back, as he sets his empty glass on the bar, his tone flirty.

"I know so," I retort, winking at him.

"You're a cheeky girl, Campbell. I can see why Ben's still hung up on you." His words catch me off guard and I cock my head to the side, giving him a questioning look. Next thing I know he's setting a shot down in front of me and the moment has passed.

I hold up my glass, my eyes lingering on him for a long second, a loose, but sad smile on my face, "Here's to new friends," I say, and we put it back together.

An hour passes quickly and I'm far drunker than I planned on getting, but Alex keeps serving them and I keep drinking. He has me laughing so hard at one point that tears stream from my eyes. As much fun as I'm having, I know I still have no place to stay. Benji hates me, and I'm almost nine hours from home.

"You weren't supposed to get me drunk," I say, as a hiccup escapes my mouth and causes Alex to laugh out loud.

"Same goes for you," he says argumentatively, but still playful. I watch him pick up his phone, holding up one finger as if to signal he'll be back, he steps away from the bar.

He returns again with another shot, his face flushed, and is now wearing just a t-shirt and jeans; losing the wool sweater he was originally wearing. He holds up his glass and says, "Last one of the night."

I giggle; I'm too drunk to care that I have no place to sleep tonight. "Cheers!" I slur before adding, "Here's to sleeping in my car!" And Alex lets out a deep laugh that I find terribly adorable. After what happened with Carson and then Benji, it feels good to have a guy just enjoy my company and laugh with me.

In the next second, the door to the bar swings open and Benji is standing there.

I look quickly at him and then to Alex before shouting, "Oh my god, I know him!" My finger is pointing in the direction of where Benji is standing and my words come out a garbled mess, but that doesn't stop Alex from laughing again.

"She's all yours, dude," he says to Benji.

"What the fuck, Alex?" I demand, realizing in this drunken haze that he called Benji to come get me. "I thought we were friends?"

"We are, Campbell, which is why I'm not letting you sleep in your car." He winks at me and Benji scowls at him and after what Alex said, I wonder if Benji is jealous. In the past it was never hard to make him jealous; I always belonged to him.

When I step off the bar stool, I find that I'm far drunker than I thought, I mean I know I'm drunk, but paired with the small amount of food I've eaten today, I'm pretty much shitfaced. I stumble and grab the back of the chair to steady myself and in that instant, Benji's arm slips around my waist, pulling me into his side.

"Come on," he says quietly, and his voice makes me weak. It's been so long since I last heard it and right now it's exactly as I remember. No animosity or uncertainty behind it, just kindness.

"Wait," I practically shout, clinging to Benji's arm for support, I turn to look at Alex. "I need to pay my bar tab." I flash him a wicked grin and he chuckles.

"It's on me," he says, shooing me out the door with a dismissive wave, his smile never fading.

"See, I told you I'd drink for free."

"And I told you, you were cheeky." He tosses a hand up wishing us goodbye as he says, "Good luck to you, Ben. She's a handful."

"Don't I know it," he mutters back as he pulls me in close to him again.

He loosens his grip around my waist when we reach his truck as he opens the door and practically shoves me in.

"What about my car?" I ask, my voice soft as I grow tired.

"Don't worry about your car."

A few minutes later, I feel myself being lifted from the truck; my eyes too heavy to open and I give in without fighting him. With my cheek against his chest and the warmth of his body soothing me, he sets me down on a bed and removes my shoes as I fall back against the pillows.

I feel his hand brush my hair back off my face and he presses a kiss to my forehead. "You can't keep doing this," he whispers and I don't know if he's talking to me or thinking out loud, but something in his words fills me with sadness.

"I'm sorry," I murmur, the tears already spilling from my eyes.

His hand strokes my hair; I feel his lips rest against the top of my head. "Go to sleep, baby," he says, and it's the last thing I remember.

I wake the next morning, the same way I have for a while now with a familiar throbbing headache that seems to have become a part of my daily routine. The difference this morning is that I'm calmed by the smell of cedar and cinnamon and a beautiful silence. There aren't any honking horns, sirens, or the background noise of cars passing on the street. The sun is peeking through the slats in the blinds as it warms the already comfortable room, and for a brief moment I forget where I am and what happened last night. It's like I woke up in someone else's life and it's perfect.

But as soon as I sit up, I'm reminded of exactly what happened yesterday and like the last nine years, it's a shit show.

I had a screaming match with Carson that led him to admit he cheated on me. Then a screaming match with Benji that led to me getting drunk and now I'm waking up with a brutal hangover.

The house is quiet, so I slip out of bed wearing nothing but a t-shirt and my underwear. But before leaving the bedroom, I call Benji's name and get no response. Part of me is relieved because with the way I'm feeling right now, I'm not sure I'm up for an argument. Yet I'm disappointed because just seeing his beautiful face yesterday brought back a surge of memories and reminders of how much I truly miss him.

I hate feeling this way, torn and confused. I don't even know where to begin or how after nine years of being apart, that I'm even going to be able to fix any of this.

I drag myself into the kitchen, my bare feet cold against the wood floor and I stop dead in my tracks when I see what is sitting on the kitchen island.

A chocolate donut, a bottle of grape Gatorade and two aspirin, along with a note that reads:

C-

Had to go to work. Stay as long as you need.

-B

I read the note over and over, searching for something in it that gives any indication that he still cares, that he doesn't hate me. I guess him remembering what I like to eat in the morning when I wake up with a hangover is a slight indicator and it makes me smile a little.

I walk around his house, and it is unreal. A huge log cabin with cathedral ceilings and exposed beams; it smells amazing and everything about it looks like it was taken directly from a magazine. I look out the massive floor to ceiling windows at the back of the house, taking in the towering pines and the small pond: the landscape like a picture.

I sit down in an oversized leather chair that looks out on to it all as I finish my donut and Gatorade. And in a moment of sheer blissfulness I let myself believe I live here...with Benji.

An hour later, I'm showered and dressed, my suitcase somehow managed to get back here with me and I'm sure I have Benji to thank for that. I'm feeling a little better and as I step outside onto the large wrap around front porch, I find my car sitting in the driveway.

I could leave and never look back, but that's not why I came here. And despite being terrified to confront everything from our past, it needs to be done. But how do I even begin?

I can see Benji's shop at the end of the gravel road. It's about a mile away and I could drive, but I decide to walk it, hoping the cold air will clear my head. And maybe, just maybe, it will give me some insight on what the fuck to do next.

Chapter Twelve

Turns out I was wrong; the walk was just cold and windy. Being in the middle of nowhere didn't give me nearly the clarity I thought it would and now I'm just nervous as hell to meet up with Benji, sober and defenseless. I thought after all this time he still wouldn't have this affect on me, but the moment I saw his face last night, heard his voice, it was like I was eighteen again. I'd do anything to belong to him. But even more, I'd do anything to forget what destroyed us.

I'm standing outside of his shop, the store is dark, but I can see light radiating from under the door of the pole barn. Up against the silence of my brain, I try to come up with something to say to him, but like everything else that has to do with these last nine years, the accident and the guilt I feel over it all, nothing forms.

My hand on the door, I close my eyes and pull it open, sort of praying he isn't armed with a shotgun again. While I knew he wouldn't shoot me, the whole thing was slightly unnerving.

The barn is far bigger than I imagined and Benji is near the back sanding what looks like a dining room table. His chin length brown hair is hanging down in his eyes as he sits on a stool in a pair of worn out jeans and a white t-shirt. And fuck me if he doesn't look incredibly hot. So hot in fact, I feel my face flush at the thought. I don't even know what's wrong with me. This is not what this is about. This is not why I'm here.

I open my mouth to speak, but he silences me as his voice echoes in the large room. "I didn't hear your car," he says, never looking up or stopping what he's doing.

"I walked."

He looks over at me, giving me a quick once over and shakes his head a little. "You cold?" he asks.

"A little," I admit, rubbing my hands together. "My feet are freezing," I confess almost immediately. "Actually, I'm really fucking cold."

Although he isn't looking at me I can see a faint smile on his face. He waits a second and then sets the sanding block down. "Come here," he says and for a minute I have to make sure I've heard him correctly, but when he signals with his head, I walk over slowly.

I stop about a foot away from him and he turns on his stool so he's facing me. Before I even realize what's happening, his hand reaches out and rests on my hip, his fingers pressing into my butt as he pulls me closer so I'm standing between his legs. I swear to god I'm going to fucking melt into the floor. My heart begins racing in my chest and I hope with everything in me that he can't see how I'm reacting to his touch, what being this close to him again is doing to me. Then he takes both my hands in his, bends his head down and lets out a long slow breath into our cupped hands, and I know I'm going to fucking die right now.

I feel his hot breath against my cold skin as he breathes into our joined hands several more times. Goose bumps line my skin and I feel my entire body start to tingle. Despite his hands being wrapped around mine, mine are trembling. It takes everything in me not to take his face in my hands and kiss him. Hard.

But in that instant, he drops my hands and asks, "Better?"

I can't even form a coherent sentence so I just nod my head and step away from him, nearly stumbling backward, knowing if I don't move I'll do something both of us will regret.

"If you're still cold," he says, returning to his work, "there's a blanket on the table over there." His eyes looking up briefly to indicate where I should look for the blanket, but then as if he's unsure of what he's just said, he adds, "That is if you want to stay."

"Do you want me to?" I ask, not meaning for it to sound smug, but that's exactly how it comes out. I almost shake my head at my own stupidity.

He lets out a huff and sets the sanding block down. "What are you doing here, Campbell?" he asks, returning to the Benji I confronted last night, a sudden irritation to his tone and his eyes almost glaring at me.

"Your work is beautiful," I toss out there hoping to change the subject and avoid telling him why I'm here. I'm honestly not sure why I'm here; there are so many reasons and suddenly all of them seem invalid. Idiotic. I shouldn't have come here.

"Thanks," he says after a long second and I finally breathe out. "I don't do a lot of local business once tourist season is over. The store is closed until spring." While he's at least talking to me, the conversation is still awkward and it makes me hate what these nine years apart have done to us.

There were times we could talk for hours without a lull in the conversation or just sit in silence, yet it was never uncomfortable—companionable and comforting. I miss it. I miss him and what we had.

"So what do you do during the off season?" I ask, even though it feels like I'm forcing a conversation.

"There's an online component to the business. I ship nationwide and take custom orders through it. There are times that it does better than the retail store because I can reach a wider clientele."

Talking about his work and his business seems to ease the tension, like talking about something that isn't linked to the two of us and our past, is safe.

"Wow," I say, and he smiles at me. It's that perfect heart-stopping smile I can remember as far back as age five. He's always been beautiful and nothing about that has changed. He might look rugged and scruffy now, but underneath it all are the shining blues eyes of a boy I fell in love with long ago.

"How about you?" he asks and I can't help but notice him subtly glance at my left hand. "You seem to be doing well for yourself. A Mercedes?" he says, as he tosses his head in the direction of his house.

"I'm an investor. Well, actually, I research failing companies and purchase them at a loss and hopefully turn a profit after restructuring. It's quite lame, honestly." Benji looks up at me, his eyes holding my mine for a split second before I begin to grow nervous and awkwardly interject, "I work for Jack."

At this comment Benji literally laughs out loud. "You work for Jack? Your brother?" The whole exchange makes me smile, and the nervousness I feel slowly begins to fade.

"Yep. It's his company, so he's actually the investor, the money end of it. I just make him the money."

He shakes his head and the tension between us eases as a light smile forms on his face. "Never thought you'd work for Jack," he says chuckling a little.

"Yeah, I know. Neither did I. But he's not too bad to work for." I find myself pulling a stool over so I can sit down near where Benji is working.

"As a brother, he's still a douche bag," I add, and again Benji laughs out loud.

"Guess some things never change."

"Yeah," I say, and the room falls silent again. Both of us are not sure what to say and I don't know what comes over me, but I lean across the table and place my hand on the side of his face, my fingers brushing softly against his beard.

"This looks good on you," I say, but my voice comes out in a hushed whisper and I feel him lean into my hand. And when his hand covers mine, I step off the stool until I'm standing in front of him. His other hand instinctively moves to my hip and I step even closer and like before, I'm standing between his legs. But this time he stands and I can feel the warmth radiating from his body. Our breathing grows labored and I realize my hands are now clutching his t-shirt, while his other hand is now gripping the back of my neck. If his hands weren't on my body right now, I'd have fallen to the floor.

He presses his face to the curve of my neck. My eyes close slowly and I almost moan out loud. I've missed what he does to my body, the way he makes me feel. I miss everything about him.

"God, Campbell," he whispers, but it's strained. Like he's struggling to control himself.

When he pulls back, I know I'm crying and it's the last thing I should be doing. I don't want him to feel sorry for me.

He cups my cheek and wipes away a stray tear with his thumb before pressing a kiss to my forehead. "I have to get back to work," he states, but it's almost as if he says it because he knows what we're doing here will lead to more than either of us are ready to confront.

"Okay, I'll go," I respond, turning toward the door, but his next words stop me.

"Alex usually brings me lunch in about a half an hour. You could go pick it up. Save him the trouble."

"Alex, my new best friend?" I ask mockingly and Benji grins at me.

"Yep. He's everyone's best friend." And again the tension in the room diminishes. "So, what do you think? Have lunch with me?"

"Of course."

I'd never turn him down.

He hands me the keys to his truck and shoots me a threatening look. "Take it easy, okay? I watched you back out of my driveway last night."

"I can walk back and get my own car," I retort, pretending to be insulted as I give him a dirty look.

"Just go get our lunch," he quips back, winking at me before returning to sanding the table.

I walk into the bar and Alex is nowhere to be seen. There's a girl about my age behind the counter and she gives me a quick look and returns back to what she was doing, before her head springs back up quickly and she greets me with a smile.

"Hi, sorry about that. I just figured you were one of the regulars. What can I help you with?" She has a sweet voice, soothing and calm, and the way she greets me makes me feel as if she doesn't normally greet customers like this.

"Hi. I'm here to pick up an order for Benji," I say and she gives me a look that says she has no idea what I'm talking about.

Luckily Alex, who comes from the back of the bar, saves me and I realize I called him Benji, which clearly is no longer the name he uses.

"Campbell," he says, his voice a mix of playfulness and questioning. "I didn't think I'd see you before at least noon." He looks over at the girl behind the bar and she raises her eyebrows. "Sorry," he says, and looks back over to me. "I guess you've met my lovely wife."

"Not exactly," I say, and she laughs a little. "Guess her lovely husband forgot to introduce us."

"Campbell, this is Annie," he says, pulling her close and kissing the top of her head. She's a tiny little thing with gorgeous blonde hair and Alex towers over her, making her look even smaller.

"Ah," she says, her eyes wide. "You're Campbell." She looks up at Alex and he shakes his head almost imperceptibly as if to tell her not to do what he thinks she's going to do, and the cynical, private person I've become immediately thinks the worst. After meeting Alex yesterday, obviously Benji has talked about me. The thought has me worried to the point that my heart begins to race. How much has he told them? I've never told anyone what happened with us. It's always been a secret I assumed stayed with all of us. Never to be spoken of again.

I can tell almost right away that they notice a change in my demeanor. I can't help but let my thoughts runaway with what happened nine years ago. All of it focused on my concern with anyone knowing exactly what happened and what we did. Would he have told them? Both Kelly and Tommy died with our secret; we're all that's left of this mess.

I can feel their eyes on me and not that I have a reason to turn defensive, but I still do. "I'm just here to pick up lunch," I say, my tone suddenly formal.

"Okay," Annie says, again looking up at Alex, both with looks on their faces that seem far too suspecting for me. "I'll get that for you." She disappears and Alex gives me a weak smile.

"Everything alright?" he asks, and it almost feels like he's feeling me out to see if I realize what is going on.

"Yeah."

A few seconds later Annie returns with a large bag and walking around the bar, she hands it to me.

"Here you go," she says, smiling at me despite the severe look on my face.

"Thanks," I tell her, but it comes across cold.

When I climb into Benji's truck, I'm immediately pissed off. I hate the fact that my past has turned me into a paranoid bitch.

It only takes about ten minutes to reach Benji's shop and by then, my anger is through the roof and about to be directed at the only person whom I believe honestly deserves it.

I storm through the door, but Benji's lost in his work. He doesn't see or hear me until I toss the bag of food onto the table in front of him. He stops what he's doing and as soon as he sees my face the realization that something is wrong hits him. He doesn't even have a chance to ask.

"You fucking told them!" I scream, and the confused look on his face only adds to my rage. "I can't fucking believe you!"

I don't give him time to respond. Leaving him confused and speechless, I start walking back to his house.

I'm hurt and angry, as tears prick my eyes and run down my cheeks. The cold air hits me in the face, making my nose run and my tears dry almost immediately. I don't care what he has to say. It might have been nine years ago, but we all agreed to keep everything a secret. I used to think he was different, that out of all the horrible people in the world, he was perfect. He was my perfection. But he's a liar too.

Chapter Thirteen

"Campbell!" Benji screams, and it reverberates in every direction, nothing to stop the sound from carrying. There's nothing but emptiness.

I can hear his feet crunching on the gravel of the road as he tries to catch up to me. My mind is begging me to get away from him and all the feelings that seeing him brought out in me. I can't deal with any of this.

He screams my name once again, his voice unnaturally loud and for a second I'm actually frightened thinking about what all of this means. Am I scared of him? Scared of what we've done or the fact that someone else now knows? It's become too much.

I suck in a deep breath, the cold air rushing into my lungs and making them burn, but I don't stop walking.

I know he's getting closer, my body can sense his closeness and I begin to cry even harder when I feel his hand grab my elbow. Spinning me around, his fingers tighten on my arm, not allowing me to pull away.

"No! You don't get to do this!" he yells, his fingers digging into my skin despite the fact that I'm wearing a coat. "You don't get to show up here and remind me of everything all over again!" His face is red and his breaths are coming hard and fast as I watch his chest heave with each word. "You don't get to run away again, Campbell!"

"Let go of me!" I shriek, pulling away from him, but he never loosens his grip. I struggle against him and by now I'm sobbing. "You told them!" I scream and he finally drops my arm. There's a look of shock on his face and I almost want to believe what comes out of his mouth next.

"I haven't told anyone. I've never told anyone," he says shaking his head, a desperate plea to his words.

"Fuck you!" I scream and it's loud and booming, but it doesn't stop him as I walk away.

"Campbell! Stop! Now!" And I can hear him jog to catch up to me. This time both of his hands clutch my upper arms. "You're not running away from me. We're going to talk about this." By now he's stopped yelling, but our anger is still very much real.

"I don't want to talk about it!" I yell in his face, and again it does nothing to shake his composure or his hold on me.

"I don't care if you don't want to. We have to!" he screams back, his breath coming out in short bursts, the air so cold each one is a puff of white. "I'm not letting you walk away. You don't get to disappear again," he says, but now his voice has turned quiet, a near whisper, almost lost in the air and the openness. "It will kill me, Campbell. It will ruin what is left of us."

I swallow hard at his words, unsure of what to do or say and for a moment I don't have to think about it. Benji's lips crash into mine, hard and desperate and just their touch causes a whimper to leave my mouth.

I melt into his body, as our kiss turns soft, my hands running up the hard muscles of his arms until I'm holding on so tightly, like I'm scared he'll disappear. When his lips leave mine, I almost cry out in protest. He pulls back slightly, his forehead resting against mine, but I can't bring myself to open my eyes. This all feels like a dream and I nearly forget all the awfulness that surrounds us and why I'm even here in the first place, especially when he whispers, "I've missed you so fucking much, Campbell."

"I've missed you too," I stutter out, my admittance more honest than I've been in years.

"This is far from over, but right now I'm starving," Benji says and it makes me laugh despite being furious with him only minutes ago. "It's freezing out, your nose is so cold," he says shuddering dramatically, "and I'm not wearing a coat. So let's take this back inside."

He motions with his head toward the barn as he starts walking. I fall in line next to him, but fight the urge to link my arm with his or hold his hand. As much as I want to fall back into our old habits, we aren't the same people. If anything, I'm more fucked up right now than I have ever been in my life.

I hear him take in a deep breath before he lets it out slowly. I look over at him as he runs his hand through his hair and says, "I know you're finding it hard to believe me, but I never told anyone what happened."

I nod my head unable to respond because a part of me knows what he says is the truth. I think I used to like to believe that who he became after the accident was who he really is. But the truth is, we all became someone else; we all fell apart. We all became liars and secret keepers, bitter, jaded and lost, and I'm not sure we can ever go back to the people we were.

Although we both agreed to talk about what just happened, neither of us broaches the subject. At first we eat in silence and then the conversation turns casual as if we're two people just getting to know each other. And in a way, I guess we are.

"Where are you living now?" Benji asks.

"I'm in the city, in Lakeview," I tell him, and he widens his eyes.

"Swanky."

"Oh, like you have any room to talk. Look at your house."

"There's a story behind that," he says casually, like it's insignificant.

"I'd love to hear it, Ben," I say, and he smirks at my use of his name but doesn't comment.

"I'd love to hear more about you," he says, and it makes my heart flutter in my chest.

I begin to chew my lip, nervous about what he might ask. There really isn't much to tell considering I tried to be as invisible as possible after the accident.

"You finish school?" he asks, although I can sense some hesitation in his voice.

"I did. After…" I trail off realizing I was about to say after the accident. My life is measured in before the accident and after the accident, a time when things were good and a time when my whole world went dark. "I finished up at DePaul and then went to work for Jack right away." I don't want to talk about myself, because the more I tell him, the more he's going to figure out that I've spent the last nine years depressed, lonely and guilt-ridden. "How about you?" I ask. "You finish school?"

"I did," he says, pausing as if he's about to reveal something he's not entirely sure about. "I finished abroad. Met a girl and followed her to Sydney."

"Australia?" I question, as I think about exactly how far that is from Michigan—a completely different continent, a different world, a million miles from everything.

"Yep, the land of Oz. I met her after you…" It's him who trails off now and I wonder if he measures his life in befores and afters. "I needed a change, so I went with her. It didn't last," he adds, quickly looking away from me as he runs his hand through his hair. "She's was the only relationship since you," he suddenly says, and his confession breaks my already shattered heart.

He looks back at me as if he's waiting for a response, waiting for me to admit something too.

"I was living with someone until just recently. It didn't work out," I share rather quickly. I can feel this conversation leading in a direction that will possibly have both of us screaming at each other and me crying again. I can't keep doing this.

"I'm not really feeling that great. I think I'm going to head back and take some more aspirin." It all comes out in a rush, almost too quickly to understand, and I don't wait for Benji to respond before I start for the door.

"Will you be there when I get home?" he asks, and I can hear a small cry of desperation in his voice.

"Do you want me to be?"

"Yes," he says, but it comes out as plea as if he knows I'm thinking about leaving.

"Okay," I tell him, my eyes locking on his and he smiles.

"Good. And Campbell?" he says, "Take my truck. I'll walk back."

"Thanks, Benji, but I kinda want to walk."

"Then at least take my coat," he says, motioning to a hook by the door. Just as I'm about to protest, he smiles again and this time it stops me, a reminder of how beautiful he really is. He's absolutely gorgeous and I almost miss his words when he says, "Don't be a stubborn pain in the ass, Campbell."

I smile back at him and take his coat from the hook. As soon as I put it on, I'm hit with a smell that I'll never forget.

Benji.

Yet with the smell, returns the memories of all the things I love and everything I hate.

It's not my house, but it doesn't take me long to get comfortable in it. The next thing I know, I've fallen asleep on Benji's couch. Exhausted from last night's drinking and its subsequent hangover, in addition to all the arguing today that seems to be coming in short, but really intense bursts. I can only act like I'm okay for so long before it all catches up with me. Sometimes just living my life is exhausting.

I wake to the sound of cabinet doors closing and the smell of cooking food. I don't know what it is, but it smells delicious. And again, I feel like I'm waking up in a life that belongs to someone else. It can't be mine.

Yawning groggily, I shuffle into the kitchen to find Benji at the stove giving a pot of noodles a quick stir before returning to a pan of chicken.

"Sorry, I didn't mean to wake you," he says.

"You're making me dinner?" I ask, and I don't know why but I feel my stomach tighten into a knot. This is wrong. We were screaming at each other, then he wanted to talk about it, and now he's making me dinner as if everything's fine. He shouldn't be this nice to me. He shouldn't act like nothing's changed. But he does. I hate it.

I want to ask him how he can carry on as if nothing has happened. How he can wake up in the morning and not hate his life, not want to stay in bed. I wonder if like me, his heart feels like it's been ripped from his chest. Are there times that he struggles to breathe or wonders what it would feel like to end it all? The crippling pain of secrets and death and lies that consume you; it never ends. Even after nine years, everything is still raw. He can't possibly feel this way, or he hides it well.

"I can't do this," I say, a mixture of anger and sadness weighing me down.

He stands there looking at me and I want to scream at him again. Yell in his face and tell him I hate him, blame him for the way I've felt for the last nine years, for the way I feel right now. I need someone else to blame. I'm angry with myself for coming here, angry with him for acting as if nothing has changed, that we aren't a gigantic fucked up mess.

But worst of all, I hate the fact that I need him. I don't want to need him because it makes me pathetic. Nine years gone and I still need him.

I want to confess everything to him. I want to tell him how lonely I am and how I never stopped loving him. I want to show him Tommy's letter and tell him how it ripped my heart out and left me a mess. I blame myself for it all, but saying it out loud is a risk I can't take, because it's what hurts the most. I can't let him in, only to lose him all over again.

And the tears start again. I don't want to cry anymore, but my body forces me, a never-ending betrayal. I don't even know what's going on anymore. *Is this really my life?*

But without acknowledging my words, without a word spoken from him, I find myself in Benji's arms. The tears are falling hard and fast as I bury my face in his chest, soaking his t-shirt with each ragged, muffled cry that leaves my mouth. I feel his arms tighten around my body; I can smell him, and feel him, his heart beating against my ear. I should find comfort in all of this, but all I can think is, *What if I lose him too?*

I don't know how long we stand like this, me wrapped in Benji's arms, neither of us saying a word. The time passing slowly, but quickly all at the same time and I long to have him hold me forever.

Benji's the first to speak. I hear his hushed voice shushing me as I continue to cry, wondering if my tears will ever run dry.

"It's okay," he says. "We'll be okay." And while there's no truth in his words, they're the words I longed to hear him say nine years ago when this whole thing started. It wouldn't have corrected everything that was wrong or everything we did, but it may have been the one thing that could've saved us.

Chapter Fourteen

"I'm sorry," I say eventually pulling away from him.

"Stop, Campbell. You have nothing to be sorry for," Benji says, his fingers softly brushing my cheek as he tucks my hair behind my ear. When I look up at him, my heart breaks. His eyes are filled with tears and he looks like being near me is painful, but I also feel like he'd do anything in the world to make all of this disappear. Not just for him, but for both of us.

"Take a few minutes," he says, his voice sympathetic. "And then come have dinner with me. You need to eat."

I nod at him and head back to the bedroom I found myself in this morning. I start to wonder why Benji lives in such a big house. The bedroom I'm staying in is one of four. It has a huge attached bathroom with a steam shower and a soaker tub, and as I look around, I feel like I don't ever want to leave. All of this an escape from what my life has become.

I quickly wash my face and brush my teeth, not wanting to keep Benji waiting, but as I look in the mirror, it's obvious I've been crying. And not just ordinary crying, it's the kind that makes your lips swell and your eyes red and puffy. I look like shit.

I run a brush through my hair and sweep it into a ponytail, pulling it off my face which probably only accentuates the fact that I look like hell.

As I turn to the leave the bathroom, something catches my attention. There's a small bottle sitting on the ledge along the side of the bathtub that wasn't there before. I pick it up and smile. A bottle of eucalyptus oil.

Did he know I was going to be here? How long has he had this? Why would he hold onto something like this after all these years? It's the exact brand I use, it's impossible to find, and to this day it still makes me think of him.

I take the bottle with me and when I enter the kitchen Benji is setting the table.

"What's this?" I ask him, and he turns to look at me.

"It's for you," he says, shrugging his shoulders as he returns to setting the table; acting like this is a casual conversation and I wasn't just sobbing uncontrollably into his t-shirt. I find his ability to forgive me and forget that I've lost my shit too many times a relief. I don't know how he's able to, but it makes me love him all over again.

I don't push it anymore, I just set the bottle on the island and take a seat at the table.

"Thank you for doing all this," I say, as he sets a plate of chicken marsala and angel hair pasta in front of me. I shake my head and add, "This is my favorite."

"I know," is all he says as he sits down across from me.

We begin eating in silence, but this time there's nothing uncomfortable about it. Actually it's strangely comforting, and for a minute I start to imagine what our life would've been like had everything not fallen apart. But I can't go there and I won't start crying again. I look away from him and out the window as I try to regain my composure.

"You don't have to try so hard to be normal," he says, his hand sliding across the table to cover mine.

Without looking at him I ask, "Why are you being so nice to me? I've been horrible to you." I free my hand out from under his, not ready to be this intimate with him again. Just his touch can be too much for me.

"Campbell," he says, but it comes out faint and he clears his throat. "Despite everything that's happened, it's never changed the way I feel about you."

And fuck me if the tears aren't back. Will this shit ever end? I wipe at my eyes determined not to cry again. I take in a deep breath, my eyes still focused on the landscape outside.

"How'd you end up here?" I ask him, and he laughs a little. I'm not sure if it's because of the sudden change in conversation or if the story of how he got here has something funny attached to it.

"Alex," he says, and when I cock my eyebrow at him, he continues. "I met Alex in Sydney. We were roommates and when his dad died and he came back to take over the bar, I went with him. There was nothing holding me in Sydney. No real job, no girl." He stops and winks at me and it makes me blush.

I love the way he can still make my stomach flutter and my heart race with just a simple gesture. I'm drawn to him like I've never been to anyone before, but as much as I'd love to fall back into our old habits, we aren't the same people we were back then.

"So I moved in with him." He leans over slightly, looking out the window and I follow his eyes. "See that small cabin? That one." He points out past the pond and I nod my head. "That's Alex and Annie's house. All of this is theirs," he says, and I give him a confused look.

"I thought this was your house?"

"It is, but this is their land. I just live on it. Run the business out of their barn. They had no use for it, and when I told him I was going to buy some land out here and build a house, he suggested I just pick a spot on his twenty acres. And that's exactly what I did."

I admire his ability to live like this, in the middle of nowhere; doing something he obviously loves without worrying about the predetermined norms of society. I wish I were him. I wish I could disappear and live a quiet existence that isn't ruled by my job or my ability to turn a profit or my incessant need to feel numb.

"This had to have taken forever to build," I say, looking around.

"It took me four years," he responds, and again I find myself giving him a questioning look. "I built it myself." I watch him quickly look away from me as if he's uncomfortable talking about it.

"Benji, it's amazing. It was beautiful before I knew you built it, but now it's just…" I trail off unable to find the right words to describe it. "I don't even know what to say."

He finally looks back at me, a forced smile on his face, and behind his eyes, I finally see sadness. He isn't okay and the thought breaks my heart.

"Sometimes you just need a distraction," he says, and doesn't elaborate. He doesn't need to; I know exactly what he means.

After I left Ann Arbor, after I walked away from Benji and Tommy, thinking I'd left the mess behind me, it was far from the truth. It haunted everything I did and everything I was. I threw myself into school, taking far too many classes and when I graduated early, it only reminded me of how awful my life had become. Lonely, but unable to let anyone in for fear I'd admit the secret I held inside, afraid the lies I'd spun would eventually sell me out. So, I started working for Jack and each day that passed, I found myself working harder, working longer hours, desperate to find a distraction, desperate to forget. And when I couldn't quiet my brain in the evenings, long after the workday was done, I'd drink. A lot. None of it worked. It was all just a Band-Aid, but I still do it. And it still doesn't work.

"Did it work?" I ask him, even though I know the answer.

"Never."

We finish dinner without our conversations taking a turn for the depressing, even though it's still there just below the surface. It never fades. But like the last nine years of our lives, we're exhausted and raw with regret. It becomes too much and we both realize that we are in no shape to dissect it right now.

As I'm washing the dishes from dinner, Benji gets a fire started in the fireplace. He doesn't ask me to stay, but there's an unspoken invitation as if saying it out loud makes what we're doing real.

I join him on the couch, sitting strangely far from him and he chuckles as he stretches out, laying down and resting his feet in my lap.

"I've spent all day working and if you're only going to take up a corner of my couch with your tiny ass, then I'm gonna be comfortable," he says smugly.

I give him an annoyed look as I stick my tongue out at him. I watch him fold his hands behind his head, an arrogant look on his face.

"If you can't keep that tongue in your mouth, I can find something to keep it busy."

I feel my face heat up almost immediately and when he sits up, leaning close to my ear, my entire body feels like it's on fire. I can feel the warmth of his skin, his hot breath tickling the sensitive spot below my ear as he whispers, "I love that I can still make you blush. It's so fucking hot."

"It's hot in here," I respond back, shakily, and he laughs, falling back onto the pillows as he settles himself where he once was.

"You wish that was all it was," he retorts. He's teasing me and I love it. Everything about this is so natural and both of us are smiling now.

We spend a few minutes flipping through the channels on TV, only to find there's nothing on, so he switches over to his DVR.

"Oh my god, why do you have an entire season of *The Walking Dead* on here?" I ask, shocked that anyone could let it sit unwatched. "What the hell is wrong with you?"

"Relax," he says sarcastically, giving me a poke in the side with his foot. "I just haven't had time to watch it."

"Well, what are you waiting for? We've got nothing but time tonight." I smirk at him, giving his foot a squeeze as I slide my fingers up the leg of his jeans, letting my fingertips trail along his skin. And now I watch his cheeks turn a slight shade of pink and I'm shocked that I've made him blush now.

We blow through the first two episodes of the season rather quickly, even though Benji would not stop asking me questions. And as we begin to start episode three, I can't take it anymore.

"Would you shut up!" I finally yell and he laughs.

"Just tell me what's going to happen!" he screams back.

"No!"

"You're going to pay for this later," he says firmly, giving me a long serious stare and it makes me swallow hard. I hope he does make me pay for it later, the same way he used to. I have a sudden image of him pinning me to the bed, the weight of his body pressed against me, my arms above my head, his hands locked around my wrists. The thought makes me squirm and right now all I can think about is Benji.

Suddenly he pauses the TV and practically jumps off the couch, a huge smile on his face.

"I forgot something," he says and I can hear the happiness in his voice. I turn around on the couch, looking over the back and watching him as he opens the refrigerator and takes out a bag.

"What is it?" I ask, excitedly, now sitting up on my knees, practically bouncing up and down and he shakes his head.

"Be patient."

"Stop teasing me."

"Stop being so fucking adorable."

That's all it takes to silence me. My words caught in my throat, my heart racing as I suddenly can't control myself. Since I arrived here, I've felt the intense connection we once had and I think he feels it too. When he warmed my hands, when he pressed his face to my neck, when he kissed me; it brought back everything I've missed about him, everything we once had. As much as I've fought it, I can't any longer.

He finally stops in front of me, his hands behind his back; he pulls out a red velvet cupcake. He's smiling and while I love that he remembered I love red velvet cupcakes, I don't fucking care right now. I know what I want and I'm not thinking about anything else. He's all I want.

"I don't want that cupcake," I say, my eyes locked on his and he seems put off by my words. He takes a step backward, but I step toward him, taking the cupcake from his hands and setting it on the coffee table.

"What do you want?" he asks, as if he's unsure and his voice trembles, almost like he's anxious about what my answer will be.

"I want you," I say, closing the small distance between us, and when I press up on my toes, my mouth close to his ear, I whisper, "Be my distraction."

No more words are spoken between us as he backs me up to the couch slowly, his hand sliding into my hair, his arm wrapped around my waist. I find myself lying back on the couch as Benji's body covers mine, the weight of his body calming me, as the touch of his skin to mine, excites me.

I feel his lips against my neck and my body is covered in goose bumps; I tangle my hands in his hair, pulling him closer.

This is something I never thought I'd feel again. The intensity and intimacy of it all almost overwhelming, but somehow what I've needed for so long. Being here with Benji, in his arms, and even though I know all the reasons I'm here and all the painful memories are still hidden, I don't want to feel them right now. I silently wish for this to never end and as if he hears me, he presses closer to me, until his body completely covers mine.

"Campbell," he softly moans against my skin and I shudder, my body overly sensitive. "I've missed everything about you," he says, leaving a trail of kisses along the line of my jaw. "I've missed the way you smell, the way you feel in my arms, the way you taste," he whispers, as he sucks at my neck.

His lips press a series of soft kisses along my neck and cheek until he reaches my mouth, pressing a slow, gentle kiss to my lips. Everything about this moment feels so perfect, like this is the way our life should've been. Nothing in my life has been this right, this real since the accident.

He pulls back slightly; his fingers brushing my hair back off my face and I lift my eyes to meet his gorgeous blue ones.

"You are so beautiful," he says and a shiver runs down my spine. My arms wrap around his waist, holding him to me as if this is all a dream, if I let go, if I'm not touching him, it will all vanish. "It's been a long day," he says, and I nod as his lips connect with mine once again. "We're both exhausted, let me put you to bed."

As much as I want him, he's right. I just need to be near him at the moment, so without another word spoken by me, I nod my head and he says, "Stay with me, in my bed."

Chapter Fifteen

I roll over the next morning to find Benji gone, but in his place is a note. I pick it up, a smile already on my face. I haven't woken up like this in years, completely rested and happy. And after I read his note, my day is pretty much made.

C-
Sorry, I wanted to be there when you woke up.
But I have a ton of work to do.
There's a surprise for you downstairs.
Love
-B

I scramble from the bed, untangling myself from the sheets, smiling the entire time. Wrapped in a blanket as I make my way down the stairs, I find another note on the kitchen counter next to the coffee pot with a cup of coffee waiting for me.

Look out the window.
PS...it snowed. A lot.

I run to the window my smile literally hurting my cheeks and find there's at least eight inches of snow covering the ground, I can hardly see my car parked in the driveway.

The wood floor is cold on my bare feet as I take my cup of coffee and the blanket, and curl up in the oversized leather chair that looks out on the picturesque view of Benji's yard. I tuck my feet underneath me as a feeling of blissful contentment washes over me, and I realize I never want to go back home. What if this became my life? Maybe there's still a chance for Benji and me to have the life we once dreamed about.

I finish my coffee and as I'm about to put my mug in the sink, I notice the eucalyptus oil still on the island, but this time there's a note under it. I'm certain at this point nothing can remove this smile from my face.

Take a bath, relax, and when you're
done meet me at my shop. Make sure you walk.

This is all too much and I'm now trying to figure out a way to thank Benji for everything. Not just for the notes and the food, but for making me happier than I have been in years.

I do as I'm told and take a bath, the water ridiculously hot and smelling of eucalyptus as I sit in the darkness of the bathroom trying to remember every detail from yesterday and today, committing them to memory. I don't want to forget there was a time when I was happy, truly happy, should for some reason it all turn ugly again.

After I get dressed, I find another note taped to the front door and I almost laugh out loud at how fucking perfect he is.

Put these on and take the bag with you.
Finish my snowmen along the way.

I look down and find a pair of snow boots and a bag filled with a bunch of random stuff. Two scarves, a hat, strawberries, a small bag of birdseed, scraps of wood, some carrots and a bunch of other things I haven't had a chance to look at. I have no idea what he's done, but I'm dying to find out. I quickly kick off my shoes and put the boots on, taking the bag with me, I leave the house practically skipping out the door and begin my walk to Benji's shop.

After about five minutes of walking I come across three large snowballs stacked on top of each other, the snowman about my height and I set the bag down and get to work. I step back and admire my work, laughing knowing Benji will love it.

Eventually I come across another one and while I'm having a blast, I'm hoping this is the last one because I'm freezing. I quickly add a few things to it and take the bag with me. By now, I'm only concerned with finding Benji and showing him exactly how happy he has made me.

When I finally make it to his shop, I'm cold but ecstatic, and I fling the door open and find him sitting in front of the same table he was working on yesterday. My smile is so huge I'm sure he can see it from where he's sitting.

"Guessing you had a good morning?" he says smiling back at me.

I don't even answer; I run to him and throw myself into his arms. I can feel myself begin to cry, but this time it has nothing to do with being sad. He lifts me off the ground, burying his face in my neck, as I hold on as tight as I can.

"I had the best morning ever," I say, pulling back to kiss him furiously, my lips touching every part of his face. "You are so fucking perfect."

"I just want you to be happy, baby," he whispers, his hands holding my face as he looks at me with his beautiful blue eyes and lets out a contented sigh.

"I am now," I say as my lips gently meet his and when I let out a soft moan, his tongue slips in and slowly moves against mine. I can taste him; feel his soft lips as they press against mine. I don't want this to stop; my body silently begging as every nerve feels like it's on fire. When he finally pulls away from me, his forehead resting against mine, his eyes closed, I feel like my whole body is humming.

"Campbell?"

"What?" I ask breathlessly.

"I love you," he says, his eyes now open and looking right at me as if to make sure I've heard him, to make sure his words aren't lost somehow. "I've never stopped loving you."

I don't say anything for a few seconds and it's not because I don't love him back. I'm hit with the memories of all the times we said these words to each other. I always felt like it was a lot, maybe too much sometimes, like we didn't mean it, like it was just something we said. But now I feel like I can't say it enough, like all those times before this were meaningless. This connection is far more intense than anything I've ever felt before, even with Benji and I can tell he feels it too.

"I love you too." And as the words leave my mouth, Benji takes me in his arms, whispering I love you, over and over again.

I stand clinging to him for what feels like forever, memorizing the way he feels in my arms, the way he smells, and the sound of his voice. It all feels surreal, but for once I don't dwell on what could go wrong, I just let myself fall even more in love with him.

"Do you have any plans today?" he asks and I laugh out loud.

"What do you think? I have no idea where I am, I know no one, and considering my car is pretty much buried, I don't think I'm going to be leaving any time soon."

"Good," he says, smiling at me. "I have to head up to Canada to ship some things. You wanna come with me? That is, if you have your passport."

"Funny, I actually do have my passport. I grabbed it just in case, figuring I wouldn't need it, but I guess it's a good thing I did."

"Great. We have to walk back and get my truck, but then we should be all good. Now let's go have a look at those snowmen," he says winking at me and taking my hand.

I watch him put his coat on, the lean muscles of his arms flexing as he slips his arms in. I look around his shop knowing his body built everything in here. There's a reason he looks the way he does; his well-worn and calloused hands, his muscular arms, defined to almost perfection; it's all unbelievably amazing. My eyes follow him as he bends down to tie his boots and he smirks up at me.

"Stop checking me out," he says, feigning like he doesn't enjoy every second of it.

"I can't help it," I tell him teasingly, as I shrug my shoulders.

"Come on," he says, taking my hand and pulling me out the door and into the snow-filled abyss.

Trudging along, our feet crunch under the snow and gravel as we approach the first snowman. Benji stops and looks at me, his eyes wide and questioning, but a huge smile plastered on his face.

"You didn't," he says, and I giggle.

"I did," I tease back playfully.

"Campbell, you naughty girl. You made dirty snowmen," he says, pointing at the carrot, which is placed in a very obvious spot. "You never cease to surprise me," he says, as he reaches for me and pulls me into his arms. I know he wanted it to be something fun for me to do and I, in turn, wanted to make it something fun for him to look at.

"The other one has snow boobs," I whisper, my cheeks turning pink as he laughs at me.

"Come on, crazy girl," he says shaking his head, and I follow him, my hand linked with his, my other arm wrapped around his bicep. No matter how close I am to him, I still can't get close enough. All this time apart has made me desperate to be near him and the more time I spend with him, the more the loneliness fades, and I start to forget how miserable I used to be.

About a half an hour later, we're in Benji's truck on our way to Canada. Because of where he lives, he has to cross over into Canada to ship any orders that are placed online. Although, Hessel has a post office, it can't accommodate the size or the quantity he ships. All of this is explained to me in the short amount of time we've been in the car.

I admire his drive to continue to help his business grow. Most people would've quit given the effort that goes into it all. Not just the shipping, but also the amount of time and effort that goes into creating his work. I've only been with him for two nights, but he obviously wakes very early and I can't help but think he probably finds himself working well into the evening. And unlike me, he spends the time because he loves what he does, and that shows in everything he makes.

We drive along quietly, only the sound of the radio to fill the silence and when I hear Benji's voice begin to sing along softly, I close my eyes. His voice is exactly how I remember it, deep and raw, it's always been beautiful.

He reaches over and takes my hand in his, bringing it to his lips and kissing each one of my fingertips.

He looks over at me and when our eyes connect, I see sadness in his and I'm about to ask what's wrong, but he speaks before I can. "I'm sorry, Campbell," he says, and a moment of panic rips through me.

What is he apologizing for? It should be me apologizing to him. Did he ask me to come with him so we can finally talk about the accident? He has me trapped in the car so I can't get away from him this time. I don't want to do this, especially after how well everything has been going. We can just keep acting like we're okay. We can be fine.

His hand tightens in mine and my heart begins to race. I watch as he wets his lips and looks away from me. I want to say something, but nothing will come out. I'm silent.

"I'm sorry for the way I treated you after the accident," he says quietly, and I breathe out in relief. "I know we have a lot more to discuss, but you need to know, I never meant to hurt you and I know I did."

I shake my head, not because he didn't hurt me, but because an apology isn't necessary. We both did things we regret, actually all four of us did and it made us so resentful and broken and filled with guilt that we couldn't deal with it.

"I'm sorry, too," I tell him, and he brings my hand to his lips once again, kissing it, but this time letting his lips linger. "I shouldn't have run away the way I did."

"It was your coping mechanism and I don't blame you. We all do things to cope and I drove you away because I couldn't..." He stops short and grips the steering wheel tighter as I see his hand shake. I can feel his other hand trembling in mine. And inside, I feel my heart breaking, tiny pieces shattering for all the pain we've endured alone.

"No more lies. No more secrets," Benji says, his voice nearly inaudible over the sound of the car. I nod my head slightly, but enough that I know he sees it. "I couldn't... It hurt to be near you," he says quickly, letting out a long breath as his words cut right through me.

"I hated what it did to us," I say, the words almost too painful to get out. "To all of us."

I watch a tear roll down his cheek and it's almost more than I can bear. I can't see him cry over this, it will be my undoing. I wrap my arm around his and rest my head against his shoulder.

"I still hate it," he whispers roughly, and I want to respond, but my words get caught in my throat, painful and heavy. He holds onto the steering wheel, his hands still shaking, his breathing erratic.

I leave my head against his shoulder, his lips occasionally leaving a kiss on the top of my head as we drive once again in silence.

I want to tell him about Tommy, but I can't even work out how to break it to him that he's lost someone else; that this horrible situation, that this accident is still ruining our lives. I can see he's already fragile and I don't want to be the one to break him.

We said no more secrets and lies, and I won't keep this from him, but I need to be looking at him, holding him when I tell him. I need to feel him in my arms so he knows I'm not going to run away again. That we'll deal with it together.

"I love you," I murmur, kissing his neck and his shoulder and then taking his hand from the steering wheel, I kiss every one of his fingers, and they finally stop shaking.

"I love you, Campbell."

Chapter Sixteen

As we're driving back, Benji's phone rings and it dawns on me that I don't have his phone number.

"You know, I don't even know your phone number," I say, before he answers it.

"And I don't know yours," he responds, holding up one finger as he answer his phone. "Hey Alex," he says and they talk for a few seconds before he turns to me and asks, "Do you want to have dinner with Alex and Annie tonight?"

"Sure," I say, but even as I answer, I worry about the last conversation I had with them. I overreacted; honestly, I acted like a fucking bitch and a paranoid one at that. And after Benji admitted to me that he hadn't told them anything, I'm not sure how I'm going explain myself. All I know is that I definitely owe them an apology.

He hangs up and hands me his phone with a smile on his face. "Your number, please?" he says and it makes me giggle. He's so fucking adorable. I enter it and hand the phone back to him and only a second later does my phone begin to vibrate in my bag.

I haven't looked at it since I arrived and I still don't give a shit what's waiting for me, but I pull it from my bag, ignoring all the missed calls and text messages, I find Benji's text waiting. "So we never lose each other again", it says, and it makes me smile.

I quickly add his number to my phone and turn my attention to him.

"So," I say, and he laughs, answering back by echoing my 'so'. "Don't make fun of me," I quip, and he reaches for my hand, but I pull it away dramatically.

"I'd never," he says, shooting me an innocent look.

"Benji, I need to apologize to Alex and Annie for the way I reacted the last time I saw them," I tell him, but it comes out rushed and embarrassed.

"No worries, Campbell," he says casually. "I get why you were defensive. We have a secret that could ruin relationships and friendships, it could ruin everything, but I told you before, I never told them."

I often think about why I never told anyone and while the four of us agreed it was a secret we would all keep, I figured one of us would've come clean by now. But knowing that Benji hasn't said anything and Tommy never told his wife, it's a safe bet to think that it's still a secret. There were so many times when I was struggling that I wanted to admit it to someone, anyone, but the guilt over what we did always stopped me. How would I be perceived? I was always sure that I couldn't stand the judgment that would've come with my admittance. And in the end, it never felt like it was mine to share. It was never my secret alone.

"I know you didn't and I'm sorry I reacted the way I did."

Benji stops and looks over at me, like he wants to say something. My hand now resting in his and he starts and stops several times before eventually saying, "But I did tell them about you...and some of it wasn't good."

"I deserved it," I say and he shakes his head.

"No, you didn't, but I was angry and bitter and hurt at the time and that was the way it all came across." With a sad smile on his face, he clutches my hand tightly. "I'm sorry, I said some horrible things about you and the crazy thing was, Annie saw right through it all. She knew I still loved you despite everything I said."

Both of us have a million things we could be apologizing for, but in the end, I've always loved him. It doesn't matter that nine years have passed, and it doesn't matter what was said or what we did. What matters is that we've found each other again.

"It's okay, seriously," I tell him. "I owe you an apology, too."

"For what?" he asks, confused.

"For staying gone. For disappearing without telling you I was leaving and for all the years we've missed together. I was being spiteful." I stop because I don't want to tell him anymore. All of this is too painful, the memories, the reminders of what we did, and what it did to us.

"It doesn't matter what we did," Benji says, but we both know that's not true. It might not matter what we did or said in terms of our relationship, but what happened with the accident still matters and it's a topic we have yet to fully discuss. I feel like both of us are skirting around the bigger issue here and we probably will because we know the severity of it all and what it could possibly do to our already unstable lives.

Our conversation falls silent and it's like we both know that delving too deeply will bring to the surface all the things we keep hidden. There's a reason we spent nine years apart, but there's also a reason we've found each other again.

An hour later and we're pulling into Alex and Annie's driveway and my hands begin to shake. I'm nervous as hell to see them again. Clearly they're very important to Benji, they're like his family and the last thing I want to do is embarrass him or have them not like me.

I begin to chew my lip, stressing about how I'm going to apologize without coming across like a paranoid asshat. Normally this shit wouldn't bother me; given my job I'm pretty much hated by everyone I come in contact with and I usually let it roll off my back. Sometimes I actually find it gratifying to know these assholes I do business with hate me. It keeps me emotionally detached from it all.

But in this case, that's the last thing I want.

Suddenly Benji is standing at the door to the truck, laughing at me and I flip him off, a crabby look on my face, as he asks, "You gonna stay in here the whole night? You'll freeze your ass off."

"No."

He opens the door, his hand held out for me to take and as I do, he pulls me close; kissing me so hard it takes my breath away. His beard rubs along my cheek as his mouth finds my ear and a shiver runs up my spine. It has nothing to do with the cold air. Just being this close to him is all I need and everything around me disappears. He becomes all I can see.

"Stop," he whispers in my ear, his voice deep and sexy as hell. "As beautiful as you are when you're nervous, you're hot as fuck when you're being indignant." His hand is pressed against my lower back as he pulls us closer together. I'm breathless and ready to get back in the truck so we can go home together, right now.

He's kissing and nibbling at my neck now and while I'd normally be freezing standing in the snow, right now, I feel like I'm on fire.

"Your friends are waiting," I murmur, my voice failing to convey my message. It's obvious that both of us wish we were doing something else at the moment.

"Fuck them," he says, and it makes me laugh out loud.

I push him away slightly, taking his hand; I tug him toward the house as he grumbles and pouts behind me.

Annie greets us at the door with a huge smile on her face and as we step in she hugs Benji and then me. I have a hard time with intimacy of any kind, especially with people I don't know well. I've been so closed off for years that it catches me off guard and I stand awkwardly as she wraps her arms around me. It takes me a second to realize what's happening before I respond and I try to return her hug without it seeming strange.

"Nice," Benji whispers, laughing, after Annie pulls away and walks into the kitchen.

"Piss off," I snap back. "I know I'm awkward. She caught me off guard."

"It gets easier," he says, smiling sympathetically as if he understands. "I'm just giving you shit."

We follow Annie into the kitchen and find Alex at the stove cooking, and it smells delicious. Without asking, Benji walks to the refrigerator and takes out two beers, handing one to me and then asking if Alex needs help with anything.

Their entire dynamic is so normal and natural, and it makes me crave what they have. It also makes me remember what Benji and I once had with our small group of friends and that dull ache in my chest returns. Can I let these people in the way Benji has? Can I be happy again? I want it, but I fear it, all at the same time.

I take a quick drink before clearing my throat and saying, "Hey Annie?"

"Yeah?"

"I'm sorry about the other day at the bar. You too, Alex," I add, looking past Annie as Alex turns to look at me. "I was rude and I shouldn't have been."

"No worries," Annie says, brushing me off, but giving me a kind smile.

"I get it," Alex adds. "You knew Ben told us about you, but don't worry, we won't hold it against you. We know Ben can be a dick sometimes."

I laugh and Annie smacks Alex on his shoulder as she rolls her eyes.

"He's terrible," she says.

The four of us take a seat at the table, eating and talking. The night goes by quickly with Alex and Benji telling stories from when they lived in Sydney. It turns out Alex and Annie met in high school, but broke up when he left for Sydney. He was miserable and after meeting Benji while looking for a roommate, they spent most of their time drunk and miserable together. Benji pining after me or hating me, depending on the day, and Alex whining about missing Annie. Although the two of them tell it a little differently, I believe Annie's version.

"They were a mess," she says, looking at me. "I'd call and Alex would tell me he was coming home and that he loved me. It was pretty pathetic."

"It sounds sweet," I say and she laughs.

"It was, actually."

"So how'd you two end up back together?" I ask and Annie looks at Benji first and then to Alex.

"Well, they got arrested and I had to bail them out."

"You're fucking kidding me?" I say, looking at Benji and he nonchalantly shrugs his shoulders like it's an every day occurrence that someone's ex-girlfriend bails him out of jail.

"Nope. Everyone loves a phone call at six a.m. from an Australian police station asking if you can wire money to bail your ex-boyfriend and his friend out of jail."

"What did you do?" I ask, appalled. And while I'm sure this story has some humorous qualities to it, I can tell by the look on Benji's face, the whole thing makes him uncomfortable. Our past isn't exactly normal and since it's all a secret, I'm sure he's struggling with the memories of what happened with the accident and being questioned by the police.

"We broke into someone's house," he says, mortified. "But that wasn't really what happened." I give him a questioning look and Alex begins to fill in the missing details.

"We had just moved and neither of us could remember where we lived…"

Benji cuts Alex short and adds, "We were drunk," like it wasn't obvious. I know Benji would never knowingly break into someone's house. Although he did pull a shotgun on me.

"Yeah," Alex says, and continues. "All the buildings looked the same and then neither of us could find our keys, so we picked a door and hoped it was ours."

"It wasn't," Benji says, glaring at Alex, like this is somehow his fault. "And the rest you can figure out on your own," he adds sharply.

"That's pretty horrible," I say, my hand stroking the back of Benji's neck and I watch him relax at my touch. I love that I have that effect on him. It's the same thing his touch does to me, comforting, calming.

The night comes to an end and I've had a great time getting to know Alex and Annie and laughing with them. We've all had a lot to drink and I'm definitely feeling the effects as Benji and I make our way to the front door.

We thank them both and wish them good night as we step outside into the cold air. I'm giggling as Benji pulls me into his arms the moment the door closes. He can't keep his hands off me and when he presses his mouth to mine, I respond immediately, parting my lips and letting his tongue slip inside. The combination of the cold air and his warm mouth makes me dizzy and I hold onto him tightly. It's an amazing feeling being this close to him. I love everything about it.

"I'm drunk," he mumbles into my neck, and I laugh again.

"Me, too."

"I think we should walk back," he says, and his words stop me. His hand is in mine as he gives my arm a little pull. "Come on, Campbell." But I don't move. I feel my heart begin to race in my chest as I relive the moment we climbed into Sam's car feeling this way, drunk and giddy.

He looks back at me, realizing I'm not moving. He shakes his head and steps closer until he's directly in front of me. "No," he says, and shakes his head again. "Don't overthink this, Campbell. It's not the same thing."

He's right. It's not. We've learned from our mistakes. No one is going to die tonight. I won't let the horribleness of the accident ruin this otherwise perfect evening. It won't take control of my life again. It won't drive us apart.

With my hand still in his, I'm the one who pulls him along this time, as we start to make the snowy trek back to his house.

It's cold and our breath is coming out in short, ragged bursts of white air as we both trudge through the snow. As if Benji can sense it's all still weighing on my mind, both of us quiet, he stops a few feet shy of the house. His breathing hard and labored from the cold and the long walk, he looks at me and smiles before scooping up a pile of snow and throws it at me.

It hits me in the chest and my mouth falls open in mock surprise and Benji does it all over again. Before I know it, we're throwing snowballs back and forth at each other, most of mine missing him by miles and his connecting until I'm almost completely covered in snow.

"You win!" I yell, sounding winded as I hold my hands up in defeat.

"Did you seriously just quit?" he asks.

"I did," I respond, walking over to him, but as soon as I reach him, I lock my leg around his and take him down with a technique he taught me when we were only ten. It still works like a charm.

Benji falls flat on his back in the snow as I climb on top of him, straddling his hips, I try to pin his arms down with my knees, but he's too quick.

"You're a cheater!" he screams, and I'm squealing with laughter as he reverses our positions and it's now me flat on my back and him straddling my hips. My arms are pinned above my head as I squirm underneath him, but he silences me with a kiss.

It only takes a second for him to deepen the kiss and I can feel the heat radiating off his body despite the coldness all around us. His tongue entwines with mine and I taste him once again, a mix of beer and warmth, his lips soft and smooth as they press into mine. I moan into his mouth, my arms around his neck, dragging him closer to my body. I need to be closer and as if he can hear my thoughts, he lifts me off the ground and I wrap my legs around his waist.

"Take me home," I whisper into his mouth, breathless and needy.

Chapter Seventeen

Benji pushes the door open, my body still wrapped around his as I slide out of his arms and down his body. Without words, I walk up the stairs to his bedroom with him following behind.

When I turn to face him, his eyes are dark, his pupils wide and I can see all the want and need I feel reflected in his face. My hands begin to shake as I step closer to him, closing the distance between us, my heartbeat drumming loud in my ears, as I'm flooded with warmth.

I need to touch him, to be close to him, and this can't be like all the other times we've done this. There is so much more meaning in it now than there ever was before.

I love him.

I've always loved him, but now, I know I can't live without him.

I watch Benji lift his shirt over his head; his flat, toned stomach and his perfect chest exposed to me and I suck in a ragged breath. There's a tattoo that runs down his right side and my hand shakes as I reach out and run my fingers over it. His skin is warm, but his body lines with goose bumps from the touch of my hand and I hear his sharp intake of air as I go back and trace each letter of his tattoo.

tu me manques

It's all in lowercase letters and when I look up at him, he tucks my hair behind my ears, his mouth only inches from mine as he whispers, "It translates to *you're missing from me*."

He doesn't need to say any more, I understand the significance behind it, the words holding more meaning than anything he's said to me. Without each other we're incomplete and not just the two of us, but our group that was once five.

I don't want to cry anymore, but the tears escape slowly and Benji's fingers wipe them away as my hand rests on his chest. I can feel the steady beat of his heart calming me and I close my eyes, stepping closer to him until I'm wrapped in his arms.

I lean back, lifting my head and he lowers his to meet my mouth. We kiss, slowly, passionately and behind it are all the feelings we tried to forget, feelings we both buried deep inside because the loss hurt more than anything.

But here in the darkness of his bedroom, the room quiet, our bodies on fire, our labored breathing coming hard and fast, I want him. I want to feel everything; everything I've shut out for so long. I want the rush of emotions that comes with being this close to him again. I want it all.

I step away from him and run my hands down his chest, my fingers undoing the buckle on his belt, but he doesn't move. His eyes are closed and every time my fingers graze his skin, his breathing grows ragged and a soft moan escapes his lips. I undo the button on his jeans as my lips kiss a line of soft kisses across his chest.

Moving away from him just slightly, I lift my sweater over my head and unbutton my jeans, kicking them off with my boots and tossing my sweater to the side, his eyes locking with mine as I do.

Once again I'm pressed against him, this time my bare skin against his and the feeling causes my body to ignite, warm and aching. I'd forgotten what it feels like to want someone like this, to be completely connected to someone and to feel it everywhere. My body is on fire, his touch is the only thing I can feel, hot and burning as his hands explore every inch of me.

I'm shivering under his touch, my body trembling as he touches me, his fingers trailing along my overly sensitive skin. Each touch is like sparks of electricity and my heart races. I need to be as close to him as possible.

"Please," I beg, and his mouth, soft and pleading, runs along my jaw and down my neck, stopping to kiss and bite gently until I'm needy and desperate.

I feel like I'm drowning and I don't care. I want to get lost in him, I want to lose myself and remember what it's like to have him love me, to feel him inside me.

My hands on his chest, his heartbeat matching mine, fast and rhythmic; the anticipation intense and when his mouth meets mine again, I grow weak. I feel myself push his jeans to the floor and he slips off his boots, kicking his jeans off with them as he backs me up against the bed. My legs brush the duvet and I lay back on the bed.

I grow lightheaded as I watch his eyes rake over my body and when he lies down, the weight of his body on me, I gasp out loud. I pull my bottom lip into my mouth and his pupils dilate, showing me exactly how he's feeling.

He begins kissing me again, his lips soft and slow. Taking his time, he kisses my face and my neck, my shoulders and my lips as his fingers run down my arms. Each touch brings a shiver to my skin, but I need more. I need him.

Benji kisses a line up my neck until he reaches my ear. I can hear his breath coming fast and ragged as he whispers, "You've always been my light, Campbell."

"Don't stop, please," I beg, and I feel like I'm melting. His words, his touch, the way he kisses me; it's all more than I ever thought I would feel again. It's perfect.

My fingers trail up his arms, caressing the tight muscles in his biceps, and when I reach his neck, I cradle his face in my hands. Bringing his mouth to mine, I exhale slowly as I whisper, "I love you."

Running up the sides of my body, his hands slip around and undo my bra, but he's slow and deliberate, taking his time as he slides the straps down my arms. Each brush of his fingers causes my body to respond. My pulse rapid, my breathing labored, as my body tingles. And when his lips press against mine, his tongue urging my lips apart, I open to him and feel the warmth of his mouth meet mine.

I'm ready for him.

And then it's just us as I feel him push inside me.

The soft moan that leaves his lips is nearly my undoing.

I love him and this is perfect, despite all the awfulness that still surrounds us.

Afterward, my head is cradled in the crook of Benji's arm; his fingers are tracing a light pattern of circles on my back as the silence of the room consumes us. It's only us, no words being spoken, just a remembrance of what we once were and what we can become again.

"Thank you," I whisper, my voice quiet and weak. He has no idea what he's done for me, and my words don't even begin to express how I feel. They will never be enough.

"For what?" Benji asks, his hand now stroking my hair softly.

"For reminding me what it feels like to live again."

"Campbell," he says, my name rough on his lips as if it hurts to say it. "I never want you to feel like that again. When I saw you, all I saw was the pain you felt and it broke my heart."

I owe him so much more than just a thank you, but I don't even know where to begin. I know he's hurting too and I want to make everything go away. I want us to be normal.

"Are you okay?" I ask him, the question vague, but he knows what I mean. There's no need to elaborate. And even as I ask the question, I wonder if we'll ever be okay. Will we ever know normal again?

"I am now," he says, stopping to kiss my forehead. "But I haven't been for a really long time."

I press against him even more, my skin against his, the warmth of his body, calm and soothing. How long can we last like this? My life in Chicago still exists even if I want to act like it doesn't. We haven't discussed anything and I can't help but wonder what will happen when I have to leave.

"What happens now?" I ask, although the apprehension I feel is stifling. I don't want to ruin the moment and I'm suddenly pissed at myself for even asking.

Benji pulls away from me, looking down at me, his beautiful blue eyes soft and his lids heavy. He looks peaceful, sated, and I want him to stay this way forever.

"Anything you want," he says, kissing me gently. With his lips still touching mine, he murmurs, "Stay forever, marry me, just don't ever leave."

I giggle, but I know there is no practicality to his words. Can I really stay? Give up my job and everything I've known? And before I can think about it anymore, I know the answer. It's yes. Nothing makes me happier than being here with him. My life up until this point has been nothing but emptiness and disappointment, sadness and grief. It ends now.

"Yes," I whisper, pressing a few soft kisses to his lips and then his neck and his chest.

"Yes, what?" he asks, and I know he's smiling. He wants me to say it out loud, to tell him everything I want and everything I feel. And for once in my life, I want to feel all the happiness and nervousness and fear that comes with it.

"I'll stay forever," I say as I kiss him. "I'll marry you." I kiss him again. "I'll never leave," I whisper against his lips, and he pulls my mouth to his, his hands holding my face as he kisses me fiercely.

And all I can think is, *Please don't ever let me go.*

I never expected us to fall back into being this intimate and this comfortable with each other so quickly. Honestly, I had no idea what would happen when I first showed up here. It definitely wasn't this, yet surprisingly, it feels so right.

"Nothing would make me happier," he says, and it's all I need. We deserve to be happy and maybe this is our chance.

I wake the next morning, the sun streaming through the open blinds and with Benji asleep beside me. I smile when I see his face.

He stayed.

I cuddle into him, wrapping my arm around his waist and my legs tangling with his. I love the way he feels in my arms, the way his body is warm and smells like cedar, something that will always remind me of him. I love it.

I love him.

"Mmmm," he mumbles, his voice hoarse with sleep as he nuzzles my hair, his arms encircling me and pulling me even closer. "I love waking up with you in my bed."

Everything about this feels new, yet somehow exactly the same as it once was. We're different people now and I wonder if without the accident we would've ended up here. Would we have been this happy?

I'm kissing his chest as he slowly wakes up and begins to run his fingers up and down my spine. I shudder at his touch, everything about it is perfect and I'm incredibly turned-on.

I find myself straddling his hips and bringing my mouth down to meet his. I can't get enough of him and as his hands explore every inch of my body, I know he feels the same way.

"What do you want to do today?" I ask, pulling back from his mouth, still breathless from his kiss.

"You," he says, pinching my side and I laugh, burying my face in his neck, his beard scratching the side of my face.

"Don't you have to go to work?"

"Nope. I just want to stay here with you and do exactly what we did last night, all day today."

I don't answer him. I can't because my mouth is busy trailing kisses all over his beautiful body, my actions the only answer he needs.

Chapter Eighteen

Benji keeps his word and we spend the entire day in bed together. It doesn't stop either of us from enjoying each other over and over again. It doesn't matter how many times I've had him, I can't get enough. Nine years is a long time to be without the person you love, and we have a lot of time to make up for.

"Can we really do this?" I ask, and Benji rolls onto his side and props himself on his elbow.

"Do what?"

"This," I answer, motioning between the two of us with my hand.

"Um, I think we just did...many times," he says, a cheekiness to his tone.

"Be serious," I say, swatting him on the chest with my hand. "Can we really make this work?"

"Yes," he responds definitively, like there's no reason to question it.

"Benji, I have a job and a home in Chicago..."

He cuts me off. "You can have a job here if that's what you want. If not, I'll take care of you. You have a home here, I'm here, our life together is here. It's quiet and peaceful. It can be just us, Campbell."

I nod my head, each one of his reasons pushing me closer. The biggest reason being him. It's what I've always wanted and right now, it's exactly what I need.

"Stop overthinking it," he says, kissing my fingers as they lace with his. "I know this seems fast, but we've been together since we were five. I loved you then and I still love you now."

Why is there a part of me that's holding back? He's right about everything and although I've learned to take care of myself, to rely on no one, I can't help but relish the idea of Benji taking care of me, to once again belong to him.

"Okay, let's do this," I say smiling, but a part of me still knows we've solved nothing that drove us apart the last time. The accident will always be a broken bone hidden under the skin. You can't see it, but the pain is there, and despite the fact that it might have healed, it never healed correctly. It will always be flawed.

"Nothing has to change right away," Benji says. "I know you have things you need to take care of and I'll be there to help you."

We're still avoiding it all, the reason I came here in the first place and as much as I know we need to discuss it, I can't bring myself to start the conversation. We can just go on as if it didn't happen. We've survived this long without any discussion of it, among each other and with people we've met. But, in the end, we haven't really survived it, we've both just floated through life, ignoring and denying, only to find out we've lost another friend because of it. It's a secret I'm now keeping from him.

"Benji," I say, my voice soft and a knot forms in my stomach. I need to tell him even though I know it's going to hurt and there's potential that it will push us apart. I begin to relive it all; Tommy's letter, the funeral and his burial, the pain I felt through it all and how I went it alone when I didn't have to. I don't want Benji to deal with this alone; it's what made all of this so difficult in the past. We need each other to cope, being the only two who understand what we've been through.

"What, baby?" he murmurs, his deliciously warm body wrapped around mine. His hands are roaming over my skin, first my arms, my stomach, my breasts; his fingers softly brushing against my skin distracting me and making me crave him.

"I have something to tell you," I whisper, my voice breathy.

"Shhh," he says, silencing me with a kiss. "We have nothing but time, baby and right now, I want to take a shower with you."

Despite the protests my head is screaming at me, I give in to what he wants. Maybe part of me is still avoiding it all, but right now, I just want the happiness I feel radiating from Benji to last as long as it can.

Before I can answer him, he's tugging me from the bed and into the bathroom. He starts the water and the bathroom begins to fill with steam. It's warm and calming and everything about him is a turn-on as I watch him step into the shower, his body disappearing into the fog.

I step in behind him watching the water cover his beautiful body, and even though we've spent the whole day together, I can't stop touching him. I run my hands up the muscles of his sculpted back, kissing him and letting my hands run down the side of his body.

He turns in my arms and I feel the cool tile against my back. He backs us up further until his body is flush with mine, the warmth of his skin coupled with the cold tile is driving me crazy as his hands reach down and grab my ass. When he lifts me up, I wrap my legs around his waist, pulling him as close as I can get.

Our mouths meet in a desperate, urgent kiss—hard and breathless. I can't breathe, but I don't care. My body is screaming for him to never stop.

I feel him enter me and I hear the groan that leaves his mouth as he does, and it makes me want more. We're as close together as we can possibly be, but I always want more. I want to be connected to him in every way possible as I take in everything; absorbed in him and everything he does to my body. I'm on fire and it makes me want to call out his name, and beg him to never stop.

"Campbell," Benji moans, his mouth kissing and sucking on my neck. "You make me fucking insane," he says, but this time his words come out in a growl, desperate and pleading.

Neither of us speaks after that; we can't. Our bodies are consumed by each other and our breathing hard and labored. It's intense and all overwhelming.

As we're drying off, Benji comes up behind me, gathers my wet hair in his hands, and pushes it to the side, exposing my neck. I close my eyes when I feel his lips meet my skin.

"You're insatiable," I murmur, reaching behind me, my hand cupping his face. "But I love it."

"I love you," he says, his hands now pulling at my towel until it falls to the floor, his hands caressing my body. "God, I want you, but I'm fucking starving," he groans, and it makes me laugh.

"Then let's eat, I don't want you to starve."

We decide to have dinner at the bar in town, since Alex and Annie are both working tonight. Benji told me they have an amazing menu and that Annie does all the cooking, but she's rarely there during the off-season, spending only two or three days there when the weather gets cold.

We take a seat at the bar and Alex greets us with a smile. He continues serving the two older gentlemen at the other end. Otherwise, the place is pretty deserted.

"It's always like this," Benji says, shrugging his shoulders like I should be getting accustomed to the quiet of this small town.

A few minutes later, Annie comes out from the back and practically squeals when she sees us. "Yay!" she yells, and Benji smiles at her. "I'm so glad you came in. I didn't think we'd see you tonight."

"We just saw you yesterday," Benji teases, rolling his eyes at her and she reaches across the bar and swats him on the shoulder.

"Stop being a shit," she says. "We usually see you every day and since Campbell came back, you've disappeared." She doesn't mean this maliciously or even jealously; it was clear when I met them that Benji spends a lot of time with them.

She hands us both a small menu and gives me a sympathetic smile. "Sorry, there isn't much on the menu this time of year."

I give it a quick look and my eyes catch Alex's as I look up. He winks at me and I add, "Better than lukewarm potato skins and chips and salsa."

"Hey," he says acting insulted. "I helped you out when I could've just told you to piss off."

"You did, Alex," I answer back, lacing my words with sweetness. "And for that I'm grateful."

He gives me a quick nod and it makes me giggle. This whole situation is completely foreign to me. I have no friends back home, my only social interaction being at work and even there I keep everyone at arms length. Before I left I had Carson, but even that was forced and in the end turned out to be a complete lie. I know I can't recreate what I once had with Tommy, Sam, and Kelly; but Benji and I can start over, create something new.

We place our orders and Annie disappears into the kitchen leaving us alone with Alex. We chat for a few minutes before the bar begins to fill up with customers, busier than I've seen it since I first set foot in here a few days ago. But given this is the only place in town that seems to be open on a regular basis, I'm not really surprised.

We sit quietly for a little bit before I turn to Benji and say, "You spend a lot of time with Annie and Alex."

He nods and says, "Yeah, they're my family." He looks away from me quickly, like he feels badly about not seeing his own family or guilty that I was separated from that whole plan. He's made no mention of his parents since I've been here and I can only assume he's lost touch with them.

"It's okay, Benji," I say, taking his hand. "I get it. Sometimes it's easier to start over."

"You still see your parents?" he asks.

"Not really. They moved down to Florida and rarely come home. But you know how my mom always was." I run my hand through my hair and shake my head.

"Yeah," he smiles a little. "Blissfully faking her unawareness of all the shit we were doing."

"Yep, and nothing's changed." That pretty much describes her and to this day it still doesn't bother me. I often wonder if it should. Would I have shut down after the accident had she been more involved in my life? Would I have shared with her what happened? All of it there in the back of my mind, but I still believe that tragedy would have struck hard regardless. It was an awful situation.

"How about you?" I ask him, although I feel like I already know he doesn't have a relationship with them anymore.

"Nope. After everything," he says, his voice taking on a softer quality as if he says it too loudly he might have to explain himself. "I kinda just disappeared. Never really told my mom where I was going and by that point my dad had met someone new. I felt like my life was falling apart and they were the last people I wanted to share that with. And the more time that went by, the harder it became to get back in touch with them."

He looks away from me and I can sense his guilt over it all. The accident has made us do things we would never normally have done. It's made us defensive and nervous, scared and closed off. I know the feeling well.

"Eventually I learned to live without them, I learned to stop missing them." He stops talking again, taking my hand in his. "Yet I always missed you. No matter how much time passed, I couldn't stop missing you."

I squeeze his hand and lean my head against his shoulder. I feel him kiss my head and I whisper, "I've missed you every single day."

Annie interrupts us, dropping our food off and chatting for a few minutes, but leaves quickly since the bar has become busier.

I feel like this is the way it's been since I found Benji. We start to talk about things, but our conversations are short and punctuated with small moments of admissions, yet nothing ever gets too deep; we're just scratching the surface. We can't possibly go on like this, but I can't bring myself to be the one to initiate what we both know we need to talk about.

I rub my hands up and down my arms and Benji looks over at me, wrapping his arm around my shoulder, he pulls me closer.

"You cold?" he asks, and I giggle.

"Are you going to warm my hands again?" I ask, cocking my head to the side and smiling at him seductively. "If the answer is yes, then I'm absolutely freezing because watching you do that was so fucking hot."

"It was pretty damn hot," he says winking at me. "But no, that's not the reason I was asking. I was asking because you were being a stubborn ass when I told you to take my coat."

"Why, so you could freeze instead?"

"No, I could've worn another, but you, in all your independent pain in the assness, opted to wear no coat instead."

"Mine was still wet and it wouldn't have been if someone hadn't tackled me in the snow last night." I shoot him a dirty look and he laughs.

"Stop being so fucking cute. I kinda wanna eat really fast and then take you home and have you for dessert."

"Do it then," I challenge, raising my eyebrows as I watch him start eating.

"Hurry up," he tells me. "We have some place we need to be."

We finish our dinner and wish Alex and Annie a good night. I climb into Benji's truck, my teeth nearly chattering from the blast of cold air that hit me as we were leaving the bar. I'm utterly freezing, not used to it being this cold so soon.

"Hurry, turn the heat on!" I yell, and Benji gives me a filthy look.

"Should've brought a coat," he says nonchalantly back, like he couldn't give a shit that I'm cold and shakes his head at my stupidity. I love his teasing; it feels so normal.

I slide over so I'm sitting as close to him as possible, slipping my ice-cold hands up his shirt, he jumps and practically calls out in shock.

"I need you to warm me up again, Benji," I say seductively, my hand sliding down his stomach and into the waistband of his jeans.

"Anything for you," he murmurs, both of us eager now.

And I'm once again telling him to hurry, but this time, it's not because I'm freezing.

We walk in, both of us desperate for each other and I'm peeling my clothes off as I make my way upstairs. Benji is behind me and when I look back, he's shirtless already. I can't control the impulse I have to stop where I am and forget the bedroom. I kick my pants off and as if Benji can see my urgency, he loses his too. We meet halfway on the stairs and his mouth collides with mine; both of us in need and I wonder if it will always be this way.

He's standing on the stair below me, his mouth level with mine and I can't stop kissing him. This is the way we were meant to be and as he takes me in his arms, I know there's no place else I want to be. I want to be with him forever. This is our second chance.

In his arms, Benji's mouth on my neck, he walks us carefully up the stairs and into the bedroom until I'm on the bed. I watch his beautiful body cover mine and he silently enters me as I whisper, "Make love to me." And in the quiet stillness of the bedroom, dark and peaceful, he does just that.

Chapter Nineteen

The next morning comes far too soon and I know there's no way I'm going to get Benji to stay away from work for another day. He's still asleep, our arms and legs are tangled together and even though I'm warm, I can't bring myself to pull away from him. I also know I have to go back to Chicago eventually. I can't keep avoiding my life there; I told Jack it would be just a few days I would be absent. I need to go back and break the news to him that I won't be coming back permanently.

I press my nose to Benji's chest, taking in his smell as he stirs in my arms.

"I love waking up with you in my bed," he mumbles, still tired.

"I do too, but I hate to be the bearer of bad news. I really have to go back to Chicago and talk with Jack, take care of everything."

I still can't believe I'm about to do this. Benji lives in the middle of nowhere and I'm about to quit my job, rely solely on him for support, and hope that nothing will go wrong.

Nothing will go wrong.

I need to stop being so pessimistic about life, about everything. There's a reason we found each other again. It was never over in the first place. We were meant to be together.

"Can you at least give me until noon?" Benji asks, his words pleading and I can't say no to him. I've never been able to say no to him, which is why I left all those years ago without telling him. "I'll go to work after you leave."

"Okay," I answer, and he pulls me closer to him. It hasn't been that long, only a few days, but I don't know how I'm going to sleep at night without him next to me. I've already grown used to the smell and the warmth of his skin near me, soothing me and making me feel safe. I don't want to leave.

"Anyway, you can't leave yet, your coat is still wet and I'm guessing it's now smelly since we've left it in a heap on the floor."

I laugh at him, knowing he's just looking for an excuse to make me stay.

"Fine, how about you go throw my coat in the washer and I'll make us some coffee?"

"No," he responds immediately, and I push up on my elbow so I can look at him. He's smiling as he says, "I'll go put your coat in the washer and make the coffee. You stay here in my bed, naked and waiting for me."

"Sounds like a plan," I say, smiling back as I lean down and kiss him.

I fall back on the bed as I watch Benji pull on a pair of sweats and head downstairs. I listen to his feet trudge down the stairs until he reaches the kitchen and starts the coffee pot. I can't imagine anything being as perfect as this moment.

A few minutes pass and he still hasn't returned. I'm growing anxious waiting for him and even though I told him I'd wait for him in bed, I throw on his t-shirt, the smell covering me as I slip it over my head and make my way downstairs.

"Benji," I call out when I don't find him in the kitchen, and I get no response. I call again as I begin to search the house. Going toward the back, I find him in the laundry room, my jacket in one hand and a piece of paper in the other.

Tommy's letter.

The moment I lay eyes on it, I stop breathing, my heart breaking in my chest as I try to find the words to explain myself. And when I finally tear my eyes away from his hand, I'm met with a look on his face that not only says he's confused but hurt and angry too. The letter is crumpled in his grasp, his mouth set in a firm line as he looks at me with wide questioning eyes.

"What is this?" he asks, and I say nothing, just staring at him wondering what to say, wondering how to explain myself, how to explain it all. "Campbell, what the fuck is this?" he asks again, this time harsh and accusing.

"It's a letter," I say meekly, and it only adds to his anger.

"I can fucking see that!" he screams, and I startle at the tone of his voice, all of this reminiscent of the accident, the way he spoke to me, the way it made me feel back then.

"He's dead, isn't he?" Benji asks, but although his tone is still laced with anger, I see the sadness in his eyes. I nod my head and he pulls his hand through his hair as his chest heaves with each breath he takes. "We said no more secrets. You kept this from me, Campbell." The hurt seeps through into his words as he clenches his teeth.

"I... I..." I can't even begin to figure out where to start. It wasn't supposed to go down this way. I was going to tell him, but after everything we had been through, I was struggling to break the news to him that someone else died, that we'd lost someone else we both loved.

"Fuck!" he screams, and now I'm crying. "Say something, Campbell."

"I didn't want to hurt you," I sob. "I never wanted to hurt you..."

"It's too late for that," he says, my letter clutched in his hand as he pushes past me. I reach out and he avoids me, moving farther away.

"Benji, please," I beg and he says nothing, just disappears into the other room. I follow him and when he turns around, he's still furious with me, but more than that he's hurt by what I've done and what's happened. We can't keep pushing each other away. We can't keep running from this, but that's exactly what he does.

He's pulling on a pair of boots and a sweatshirt that was left on a chair as I try to figure out what to say next.

"I'm sorry," I say, trying to keep my voice even, but the shakiness and the worry come through. I can't lose him again. This time it will kill me.

"See, Campbell, you made me believe you came back because of us, because you wanted what we used to have, that you loved me. And I fucking find this."

He holds up my letter, all tattered and taped back together. I know how this looks to him and while Tommy's letter was the catalyst I needed to find Benji, it was not the reason I stayed or the reason I found myself falling back in love with him. I've always loved him.

"Guilt made you come back. This fucking letter made you come back," he hisses and again the tears begin to fall.

"No," I cry. "It wasn't like that." But right now, it doesn't matter what I say, he's furious with me and I'm sure if I were in his situation, I'd feel the same way: used, misled, and hurt.

He doesn't give me an opportunity to explain, even though I feel like after he told me he loved me, and knowing the way I feel about him, I deserve his time, deserve to have him hear me out. Instead, he leaves out the back door, and as I chase him outside, my feet bare, wearing just Benji's t-shirt, the snow and cold air stings my skin.

I stand, freezing, as I watch him turn around and glare at me. "I can't be here with you, Campbell," he growls, and he gets in his truck and drives away, leaving me brokenhearted and devastated.

I'm not sure what I expected to happen, but after everything that went on between us over the last few days, I thought we would endure this together, that we were over shutting each other out. This is the Benji I ran from all those years ago and after letting him back in, I won't make that mistake again.

My chest aching and the tears pouring from my eyes, I head back in and gather my things. I won't be here to have him scream at me when he gets back. This is why I stayed gone and why I shut everyone out. It left me emotionless and right now, after what I'm feeling and what just happened, I regret ever coming here.

I'm ready to go in just under a few minutes, tossing on my clothes and shoving everything into my suitcase, but as I head to the front door, everything in me is screaming to stay, but with my heart breaking, I leave Benji a note.

B-
I love you. I've always loved you.
-C

I take my suitcase out to the car and as I'm putting it in my trunk, Alex pulls in next to me. As he gets out of his car I mumble, "He's not here."

"Is he at the shop?" he asks, clueless as to what has just happened.

"No," I answer sharply, and when he takes in my face, obvious I've been crying, he stops in front of me.

"Campbell, what happened?" he asks, the concern flooding his words.

"Nothing," I answer back as I get in my car, my eyes falling to Alex's hand, a flash of white catching my gaze as I close the door and say nothing more.

I can't put myself through this again and although I've been happier than I've been in years, this pain is more than I can handle. I need to forget I ever came here, I need to forget Benji, but the stupid part of me still loves him.

Too much.

And as I drive away, all I can think is maybe this is the end of it all.

Chapter Twenty

It's after six when I finally arrive home, yet I still drive straight to my office. It's the one place where this life doesn't exist and I can lose myself in all the work that I know is waiting for me. It's my distraction and I need it in order to keep going.

Everything hurts as if I've been forced to run for days without stopping. It hurts to breathe, my legs and arms aching as my chest feels tight, like it's closing in on me. It's stifling and painful, and far too real for me to focus on. I need it all to end.

I'm not sure what's worse, my memories of the weeks after the accident and my remembrance of walking away from Benji, or having it all happen a second time. It's like a horrible living nightmare that won't stop, and I can't imagine what it's going to be like when I go to bed tonight.

Jack's car is still in the parking garage when I pull into my spot and for some reason it pisses me off. I think right now anything would piss me off. I park and take the elevator up to the office, hoping that for some reason, he happens to not realize I'm back. But of course that fails miserably as soon as the elevator door opens.

I come face to face with Jack as he stands in the lobby of the office waiting for the next elevator. The doors open, but he's looking down and when he looks up, his eyes grow wide.

"You look like shit," he says immediately.

"Fuck off," I reply back and shove past him, heading for my office.

I hear his footsteps following me before he says anything else. The sound of them scraping along the carpet and then clicking when we hit the tile floor that leads to the office. I focus on the sound so I can drown out the thoughts that are running through my head.

How am I going to explain anything to him when I can't even explain it to myself?

"Campbell," Jack calls, as I reach my office. "I have no idea what's going on and you've told me not to ask, so I won't. I just need to know, is this one of those times when you want me here or should I just leave?"

I look up at him, my eyes dry and itchy from crying and as much as I want to unload everything right now, I can't. I just can't do it.

"Go away, Jack," I say emotionless, yet barely holding on. "I'll be back at work tomorrow. Regular time."

He stares at me for another minute before shaking his head and leaving my office.

A long breath escapes my mouth as I collapse in my desk chair, done with this day, done with trying to figure out where things went wrong, not just with today, but with my life. It's all a fucking mess that just keeps getting worse.

I pour myself into researching several companies Jack had asked me to look into before I left, allowing them to consume my thoughts, taking excessive notes and making a plan for the three I was able to get through.

It's well after midnight but I'm not even slightly tired. I should be exhausted by now and because of that, I decide to head home. Back to my home, the one I planned to leave behind just a few hours ago. I wasn't going to come back to this life; the one where I live miserable and lonely, shutting down and only carrying on because my body just won't fucking give up. But I have no other option. I'll bury everything and continue to lie to everyone around me that my life is normal, that the way I live and the way I feel is completely normal, but deep down I'm only lying to myself.

How much longer can I go on like this? I think, as I pull in my garage, especially after the last few days I spent with Benji. The reminder of what it felt like to be truly happy is almost worse than the nine years I spent living a lie. And even worse than what I'm feeling now, is the thought of being alone, again. I hate that I long to be touched by him, to be held and comforted and made to feel safe…made to feel loved. I miss him so much more than I ever thought possible. The pain of it all is so unbelievably unending and crippling.

I walk in and find the mess that was left by Carson and I run my hand through my hair. This is the last fucking thing I want to deal with, but I also don't want his shit in my house. I don't want anyone in my house ever again. I want to get back to what it feels like to live numb and detached.

The only saving grace of it is, that it's a distraction, packing Carson's things is. If I stay awake, it can't haunt my dreams, the accident, Tommy dying, my letter, and losing Benji a second time. If I don't sleep, it won't torment me.

I still haven't stopped long enough to think about it and I won't start now.

I begin packing Carson's things, in a rather strange and obsessively organized fashion. Placing all his suits and dress shirts, still on hangers and covered in plastic into a garment bag he used when he traveled for work and then moving on to what is left in the drawers of the dresser. It's not much, but I still neatly re-fold everything and place it in the suitcase that matches the garment bag.

I wonder what is driving me to do this, because I know it's not just something that occupies my time. There's more to it than that and that's when I realize I'm crying. The tears are falling from my eyes and I understand what I've become and I hate myself.

There is nothing left in my life; that small bit of hope I let through when I was with Benji is now gone and as it left, it ripped my chest wide open. This time, my whole heart went with it. Any shred of humanity and kindness and ability to love went with it, too.

And for some reason, I think if I do this for Carson, he won't hate me. But like everything else, it's a lie too. It just makes it easier to live with myself. I'm a horrible person.

I finish packing all of Carson's things, placing them by the door so I can take them with me to work tomorrow. I'll courier everything from the office to where Carson works. This will save me the time and the stress of having to deal with him and despite the fact that he cheated on me, I'm the one who ultimately ruined everything between us and I'm not sure I can face him.

I didn't love him and I never would have, but I did love Benji and still do. Yet, I seem to ruin what I have; it all falling apart around me, slow and painful.

I pick up my phone in the hopes that Benji has given me something, but I find nothing. I won't text him or call, because that makes me seem desperate, like I'm clinging to the one bit of dignity I have left and I'm torn as to what to do. I want him back, I want to feel whole again, but I also know how quickly it can turn bad. It's not something I want to deal with, and after the way things ended, I'm certain I can't put myself through it all again.

I'm avoiding sleep, and I feel my body beginning to shut down, my eyes heavy, my head starting to ache as a feeling of nausea looms. I know I need to sleep, but my life is a waking nightmare. I can only imagine what will happen when I finally give in and fall asleep.

I climb into bed, the sheets cold and unforgiving, and in the darkness of my bedroom, the loneliness only seems to be magnified. I'm done crying, I tell myself, returning to the harsh exterior I've grown used to, I need to protect myself. I can't let my guard down again. I won't find myself here, crying and desperate, but I know I'm lying.

I miss Benji more than anything. I miss him more than I miss myself.

I find myself falling asleep, but fighting it vehemently, because each time I close my eyes I see his face. I hear his voice say my name and feel his hands on my body, comforting me, and it hurts like hell.

I wake up, a silent scream stuck in my throat. My mouth is open, but no sound comes out. I'm covered in sweat and shaking before I finally suck in a rough, hard breath. It does nothing to calm me; the visions of the accident replaying endlessly in my head, each image worse than what I remember.

This time it's Benji's body, lifeless and bloody, slumped over the steering wheel and I'm standing in front of him crying, screaming his name, but nothing happens. I'm alone and I leave him. It's horrifying and disturbing and I wonder if this will ever stop.

I can't live like this. I can't live without him.

It's still dark out, but not nearly as early as I expected. It's after five, and as if I'm on autopilot, I do what I've always done and get ready for work. Going through the motions of a regular life, but not remembering any of it and by the time I arrive at my office, I can't even recall how I got here. Dragging myself off the elevator and into the dark lobby, because I'm far earlier than most of the people who work here, I head to my office and immediately close the door.

My computer is now sitting on my desk, open and starting up, I remove my phone from my bag and see a missed called, three actually—all from Benji. All of the calls coming in after two in the morning and I wonder how I missed any of them and then I notice my phone is on silent.

And despite the rush of energy that ran through my body at the sight of his name, I'm not sure I would've answered anyway.

My only thoughts are negative. What could he have possibly said to me at this point? And while I know at one point there was hope for us, it's now gone. It's too fucked up to fix.

Shit, this is not good; it's really bad actually. Seeing his name on my phone, knowing he's trying to reach me; I just can't do it.

I toss my phone back in my bag, ignoring his calls, ignoring him and ignoring the way I feel, torn and lost, but adamant not to set myself up for hurt. I'm not sure I could hear his voice and not breakdown immediately.

As soon as my day starts I begin to function normally again, even though Jack keeps eyeing me from across the conference room table with a look of pity in his eyes. It makes me sick and his stare is now becoming uncomfortable. I look away from him as I feel my hands start to shake, frustrated with myself for ever sharing anything with him and even more upset that he can't just let it go. The more I feel his eyes on me the more flustered I become, making it difficult to carry on with this meeting.

"Excuse me," I interrupt as the president of our marketing department is in the middle of a presentation. His eyes quickly flash to me and he glares as if I've just broken his concentration. I'm sure I have, but I can't have Jack staring at me all day, especially since we are about to close a huge deal that I've been working on for months. "Sorry," I say curtly as I turn my attention to Jack. "I need to speak with you for a minute." And Jack instantly looks perturbed but I really don't care.

"Now?"

"Yes, now."

He lets out an irritated sigh before addressing the people sitting around the table and following me out of the room and into my office.

"What?" he says tersely, as I close the door behind us.

"You've got to stop. I'm fine."

"You're not fine."

My life has become all about hiding myself and right now I'm failing miserably. Jack can see right through all the bullshit and I need him to stop. He's making this far more difficult than it needs to be.

"From the moment I walked in here today, I've been nothing but professional and that should be your only concern." I look away from him not needing him to see the pain that hides behind my eyes. It's now harder than ever to hide it all.

"Campbell, please let me help you," he practically begs and it wrecks me. I wish he could help me, but this is so far beyond him or any help he could give. Not to mention the fear of what sharing all of it with him might do to my job, his view of me and our working relationship. I can't and I could never share this burden with anyone else. This is mine. I created this problem.

I shake my head as I answer softly, "No, Jack, please just let it go."

Neither of us speaks for a moment and then without warning he leaves, which has me breathing a sigh of relief, yet at the same time I'm crying inside.

An hour later, I step back into the same conference room I found myself in earlier in the day with Jack sitting across from me, but this time his face is stoic and he never once looks over at me.

He speaks firmly and professionally throughout our meeting and I eventually find myself looking over at the man sitting next to me. He's young, probably about Jack's age and I suddenly feel sorry for him. He's about to lose his company to us. I spent months researching him and his company as I watched his stock plummet on a daily basis as he tried to restructure, firing most of his staff and sinking more money in every day, only to find his company continued to fail. At this point he's so far gone, there's no way to dig his way out.

I'm certain he never thought he'd be sitting here with us as we talk money and mergers and a way to buy him out without it looking poorly for him. Jack bullshits him, coddles him almost and I hate it. This is what we've become. This is what I've become to keep myself detached from life. A hardcore bitch that takes people's hard earned businesses and profits off their loss and stupidity. It's a job that requires time and focus, and one mistake could cost Jack his entire life and maybe that's why I work so hard at it. At least one of us can be happy.

I want to tell the man sitting next to me exactly what's going to happen, because right now he's too blinded by the money end of it to see it's all going to end badly. We're going to sell off his company piece by piece to the highest bidders; salvage is what we call it, leading us to make more money than he's seen in the last five years. He doesn't want to fail and sees this as a means to an end, but when it all comes down to it; he fails and we profit.

I often wonder if I should've taken a job where I help people and not one where I ruin their lives. Would it have been my redemption for what I had done? Would the accident and all the death no longer matter if I spent my days helping others? It doesn't matter, because I would still be living a lie, carrying secrets that burden my life beyond repair.

Nothing can repair what I've done and nothing can bring them back.

Chapter Twenty-One

I've only been home for an hour and I'm already drinking, drowning in it actually. I want to block it all out.

My life.

Everything.

As much as it hurt to see Benji's name on my phone, I found some sort of sick comfort in it. Like he might still care, like he still loves me despite the awfulness that continually surrounds us. I left him that note, the one that said I loved him. What more can I do? I could call him; beg him to take me back. But then, this nagging voice at the back of my mind asks, *Who calls at three in the morning?* Drunk people, the kind who speak the truth and tell you what they're really thinking.

I should know, I'm drunk and right now, no one wants to know what I'm really thinking. It's horrible.

I wish I had died in that car accident. I wish I had the courage to take my own life like Kelly and Tommy. Maybe if I had thought to be so selfish, I could have ended all this pain.

To be happy, we must not be too concerned with others.

I come back to that quote that I always believed to be bullshit, but now I see the truth in it. Or maybe my concern for the others should have driven me to take my own life. Concerned about how all of this affected them and how with one simple change to the plan, maybe they all could've lived normally. Were Kelly and Tommy concerned with anyone else when they chose the route they did? Maybe they were thinking about everyone but themselves or maybe it was always about them? The pain too much to bear, the loss and the heartache too debilitating. I should know.

I was so distraught after the accident that I couldn't see that Kelly was dying too. Both of us falling apart, but I never asked how she was doing, not that I needed to. It was clear to everyone around us that we were all fucked up. But it was one of those stupid questions that mean nothing, there's no real concern in anything like that. It's just what people ask;

maybe I should've asked. I never did. I never thought to. I just let her die a silent death from a broken heart.

Had it been me who died in that accident, she'd still be alive and so would Tommy. Neither would have had any reason to do what they did. Their lives wouldn't have changed and after knowing what I know now, Benji's life would've been better without me, too.

The room begins to spin as I pick up the bottle of vodka and take another drink. Falling onto the couch, my foot on the floor in an attempt to subside the feeling of the room moving, yet I still keep drinking. I want to forget, but I can't. Even the alcohol can't make it go away.

My thoughts begin to swirl and suddenly I'm remembering Kelly's funeral. I'm crying now even though I didn't cry at the funeral. Numb and confused, lost and heartbroken was what I was back then.

I can picture her in the casket. They buried her in her prom dress. Who does that? Who buries their daughter in her prom dress? Who buries their nineteen year old child at all? It was a tragedy, a horrible, disgusting, avoidable tragedy.

Her mother begged me for answers, racked with grief and the idea that her daughter would never get married, have kids or grow old, she couldn't stop herself from questioning me, crying and pleading for me to give her something. I couldn't do it. I had nothing left to give.

Benji's hand felt foreign in mine as we stood together at Kelly's funeral. I couldn't seem to hold his like I once had, switching my grip, but each time finding no solace in it. We were doomed.

With Benji on one side, Tommy on the other, his was the hand I held tightly. The one I couldn't let go of and as he stroked his thumb over my knuckles, I watched the tears fall from his eyes. The three of us, ruined forever.

The room is spinning faster now and I'm having trouble seeing. I'm tired, but every time I close my eyes, I see Kelly, with her bruised neck, and wearing her pale pink prom dress. I see Sam, laughing and teasing me, but then I see him bloody and lifeless, a shell of what he once was. I feel Tommy's hand stroke my knuckles and I remember what it felt like to love Benji and have him love me back. I'm sobbing now, uncontrollable, deep guttural sobs that make my body ache.

It's too much and I cry out even though I know there's no one to hear me. The bottle is empty now but my thoughts aren't.

My letter, I think as the room moves and I climb off the couch, sliding along the wall and into the kitchen to find something to replace the empty bottle.

Benji has my letter, my letter from Tommy. The one thing I have left of him. I need to find my phone. I need to call Benji. I need my letter.

I need him.

I open the cabinet and find a bottle of scotch, but it slips from my hand and crashes to the floor. The noise is loud and shattering, the floor wet with alcohol and I collapse on my knees, crying, my tears mixing with the mess in front of me.

How did it get this bad?

As I pass out I hear the doorbell go off. It keeps happening, over and over, but I can't move. It'll stop and then it does.

I wake up in a pool of alcohol on my kitchen floor the next morning, my head throbbing and my eyes burning, the sound of my phone ringing as I try to locate it.

"Hello," I answer groggy and disoriented.

"Jesus fucking christ, Campbell," Jack shouts into my ear, and I feel my stomach forced into my throat and my head split in two. "We have a fucking meeting with Saxon about that merger in ten minutes and you aren't here."

"Shit fuck," I mumble, and Jack begins to yell again. I can't even begin to process it through this headache. "Stall," I manage to get out as I stumble to the bathroom before hanging up on him.

I down three ibuprofen and get in the shower knowing I can't show up to work smelling like a drunk. Who am I kidding? I am a drunk. A borderline alcoholic. An alcoholic.

A sad thought crosses my mind as I stand under the water. In the few days I spent with Benji, I didn't need to drink. I didn't need it to get by, to fall asleep or forget. Maybe that says something. Maybe it says a lot.

I push it from my mind and finish getting ready. I haul ass into the office, sucking on a million peppermints that I hope make me smell better and keep the vomit at bay. I'm a fucking mess, but I really need to pull it together.

I walk in only twenty minutes behind schedule with a fake smile plastered on my face, greeting everyone as if I didn't just spend last night drinking myself stupid.

"Good morning, gentlemen," I say noticing I'm the only woman in the room. "Sorry I'm late. Traffic was horrendous." I roll my eyes and exaggerate my words as I sit down in the only empty chair.

I can function normally when I need to and it's disgusting.

The meeting begins and the discussion goes along without any problems. I see Jack rise from the table, excusing himself; he steps by my chair, leaning down he whispers, "Thank you," as he leaves the room.

I can't help but feel a little bit pleased that at least someone is happy in this situation. It certainly isn't me.

I'm discussing the merging of two companies that I hope will minimize the loss for both when I hear Claire's voice call out, "I'm sorry, sir, but you can't go in there." It catches me off guard and I wonder just who she's talking to. I immediately turn my attention to the door and everyone in the room stops talking and does the same, and then I hear Jack's voice loud and booming.

"Holy shit, Benji Kennedy, what the hell are you doing here?"

My heart drops to the floor and I suddenly feel like I'm going to be sick. This can't be happening, not here, not now. I'm on my feet, staring at where the voices are coming from.

"Campbell in here?" I hear Benji's voice shout, and then the door flies open and he's standing there.

He looks like hell, not that I'm one to judge, and when he storms over to where I'm standing, I panic.

"No!" I shout, and everyone in the room stands up. My heart is racing like it's going to tear through my chest at any moment, pounding against my ribs almost painfully. "You can't be here."

"Campbell, no!" he shouts back, and I can feel my eyes fill with tears of embarrassment and frustration but more than anything, I'm completely shocked that he came. He came to find me. "I'm sorry," he begs.

I shake my head. "You can't be here right now. I'm at work. This isn't the place for this."

I forgive him, I do, but not here, not like this.

"Please go, Benji." I plead, walking toward the door with every eye in the room on me. There must be something in my words that he hears, because he listens, waking out of the conference room, leaving me alone.

I immediately regret everything that's happened. I should've told him I forgive him, that I love him and I'm sorry for everything that happened while I was at his house. But none of it would transpire in my confused and frazzled brain.

Seconds later Jack is in the room pulling me out the door.

"What was that?" he asks, the confusion in his voice pouring through. "Do you need to leave?"

I shake my head quickly, not even thinking about what I've just done. It's my instant response to think about my fucking job over everything else. *What is wrong with me?*

"Go, Campbell," Jack says, his hands on my shoulders as he gives me a shake. "Go find him." Although he's still unsure of what is happening, he's pushing me, clearly aware that Benji has something to do with all of this.

"But..." I start to protest and he cuts me off.

"No. No more bullshit, Campbell. I don't know what the fuck is going on, but go."

"Okay," I stutter out as I walk to my office, confused and trying to process everything.

I grab my bag and find myself starting to panic. What if I can't find him? Where did he go?

I pull my phone from my purse as I stab at the elevator button praying for it to move faster. I get Benji's voicemail and I leave a desperate and disjointed message, begging him to call, asking where he is and telling him I'm sorry and ending it with an awkward stuttered cry. I'm overwhelmed and unsure of what the hell is going on.

I fly out the door of the building, the sidewalk and street a sea of people and I scramble looking for Benji, but I don't see him. This shouldn't surprise me; a city this large and I expected to find him immediately, the thought is just ridiculous.

He's gone. I've lost him again.

It's my fault. I shouldn't have behaved that way. Nothing is as important as what I have with Benji, what we have together, and I just drove him away.

I sit down on a bench outside the building as I catch my breath, trying to settle myself down. I call him again, but I get no answer.

"Please, Benji," I beg, as I leave another message. "Call me. Tell me where you are. I'll meet you there. I love you." My sentences are short and choppy, but hopefully getting my point across should he listen to my message.

After a few minutes of staring at my phone, I hail a cab back to my house. I was in no shape to drive to the office today and I'm glad I didn't. The encounter with Benji was both emotionally and physically exhausting and as I fall into the cab, I start crying almost immediately.

The ride feels long and I check my phone obsessively, only to find nothing. I need to get home to the quiet and comfort of my house. Everything is accentuated, the city noise, the cab ride; I'm nauseous and I just want it all to stop.

The cab pulls up to the front of my house and I pay the driver without ever acknowledging him, and when I look out the window I see Benji sitting on my front steps with his head in his hands.

I can't get out of the cab fast enough.

Chapter Twenty-Two

Scrambling from the cab, I call his name and he looks up at me, but his face is sullen and I long to hold him in my arms and tell him everything is going be fine. We're going to be fine.

Before I can even reach him, he's standing in front of me, grabbing me and pulling me into his arms.

"I know you hate me," he says, and his voice sounds strangled. "But I can't think of anywhere I'd rather be right now than with you."

"I don't hate you. I never have and I never could." It kills me that he thinks this. He's all I have left of what was once my entire life, everything I ever knew and loved. And he was the biggest part of that.

"You should," he stutters out, and I can tell he's on the verge of tears. "After what I made you do. I made you leave the accident. You didn't want to and I made you."

"Benji," I say, taking his face in my hands. "You didn't make me do anything." I'm shaking my head, again in disbelief that he considers this to be true. We all made a choice that night, and whether we believe it was wrong or right, there's no going back now. The damage is done and I blame no one, each of us equal partners in what occurred. But that doesn't mean I don't blame myself for all the tragedy that came afterward.

I ran away from it all. I left Benji and Tommy alone and grieving, never to wonder what it would do to them, never thinking about how much they would struggle. I watched Kelly die a slow death, one that I could've stopped, but I was too far gone at that point to intervene. If the blame falls on anyone, it's me.

"It's my fault," I tell him, finally getting it off my chest; this thought that has dictated my life until now. It's almost a relief to say it out loud, but then I realize maybe we all blamed ourselves for some part in all of this. I wouldn't know, because I disappeared and it was never something any of us dared to discuss with each other.

But that all needs to change now if Benji and I are truly going to make this work. No more half-truths and avoidance, no more running and disappearing; we need each other and we need to finally grow up and face what happened.

"None of this is your fault," Benji says sympathetically, and I rest my head on his shoulder, his arms encircling me.

"Then none of this is your fault either."

We stand holding onto each other for what feels like forever, neither of us speaking, just standing in each other's arms, finding the comfort we both need. Benji presses a few kisses to the top of my head and each time his lips connect, I feel myself shiver in his arms. His touch, the smell of his body, everything about him is perfect and I'm not certain I would've lasted another day without him.

With his lips next to my ear, he whispers, "I'm sorry my first instinct was to push you away."

"I want your first instinct to be to pull me closer," I answer back, my lips pressing a soft kiss to his neck.

"It will be. Always."

It's these words that correct everything that has been wrong between us. He will always be my salvation, my redemption; the person I cling to and the one who put my heart back together. I love him.

Benji's hand slides into my hair and I trail my lips along his cheek before finding his mouth. He pulls me closer and this kiss isn't just about finding each other again or the apologies, it's for everything we both know we did wrong over the last few days and the last nine years. It means so much.

As we separate, I take his hand in mine, leading him up the steps and into my house.

Forgetting that I left in a hurry this morning and after the night I had, the place is a mess.

"Jesus, Campbell, what happened?" he asks as he looks around. The empty bottle of vodka lying next to my couch, the kitchen floor covered in glass and spilled scotch, while the place smells like a liquor store.

"My life," I tell him, and he lets out a long, slow breath as he pulls a white envelope from his pocket. I catch it out of the corner of my eye and I know immediately what it is.

"Alex?" I ask.

Benji nods his head. "How'd you know?" he asks.

I saw Alex just before I was leaving Benji's house after we had the argument about him finding Tommy's letter. I saw the flash of white in Alex's hand and for a fleeting second I thought it might have been a letter for Benji from Tommy, but in that moment, it seemed ridiculous. Like I was holding onto some false bit of hope that maybe a letter from Tommy would change Benji's view of all of this as it did mine.

"I saw Alex before I left and he was carrying something. Why did Alex have your letter?" I ask, hoping it's a letter from Tommy, one that should've arrived and explained everything, so he didn't have to find out through the secret I was keeping from him. I didn't want him to find my letter. I wanted to be the one who told him Tommy had died. But something failed and he found out the one way he shouldn't have.

"All my mail gets delivered to the bar," Benji explains. "We're the only houses outside the town limits and it's always been that way."

"Did you read it?"

"I did, but it took me a while. I wish you would've been there when I did." He stops talking, the envelope still in his hand. "I wish I would've been there when you read yours," he says, his tone hushed. I can hear the guilt in his voice and I hate it.

He pulls my torn and taped letter from his pocket, handing it to me. "This belongs to you," he states, like he somehow knows I need it. Like he's returning it to me because it's all I have left of Tommy. If anyone understands, it's Benji.

I take it from him and when I do, he takes his letter out of the envelope and hands it to me, too.

I don't want to know what it says, but I can tell by the look on his face that he needs me to read it. My outstretched hand is already trembling as I take it from his grasp and walk over to the couch. Benji sits down next to me, his arm wrapping around my shoulders as he pulls me against his body, my head resting in the crook of his shoulder.

My entire body is now shaking as I hold the letter in my hand. My palms grow sweaty and my heart begins pounding and Benji tightens his hold on me. It's not like I'm scared of what the letter will say, I'm scared of all the pain that will come with reading it.

I take a deep breath and open the letter, but my eyes are closed. "It's okay," Benji whispers, encouraging me, but my eyes remain closed.

I feel Benji's heart beating in his chest, I hear it, my ear resting closely as I take another breath. I'm still, not moving, not thinking, and in this stillness there is one sound: the sound of our pounding hearts together.

And then there were two.

Without thinking anymore, I open my eyes, scanning the page quickly, but never really reading what is written. The letter is short, just like mine, and I find myself returning to the top and reading it. Slowly and methodically, despite the feeling of emptiness that has taken hold of my body. The tears spill from my eyes as I read each line.

Benji,
She's falling apart. You're going to lose her too.

As much as she doesn't want to hear it, you need to tell her what happened. She needs you. You need each other.

I love you both.
Tommy

I'm holding onto Benji's shirt, my eyes foggy and flooded with tears until I can't see what is in front of me. The letter falls to my lap and I bury my face in Benji's chest. Once again I'm inundated with unanswered questions and they float around in my head mindlessly.

How did he know I was falling apart? Would Benji have lost me too? Was I on the verge of doing what Tommy and Kelly both did? I don't even know anymore. My life had spiraled out of control and I was no longer the one controlling it. I kept moving forward with no real understanding of where I was going or what was happening. It wasn't until I got Tommy's letter that I realized I needed to face it all or be faced with losing Benji or myself.

But how did he know any of this?

I finally pull away from Benji and he wipes my tear-stained cheeks and kisses me softly.

"We have a lot to talk about," he says, and I nod my head.

It's been a long time coming.

"You ready?" he asks, but I can see his anxiety coming through loud and clear. His hands are now folded in his lap, but they aren't still. He reaches out and takes my hand and when he does, I can feel it shake in mine.

"Yes," I say, but the answer is really no. I won't ever be ready for this. Never.

"Tommy was the only one who knew what happened before and during the accident," Benji begins, but he stops and looks at me. We're not sitting apart, but the distance between us is small, it's too much. I move closer to him, my arms slipping around his waist, hugging him to me as I rest my head on his shoulder.

"I love you," I tell him, and even though it won't make this any easier, he needs to hear it. "I love you no matter what." I mean it. Nothing he says now or anytime after this will ever make me question how I feel about him.

"I know, Campbell and I'm not afraid of losing you anymore, but everything I'm about to tell you is horrible and ugly, and it's going to hurt like hell."

This is going to be a struggle for both of us, but this time we're together and I hope it will ease some of the pain that's going to come with reliving this.

"Before Sam even started the car Kelly had passed out," Benji begins and this is something I already know, yet he still includes this detail and it's not until he continues that I realize why. "As we started to drive away, Tommy noticed she wasn't wearing her seatbelt and he leaned forward and put it on her."

"Tommy saved her," I murmur, a feeling of anxiety pooling in my stomach.

I feel him nod against my hair. "He did, but I think there were times he wished he didn't."

He doesn't need to elaborate, I understand what he's saying and there's nothing insensitive in his comment. Kelly was never the same after losing Sam and all Tommy wanted was for Kelly to be happy, which is why he stayed in a relationship with her where he had to share her with Sam. It was always about her.

"Tommy saw everything, Campbell," he says suddenly. "Sam was speeding and so was the other car and when he came around the curve, he didn't even have time to brake. We collided head on with the other car."

I didn't really need to see this to know this is what happened. It was easy to put together the logistics of it after looking at the scene. What is still unknown is how we knew people had died and what made us all decide to leave.

"You were unconscious for about five minutes after the accident," he starts to say, but I interrupt him.

"Did you think about leaving me there?" I ask, and he pulls away from me, a look of shock on his face.

"No. Never. Not even once." He swallows hard and takes my face in his hands. "Campbell, I would never have left you there. I don't want you to ever think that." He kisses my face, each time his lips touch my skin he says, "I love you."

What made me any different? Was it because I survived? He didn't have to stay; he didn't have to save me from it all. But he did. He tried to shelter me from it and even though all the secrets and lies are what drove us apart, it's going to be what heals us.

The thought still fresh in my head, I ask it even though it's strange and possibly self-absorbed, but I need to know. Why I was different than Sam or the family in the other car. I realize I survived, but why didn't he just leave me?

"Why?" I ask. "Why didn't you just leave me there?"

"I couldn't, Campbell," he says, and pauses a second, shaking his head. He starts to speak and stops. "Honestly?" he questions, and I nod my head. "Everyone else was dead and you weren't. They didn't know we left them. You would've." He looks away from me like he's horrified at his answer, at his honesty. "But it wasn't just that. I loved you, Campbell. I still do." He swallows again and I see a tear roll down his cheek. "Even if you had died, I wouldn't have left you there," he says quickly. "And that makes me a horrible person. I left Sam without giving it a second thought, but had it been you..." He trails off, unable to finish his thought and I understand.

As much as I fought Benji that day about leaving Sam, had it been him, I wouldn't have walked away. I couldn't have left him either.

His honesty is disturbing, but it's exactly what I expected. I wouldn't dare judge his choices because they were mine too.

"What I did still haunts me today. It's one of those things that if I could go back, I'd do it all differently," he admits, and with each word he speaks my heart breaks for him. All of the pain and hurt and the anguish we've both kept buried is about to finally be revealed. And it's obvious Benji knows far more than I've ever been aware of.

I curl my body alongside him, hoping that he'll find some comfort in my presence, in my closeness, and in my touch. I can't even begin to imagine what he's about to tell me, but I do know it's going to change both of us forever.

Chapter Twenty-Three

The room is silent and cold. I shiver in Benji's arms and I wonder if it's as cold as I think or if what we're talking about is driving my body into some sort of shock. Like making me relive that day is almost more than I can handle.

Benji hasn't said anything for several minutes and I don't want to push him. I need him to share only what he wants, only what makes him comfortable and then I nearly laugh out loud at my thought. None of this makes him comfortable. There will never come a time when either of us is comfortable enough with this to discuss it. With these thoughts or what we did. It will always be a struggle.

"There's more," Benji says breaking the silence as he kisses my head.

"I know. And whenever you're ready I'm here."

He chuckles a little, the small puffs of air that leave his mouth, ruffling my hair, but there's no humor in his laugh. "I'll never be ready," he says matter of factly, and I know this too, but after everything that's happened, I feel like we both need the reassurance. We both need to know this will never drive us apart again.

"Tommy and I…" he starts but stops. I feel him take a deep breath and let it out slowly. "Tommy pulled Kelly from the car and carried her away from the wreckage. She was still so drunk and confused. She kept losing consciousness…" And again he stops short, saying nothing but shifting in my arms and looking out the window. "She didn't know Sam was dead, Campbell. We didn't tell her," he says suddenly, and his voice shakes, the pain and guilt evident. "She would've never agreed to leave with us if she knew he was. We lied to her."

I remember Kelly screaming, "Where's Sam?" over and over, but at the time everything was so clouded and hazy, my thoughts a jumbled mess, that it never occurred to me to tell her. I guess I honestly didn't believe it myself. I kept thinking that maybe we made a mistake; that he wasn't dead.

It was a moment of complete surrealism and I kept feeling like I would wake up. That it was all just a nightmare.

I always wondered how they knew Sam was dead. I was unconscious and so was Kelly, how could they have been sure? And then the realization hits me.

"You checked, didn't you?" I ask, and I don't need to clarify what I'm asking; Benji understands. He nods nearly imperceptibly, but I feel it against the top of my head.

"When the car finally stopped moving, I saw you lying there, your face bloody and your eyes closed, it was the first thing I did. I shook you, but you didn't move. I kept yelling your name and you didn't respond."

I feel his hold around my body tighten and again I'm shivering. It's not from the cold, it's from everything that is being said; everything I'm finding out and everything I'm reliving.

"I laid my head against your chest. I felt you breathing. I heard your heartbeat and I started sobbing. I held you in my arms and cried. At that moment I didn't care who survived, I knew you had and that's all that mattered to me."

His words would ordinarily sound selfish, but I understand fully what he means. I'm sure I would've felt the same way had I been placed in his situation.

He continues and now it's like he can't stop, as if he needs to purge it all from his mind, from his body, from his soul, like there will be absolution in telling it.

"Tommy climbed over the seat and after he found out Kelly was still alive, he looked back at me. Sam hadn't moved at all and I think we both knew, but he still checked. It was then that he pulled Kelly from the car and away from it all."

He continues filling me in on how he didn't believe Sam was dead and despite the fact that he was terrified, he checked Sam's pulse too, actually, they both checked multiple times. While he said it felt like time had sped up, like they had been dealing with the situation for hours, only a few minutes had passed. And in those few minutes they made the decision to leave and act like we had never been there.

Neither of us has moved, still in the same position, my head resting against his shoulder, my arms wrapped around his waist, and I'm not sure I could look at him right now without breaking down. Maybe it's the same reason he hasn't moved. I can tell it's taking everything in him not to start crying.

He just admitted to me that he left his best friend, dead in the car after checking his pulse. There's so much insensitivity in it all, yet so much realism too. We were just kids, scared and confused. Our decision making skills at that moment were completely irrational and I feel like that's when everything started to fall apart. The selfishness took over. He was already dead. There was nothing we could do. He was driving, he was at fault; he was no longer one of us.

It's a sick and twisted world we live in and that day, we all saw it first hand. We saw what selfishness and fear can do to a group of people who were thick as thieves. It makes you run. It makes you forget the people who died far quicker than you ever thought possible, but more than anything, it makes you less of a person. You lose part of yourself. We all lost that day.

And just when I think it can't get any worse, Benji starts again.

"Campbell, it was all so horrible. I hated myself the instant I thought about leaving Sam, but at the time I didn't see any other option. Fear was guiding me and as I watched you lying there, you were still out, I knew this wouldn't be what you wanted."

He moves out of my arms, shifting so he can look at me, as if seeing me will remind him that he's loved, that it doesn't matter what he did because I did it with him. "I...I...I decided not to leave him." I give him a questioning look because I know how this all played out in the end. We did leave him. "I knew you'd come to and be the voice of reason. Something about seeing you there reminded me that this wasn't about just me, this was about all of us, and Sam would always be one of us."

I'm not at all prepared for what he says next in spite of knowing that we did ultimately decide to run away from the accident and leave Sam.

"Before you came to and after I made my decision," he says, his voice weak. "We realized that someone in the other car was still alive."

I gasp out loud, I don't mean to, but it escapes without warning and Benji tenses immediately. His body goes stiff and he looks away from me quickly, but I put my hand on his cheek bringing him back.

"Campbell," he whimpers, and I feel it everywhere; the ache in his words piercing my skin, making my heart shatter and my stomach churn.

"We watched him die. We could've done something, but Tommy and I stood there and watched him die."

He's crying now, the tears running down his cheeks and I pull him into my arms, his face buried in my neck. I feel the sting of his warm tears hit my skin and I cry with him.

I can barely understand him, his voice muffled with tears as it's pressed to my neck. "I used to tell myself that it was okay that he died. His whole family was dead, right?" he asks, but it's rhetorical, he isn't looking for an answer. "What kind of life would he have had? He was just a kid."

I understand what he's saying and his rationalization at the time seemed logical, but in the light of day, when the guilt creeps through and your conscience shames you for what you did, it's horrible. I hated myself and I still do, for leaving Sam, for not stepping in when I knew Kelly was on the verge of ending her life and now, for not ever reaching out to Tommy. But after hearing all of this, I know the guilt Benji carries with him is far worse than what feel. And now I know why he disappeared.

"It was never my decision to make," Benji says, his voice now a harsh growl, angry with himself and with his choices. "I chose for that kid. I never gave him a chance."

I don't know what to say. Nothing that comes out of my mouth will ever make what happened right. Nothing I say will correct all the wrongs; it will always be a burden we carry, but now he's not alone.

"I don't know what to say," I tell him. "And please don't think that's because I think what you did was wrong."

Before I can continue Benji interjects. "What I did *was* wrong, Campbell. Can't you see that? Can't you see what a horrible person I am?"

"No," I say shaking my head. "You're not. You were confused and lost. You weren't thinking rationally, but you can't keep beating yourself up over this. We have to find a way to get over it. Both of us do."

We have each other now and that should mean something. We've been going this alone, burying everything and trying to live a lie. But underneath it all, we're both a mess. Yet together we can fix this. We can find ourselves again and somehow end this guilt we carry.

"I went to the police once," he admits. "I asked them what would happen if someone was to leave the scene of an accident where people were killed." He runs his hand through his hair and wipes at the tears that have now dried on his cheeks. "They told me that if the person who left the scene was driving, they would be responsible for the death of the others. Vehicular manslaughter, he called it. I wanted him to call it what it was, murder. It was murder."

The way he says the word 'murder' makes me cringe. That's what it was. We knowingly drove drunk; while we didn't intend to kill anyone, that's a repercussion for our actions. It might have been something we'd done hundreds of times in the past without incident, but all it took was one time—one time to ruin far too many lives.

"It was like he knew what I was asking, like he knew it was me who left the scene, because he said that there really wasn't anything he could do to prove a person left the scene unless they were driving." Again Benji shakes his head, his eyes are closed now. "He also added, that the police don't generally look for that person if they have the driver. The person at fault would be the person they sought out."

"That would've been Sam," I add, filling in so he doesn't have to.

"Yeah," Benji says. "But we're all at fault. It could've been any one of us driving. It just happened to be Sam that night."

"I know. Don't you think that thought haunts me all the time? Why was it him? Why wasn't it me or you or Tommy or Kelly?"

"There are so many unanswered questions and not a day goes by that I don't wonder all these things and more," Benji adds. "You'd think I'd find some solace in what the police officer told me, but I just felt more guilty."

"It's been nine years. How do we turn ourselves in now?" I ask, and Benji shrugs his shoulders. "I don't think we do. I think we need to try to figure out how to move on, figure out how to start over, together."

"We'll never forget what happened, but we need to find a way to forgive ourselves for what we did," I say, knowing we can't continue to live this way, but knowing we need each other to survive it all.

I'm not even sure where to begin. I have so many questions and so many thoughts running through my head. Having heard all of this for the first time is overwhelming and disorienting. Trying to process it all and worry about Benji's feelings and how he's coping is more than I ever expected to encounter during all of this. Yet, as overloaded and upset as I am, I know we both need each other more than ever.

"We'll get through this together," I tell him, my hands on either side of his face, pulling his mouth to mine. I kiss him softly and slowly, my lips pressing to his as I let the tip of my tongue graze his bottom lip. I feel his hand slide into my hair, pulling me closer and he deepens the kiss. I find more comfort in his touch and in his kiss than I have felt in so long and when he pulls away, his forehead against mine, I murmur, "I love you, Benji."

"I love you, Campbell."

We sit together quietly, both of us finally calming down, but understanding that we've just scratched the surface of what we have to deal with. Discussing the accident, our letters from Tommy and our feelings about it all, is just the beginning. We have to figure out how to move on.

"Where do we go from here?" I ask, and Benji lets out a long slow breath before closing his eyes and wrapping his hand around the back of my neck. He kisses my forehead, his lips lingering for a few seconds.

"I know where we can start," he says.

Chapter Twenty-Four

His lips are still on my forehead as he begins to kiss his way to my neck. It's only been two days since we were last together, but I can sense the desperation and need radiating from him. After everything he's just shared, he needs to know we're okay, I understand. I need it too. The feeling of closeness, skin to skin, the touch of my hands, all of it will calm him and ease the stress of what we've both been dealt.

"I need you, Campbell," he murmurs in my ear.

"I'm yours. I've always been yours," I whisper back as I pull my sweater over my head. I run my fingers lightly down his chest until I reach the hem of his shirt, lifting it over his head, I toss it to the side and return my hands to his chest.

Benji lets out a soft sigh the moment my fingers touch his bare skin. He'll always be perfect to me, beautiful and caring and kind and selfless, but I know his heart is scarred. He's broken. We're irrevocably broken together.

I rest my hand on his chest, feeling his heartbeat beneath it and I know I'm lucky. I could've easily lost him, not just in the accident but also because of the accident. Not many people fall in love at age five, but we did. We've endured so much together over the years and this is just one more thing we'll deal with together. While the accident is a tragedy, it's ultimately what brought Benji back to me. It's what we both need to survive. We need each other.

My hands drift lower and with each soft brush of my fingers, Benji whispers my name. I undo his belt and then the button on his jeans. He's relaxed; his eyes are closed and his head is resting on the back of the couch. He lifts his hips as I slide his jeans and his boxers down his legs.

I kiss a path down his chest to his stomach, but before I can go any lower, he pulls me up to his mouth and kisses me, his fingers fumbling with my pants until they're unbuttoned and I'm wiggling out of them and my underwear.

I'm straddling his hips now, but he's reserved; his kisses and his touch slow and gentle as if he needs to take in everything about me. I don't want him to hold back anymore and in that moment he says, "Not here," and I take his hand, leading him to my bedroom.

I lay back on the bed and he stares down at me, but he looks tired and I'm about to protest when he shakes his head slowly. I knew he wouldn't stop now; he needs me and I love that he'll give himself to me completely.

And I will do the same.

I pull him down, lifting my head to meet his mouth with mine as his body covers me with its weight, with its warmth and the smell of him. I'm lost. Lost in him.

I feel Benji's hand slip between us and when he touches me I moan, telling him it feels good and that I never want him to stop.

I love what my words do to him; his breathing is heavy as he moans softly in my ear. He will be my undoing.

"Please," I say, and he pushes my knee up as slides inside me. He feels incredible and I whisper in his ear just how much I love him, just how much I need him, too.

I'm close, but our movements are slow and as I draw closer, I cling to him, my arms wrapped tightly around his neck. With his mouth next to my ear, he whispers my name over and over, and he could say it a million times and I would never get tired of it.

He makes everything in my life perfect.

We both wake early the next morning, but for once it isn't because of nightmares or insomnia or missing each other; it's being together that keeps us from sleeping. I can't get enough of him, even if it means losing sleep.

I snuggle against his warm body and press my face to the curve of his neck, kissing and smelling him. It never gets old and I know this time together will only add to my need to be with him at all times, to always be close to him.

It brings my thoughts to our plan before he found Tommy's letter, before we finally opened up and admitted what happened that night, and I wonder if he still wants it. I know I still do.

"I don't want to stay here," I tell him and he pulls back from me, giving me a confused look.

"In bed?" he asks.

"No. Here in Chicago. I want to be where you want to be. I want to be with you."

He says nothing, but wraps me in his arms; kissing me with everything he has, hard and pleading. "I wasn't going to leave without you," he says almost breathlessly, but with a smile on his face.

We both know we have a lot to take care of today and over the next few days, even possibly over the next year. This is going to be a lot for us to take on, but we need to start somewhere.

We haven't talked much about it all, but Benji has a plan and while it's not something I'm keen on doing, I know it's part of finding a way to move beyond all of this.

There was a time when he knew me better than anyone and what he says next makes me realize he still does.

"You're worried," Benji says, but it's not a question, he's not asking me, he already knows I am. "Nine years apart doesn't mean I've forgotten everything about you. We spent more time together, Campbell, than we ever did apart."

"What if doing this drives us apart again?" I ask and it makes my heart hurt. The thought of losing him again is something I can't even fathom, but it's always there in the back of my mind.

"It won't," he responds firmly.

"You can't possibly know that."

Benji lets out a sigh and rolls onto his side so he's now looking at me. His fingers trail across my cheek and between my breasts before coming to rest on my stomach.

"Yes, I can," he says, nodding his head and giving me a subtle smile. "My life without you was a fucking nightmare and judging by the way your house looked, so was yours."

Fuck if he isn't right. I'd honestly rather be miserable with him than ever live without him again. We're in control of the way things happen from now on and if the past has taught us anything, it's that we need to be open and honest with each other. Lies and secrets and running away solve nothing, and even if it hurts like hell, hide nothing.

We said it before, no more secrets and no more lies. We can't let fear and pain dictate the way we live our lives. This is about us and it's about healing, about finding a way to live with what we've done and somehow moving on despite everything.

I smile at Benji, not needing to argue or question the finality to his words. I trust him wholeheartedly. I always have.

I lean over and kiss him. I kiss him hard and intensely, like this might be the last time I'll ever kiss him, like we might never find each other again or like something will one day come between us again. While I know none of this is true, I hope we live like this forever. This intense feeling of wanting him and needing him, and the desire to be with him at all times, to feel his hands on my body, to need his touch to survive. To have this, and all of it coupled with the fact that we're the only people in the world who know what we've been through. We were made for each other.

It takes us another hour to pull ourselves from the bed and an hour after that to finally shower. Benji is unable to keep his hands off of me. It's like baring his soul to me, sharing everything, has freed him from this burden he carried for far too long.

I can only hope that it continues, that both of us find the redemption and solace in everything we're about to do. We'll never be able to go back in time and correct everything that went wrong, but from this point forward, we can set things right with our families, our friends and with our relationship and ourselves.

It's still early, but I send Jack a text anyway.

Me: Can you meet me at my house tonight around 9:00?

Jack responds almost immediately and I know he's already in the office. I'm sure he's trying to make up for my absence over the last few days and after what happened yesterday, he has to know I won't be in today either. I feel guilty for wanting to leave my job and leave Jack, especially after all the bullshit he's put up with from me over the last nine years. He didn't have to give me a job, he didn't have to tolerate me, but he did and he did it without question.

It's taken me a long time to realize it, but he loves me and he just might have been the reason I lasted this long.

Jack: Sure. What's going on? Do you want to meet me at the office instead?

I chose my house because it's intimate and this is now about my relationship with Jack as my brother and not my boss. He's deserving of knowing why I behaved the way I did for all these years and I also owe him an apology, one that no matter how many times I say it, it will never be enough.

Me: I'll explain tonight and nope, my house. I'll text you later on to make sure we're not running behind.

Jack: Ok. I won't ask any questions. ☺

I smile at his last text; this is the one time that I want him to ask questions, I want him to know everything.

It takes us about four hours to get up to Ann Arbor and the closer we get to the scene of the accident, the more the tension in the car builds. Neither of us has been back to the scene since it occurred and that's exactly what we're about to do. But this time, we're together and there are no lies between us, no uncertainty.

Benji reaches over and takes my hand, bringing it to his lips; he kisses it as he waits a long second before speaking. "It's okay," he says softly.

And I want it to be okay. I want to hear his words and know he means them; that we will be okay. Together.

Benji pulls off to the side of the road and it looks the same as it did nine years ago. I look down at the floorboard of the car and I'm hit with far too many memories at once. Things I've kept from myself, things that only find their way back to me in my nightmares and while they're not all bad, that doesn't mean they don't hurt like a bitch.

I can see Benji at nineteen, holding me in his arms, pleading with me to get in the car, a smile gracing his face and remembering how hard it was to say no to him. I was anxious but with it came the feeling of normalcy knowing I was surrounded by the people I loved. I don't think I told any of them enough that I loved them. Maybe I feel that way because I'll never have the opportunity again.

I said it to Kelly regularly. Leaving for class, writing her a note to let her know where I was, when she'd go home for the weekend, leaving all of us. "I love you," we'd say as one of us would part, but it became like saying goodbye. It had lost its meaning. I'd take back every single one of the times I'd said it, if I could have one more moment where we heard each other say it, where we knew it was the truth.

It always made Sam uncomfortable so I said it all the time. I'd scream it across campus when I saw him, I'd throw myself in his arm and kiss his face, telling him over and over until he'd laugh and say it back. We teased each other; it was part of who we were, part of our relationship. But I hope he knew I meant it. I meant it every time.

I can still recall the feel of Tommy's hand on my thigh when he slid into the seat next to me; the soft squeeze he gave it that made me giggle and the way his lips felt when he kissed the top of my head. I can hear his voice and feel him like it was just yesterday. His voice always had a soothing quality to it—quiet and reserved. I loved it. I loved him.

My tears are warm against my cold skin as they roll down my cheeks. I didn't intend to cry, but there are points when I no longer control my body and its reaction to things. This is one of them.

Maybe I'm crying over all the things left unspoken, for the loss I feel and the wonder if I'll ever feel whole again. Benji's return has helped, but there will always be a piece missing, three actually, in both of us. Because when I look over at Benji, he feels it too.

"You ready?" Benji asks, as he kisses my hand that is still laced with his. The touch of his lips sends a shiver up my spine and I grow cold.

"Yes," I say, nodding my head.

No.

I'll never be ready.

Chapter Twenty-Five

We step out of the car, the air cold against my already cool skin and I shudder at the sting as it hits my face. But I know it's more than that; it's not just the cold air, but all of it coupled with where we are and what we're about to do.

Benji meets me in front of the car, like he knows it's going to be a struggle for me to walk any farther without him close to me. Of course he knows this, because I imagine he's struggling too. His arm slips around my waist and pulls me against his side, kissing the top of my head.

"Can you tell me what happened?" I ask through a shaky voice, my words swallowed by the eerie silence of the road. It's deserted like it was that day, but something about its lack of noise seems peaceful, yet still somehow uncomfortably silent. The road is now repaved and the shoulder gravel packed firmly, undisturbed by the lack of cars that travel this route. All of it hiding what once happened here. Forgotten.

But not really.

Benji's arm tightens around my waist and he stops short of where the shoulder meets the road. We both look around, but I can sense he feels more than I do. I remember very little about the accident, really. I remember only a few details from the night in general. Although I can still picture what it looked like. While, what the cars looked like and seeing Sam's body is something I will never be able to forget, but the majority of it is lost. Sometimes I wonder if that's a good thing, but I also know it's not, because my brain likes to fill in the missing details and at times they are horrific.

"We were coming from the east," Benji starts, pointing in that direction as he turns our bodies to face the way the car was traveling. "The other car was coming around this curve." Again he points, angling his hand around to show the curve of the road.

In the dark of that night it all looked so different, scary and ominous, but here in the light of day, nine years gone, it looks like any old road, like it could be anywhere in the United States, like it doesn't have death marring it. It also doesn't look like the kind of road that is known for causing accidents. It doesn't have steep hills or blind curves or an extended straightaway that would make speed a factor. Yet both cars were speeding that night, both cars took the curve too fast, and one of the drivers was drunk. All of those factors played into what happened, what could've easily been avoided, but somehow came together like fate, an ugly, cruel fate.

"I only know what Tommy told me, but he said we hit the other car head on." Benji's words are quiet and although there isn't a soul around, it's like he's whispering so no one but me hears. "The car then spun around and hit this light pole." He motions to a new pole that has been put up in place of the old one. It's surreal once again, as if nothing ever happened here. They just come along and clean it all up, replace the broken parts, cart away the damage and all the broken glass becomes part of the road. Like it never happened.

Blissfully unaware.

But again, not really.

"The windows shattered when we hit the other car," Benji says continuing with the story and I interrupt him.

"I remember that," I say, and it's almost a relief that I remember something that really happened, that it hasn't been created by my mind or filled in to make the story that plays in my head complete. I look up at him and he nods his head.

I can feel Benji's breath against my hair, the cold air makes it come out ragged and labored, but I know that isn't the only reason. This is painful for him too, maybe even more painful for him because he remembers it all.

"Tommy told me that he thinks when we hit the light pole..." Benji stops shy of finishing his sentence, turning me in his arms until I'm flush against his body. Both his arms wrapped around me in an embrace that says he needs me, he needs to be as close as possible.

"He saw Sam's head hit the pole because the windows were gone. He thinks that's what killed him," he spits out suddenly. "He said he looked like a rag doll." Benji's chin is now resting on the top of my head, his arms cinched around me so tightly, it's almost hard to breathe. And as if he realizes it, his hold loosens, but returns again as he begins to speak.

"The side of his head was all bloody. I mean, it was obvious he was dead," he says with little emotion to his voice, and I don't think he's being heartless. He's trying to separate what he feels to keep it from hurting too much.

I pull him closer to me, my arms around him and I press up on my toes to kiss his neck. I leave my lips there and we stand together, silently mourning the loss of our friend, along with the loss of our innocence. Something we never did, something we needed to do.

We don't discuss what made him decide to leave Sam and there are times I think I want to know what his thought process was, what he and Tommy talked about, but then there are other times I'm glad I wasn't the one who ultimately made the decision. None of it weighs on me like it does him. I have my own issues, my own insecurities over the whole thing and maybe it's selfish of me not to want to know and not to ask, but I leave it alone. I also often find myself wondering if he even knows why we left. If it was just one of those choices that doesn't make any sense and you have no idea what drove you to do it. Fear, in this case would be my only guess.

When we finally separate, we walk down the road a few feet to the place where the other car came to rest. We both stop, but say nothing as Benji's hand slides down my arm and entwines with mine.

"It was a family," Benji says, again his voice a hushed whisper that is nearly lost in the wind. "They had two boys, I'd guess they were six and four. I don't know," he adds, but it's almost like he feels horrible for even speculating on any of it. "He would've died anyway, at least that's what I tell myself. It's a lie. Maybe he would've lived."

I look up and see Benji's face as a stray tear escapes from his eye and his jaw tenses. Without thinking, I rest my hand on his cheek, my thumb brushing away the tear and he leans into my touch.

I wish I knew what to say to ease his pain. I wish I had the words to take away everything that happened and make his world right again. But I have nothing. I can only give him myself and hope that I'm enough; that I'll always be enough for him.

"How can you not hate me?" he asks, but he's angry now and it breaks my heart.

"Benji," I murmur, the tears now falling. "I don't hate you. I couldn't. Ever. I love you. I love you more than I've ever loved anyone." I can't believe he would ever doubt how I feel about him or think I could feel that negatively toward him. "I see past all of this," I say holding his face in my hands, making sure he sees me. "And I know you're a good person and your choice back then won't dictate your life, it won't dictate our life together." I hope he hears me, hears the truth in everything I'm saying, but he turns away from me. It's crushing.

"We checked each one of their pulses, made sure they were dead," he says, cold and emotionless. "We watched that boy bleed out. Now how do you feel about me?" he asks, and I know what he's doing.

"Stop it, Benji. You're not going to push me away. I'm not leaving and you're not the person who did those things, you never were." I take his face in my hands so he's looking at me again and I can see that as much as he's trying to hide it, this is killing him. All of this is killing him. He's not angry; he's beside himself with grief and guilt. "I love you," I tell him, his face still in my hands. I tell him again and again until he's crying, his face buried in the curve of my neck.

"I need you, Campbell," he mumbles. "More than I ever thought possible. Don't ever leave me," he begs, and with each word, a stuttered cry leaves my mouth.

"Never," I whisper, stroking his hair as he hugs me tightly. "I'll never leave you again." Knowing I need him as much as he needs me.

We have one more stop to make before we head back to Chicago to meet up with Jack. It's a place Benji suggested we go and at first I was adamant that we don't. I didn't think I could handle it, but this is about facing what happened and this is part of it. Benji pulls into the cemetery parking lot and I feel my stomach drop to the floor.

"I came here once, right after the accident. With Tommy," Benji adds as we exit the car. Due to the cold weather, the cemetery is also empty.

We did our research before we left. It's strange what you can find on the internet, the gravesites and cemetery locations of the deceased. It also wasn't hard to find out their names, the accident was all over the newspapers after it happened and Benji tells me, their names will be something he never forgets.

It takes us a little while before we finally locate what we're looking for, but when we do, it's more difficult to take in than I thought. Seeing their names on the grave markers, all four together, the dates literally set in stone.

Final.

There will be nothing more for any of them and seeing it all, what we did, what we created when all five of us made the worst choice of our lives, it's scary as hell. How quickly it can all end and what it did to our lives and theirs.

There is no salvation in standing here; it just makes everything even more real. I'm not sure what we thought we would accomplish by coming here, but it has just added to our guilt and our hatred for what we've done. Maybe that's all part of coming to terms with this or maybe it's something we should've avoided. It's too late now.

Neither of us says a word, we just stare at the names on the grave markers, as we stand hand in hand. I can't look at Benji and it's not because of what he shared with me. It's because I know when I see his face I'll start to cry.

This is all extremely overwhelming and up until this point these people were just part of a memory I had that was hazy and broken. But now, seeing it in front of me makes these people real. They had lives, families and friends. We took that from them. They could've easily been Jack or Alex and Annie, people I work with, or people Benji and I know. They were someone's brother, sister, son, daughter, or grandchild. They were parents and the only solace and small bit of comfort I find in any of this is that they died together. But that doesn't mean they didn't suffer, that their families and friends didn't suffer too.

That Benji and I won't suffer with the reality of it all.

We will. We probably always will.

We say our goodbyes, as much as we can to a family we didn't know, but whose life we ruined. There's an apology in there too, but it doesn't matter. The damage is done.

The sky has begun to grow dark as the day fades to night. I shudder in Benji's arms as we walk together back to the car. The way the night falls makes it seem like it's covering everything we've done with black as if it's now behind us. I want it to be, but as much as much as I want it, I know it will always be a part of us.

Before we climb in the car, Benji takes me in his arms and we hold each other, just finding the comfort that only we can bring to each other.

"Thank you," he says, and my eyes close. "I love you."

"I love you, too."

It's been a long day, filled with regret and tears, comfort and peace, and far too much guilt, but it's not over. Far from it.

And as Benji starts the engine, I say, "You sure you're ready to come clean?" And without thinking about it, I take his hand in mine, covering the outside of his as I press a kiss in the center of his palm. I watch his eyes close and he takes a deep breath, readying himself to answer my question.

Jack will be the first person we share this all with and as much as it needs to be done, it doesn't mean it's not absolutely terrifying.

"I can't live with this secret anymore, Campbell," he says with complete sincerity. "I can't live like this."

"Neither can I."

Chapter Twenty-Six

We arrive back at my house just before nine and even though I told Jack to meet us here, I wish I'd have told him to come tomorrow instead. I'm exhausted, mentally, physically and emotionally, and I can see it all mirrored in Benji's face too.

"Come here," he says as I'm walking back out of the bedroom, my body tired, but I make my way to him anyway. When he opens his arms, I step into them without thinking as he pulls me against his firm chest.

I love how we've fallen back into this pattern of normalcy within our relationship. It happened so quickly, but in the end it's what I've always wanted. I love that he knows exactly what to do to make me feel better, to calm me and to make me feel loved.

I know most would think it's strange that I fell in love with him as a kid, but I knew from the moment I met him that we would be together forever. There was a part of me that missed him terribly when we weren't together, like I wasn't fully myself, like I wasn't whole. How I survived these last nine years without him is almost incomprehensible and honestly, I really didn't.

But as we stand here together, me in his arms, I know we're going to get through this, all of it and we're going to do it together.

The buzzer to my apartment goes off, causing us to separate, and Benji kisses me quickly before saying, "You ready?"

"I guess so," I respond, with a loose smile on my face as I try to mask the fact that I'm terrified.

Benji smiles at me, perfect and sweet and then he reaches for me, pulling me into his arms as he laughs. "I know you're scared. It's written all over your face."

"Then stop laughing at me," I say back, pretending to try to break free from his hold.

"I'm not laughing at you," he says, his fingers slipping under my sweater and pinching my side. "I'm laughing because it feels good to remember every little thing about you. Every single thing you do reminds me of how much I love you."

I melt against him, his body cradling mine like we were meant to be together, like two pieces of a puzzle, fitting together perfectly.

"I'll get the door," Benji says as I slip out of his arms. Grabbing my wrist, he pulls me back, kissing me hastily and then adds, "Go make some coffee. Something tells me we're going to need it."

He slaps my butt as I'm walking away and I giggle. It feels good to have him here, to interact so normally, nothing about it is forced and I love it. I love that he's trying to make this situation less anxious for both of us.

A few minutes later Jack walks in with a troubled look on his face. I can't even begin to imagine the horrible scenarios he has playing out in his head as to why I wanted to meet with him.

As much as I've tried to hide my problems from him and from everyone around me, I realize now that I failed miserably.

I'm curled up on the couch with my coffee mug in my hands, the warmth of the mug soothing. I set it down on the coffee table and stand to greet Jack. I wouldn't dare hug him, even that would be too much of an abrupt change from our normal. We've never been that type of brother and sister, even when I wasn't falling apart.

"Hey," I say, giving him a little smile, but it does nothing to calm his fears of why he's here in the first place.

He looks at me and then at Benji before returning his gaze to me. His head is tipped to the side slightly when he says, "You look different."

"Really?" I ask not, realizing how much different I actually feel too. With each step forward Benji and I take, it's like I get lighter, like I've been carrying around a pocket full of rocks and with each admission, with each realization, I lose one.

"Yeah and don't tell me this was about Benji the whole time. Like pining after him, lost love, and all that shit." He rolls his eyes and it makes me laugh. It wasn't just about Benji, although I was pretty wretched without him.

"Not exactly," I say, giving him a bit of a glare.

"Awww, see that, baby? I thought it was always about me," Benji says, sitting down on the couch, tugging my hand and taking me with him. Jack follows along, sitting in the chair across from us, still eyeing us with suspicion.

"I know you did," I shoot back, teasing him. "It was always about you, baby." I pat Benji's cheek and he smiles at me.

"Geez, it didn't take you two very long to get back to all that annoying baby shit I remember so well from when we were in high school," Jack quips, the humor in his voice breaking through as the naturalness of our conversation takes over.

The tension in the room begins to dissipate, but I know the real reason we're all here, and it's not going to go away with a few simple jokes.

I offer Jack a cup of coffee and when I leave the room to get it, Benji and Jack begin talking. I can overhear everything and I'm grateful to Benji for starting a conversation that may have taken me the whole night to start.

I want to tell Jack everything, but there's also the fear and the worry that telling him brings. I'm worried about what he might think of what we did, the judgment and the fear of losing him. Even though we've never been close, I still don't want him to not be a part of my life.

I know that with sharing what Benji and I did there's always a chance he won't be able to look past it, that he won't be able to see we made a mistake and that for the last nine years it's nearly killed us. He doesn't have to be sympathetic toward us. But I hope he is. I hope he understands we never meant for any of this to happen. And even more, we never meant for it to damage so many lives.

I hear Benji thank Jack for coming and explain that what we have to tell him involves both of us. He asks Jack to listen to what we have to say first before he responds, and then in a voice that is quieter than normal, he asks Jack not to judge me.

My heart clenches at his concern for me and I spend an extra minute in the kitchen trying to control my emotions. I can't start crying before we've even had a chance to explain to Jack what's going on.

When I walk back out, Benji and Jack have fallen silent and Jack looks up at me when I hand him his coffee.

He looks at Benji and shakes his head. "What the hell did you two do? Have an abortion? Some illegitimate kid running around?" he asks, and I know all of these things would be huge secrets in most cases, but they're not even close. I almost respond with, "I wish," because either one of those scenarios sound better than what we're about to tell him.

I take a deep breath and sit down beside Benji. I feel his hand slide across my thigh, coming to rest above my knee and it makes me think of Tommy. Of that day in the car, of the kiss he placed on my head and his quiet, melodic voice. Benji and I owe him so much and hopefully in death he finds the peace he needs. And I hope that with each sharing of our story, Benji and I find the support and comfort we need.

"Nine years ago, Benji and I were in a car accident," I start, and immediately Jack's demeanor changes. He sits up straighter, he sets his coffee mug down and I see in his eyes he knows exactly what I'm talking about.

"The one that killed Sam," Benji adds, but I'm certain we didn't need to say it.

"We were all there. Tommy, Kelly, Benji, Sam, and me." I suddenly look away from Jack, his eyes focused on mine and I can't help but feel exposed.

My hands fidget in my lap and Benji covers them with his as Jack sits across from us saying nothing. Benji did ask him to reserve his judgment until we're done so I know I need to continue.

"We left the scene after the accident out of fear. We were all drunk and high, our thoughts were not what they should've been and for the last nine years, we've kept the whole thing a secret." It all comes out in a rush and while I've given him the gist of it, any emotion that should be attached to it is gone.

Over the last nine years I've found myself emotionally detached from everything, including Jack. It's hard for me to expose myself to him without keeping up this wall I've had in place for too long. I worry he'll see me as weak.

"Campbell," Benji says, and I turn to look at him. His eyes are full of pity; sad and confused. This isn't the girl he knows sitting here with him right now. This is the person I became when I learned to shut down after the accident. "Don't do this," he whispers, taking my hand in his and kissing it.

"I'm sorry," I respond taking in his face, and I know I'm going to cry, but I need to be okay with it.

"We're both struggling," Benji adds, looking over at Jack and he nods his head. I can't read his expression and it makes me even more anxious. Jack has always been stoic, so it shouldn't surprise me that this is how he's responding. His business thrives based on his ability to detach himself from the emotional end of it. And given this is how I've treated him for so long, I probably deserve the same in return.

It's a lot to unload on one person, but unfortunately there's more. With Benji sitting next to me, my hand in his, he gives it a little squeeze as if he's encouraging me to continue.

"So, in addition to Sam dying in the accident, a family was killed too." Again my words come out formal and it causes me to swallow hard. I need to let my guard down and be honest with him. "It was horrible," I finally say. "It took a toll on all of us and it led to Kelly killing herself and Tommy dong the same thing."

I wish I could explain to him all the feelings and emotions I carried with me throughout all of this, but I don't think I'll ever be able to put it into words.

"It all became a part of me," I admit to Jack. "It became who I was and who I am."

After everything, I found the grief and loss hard, but what is harder is the guilt. I may have lost far too many people I loved, but the guilt took more of me away. Guilt never leaves. With grief and death, you try to carry on, but you still feel it even after it's gone. Like the sharp sting of a paper cut, it's quick and fleeting. But guilt lives on in your conscience, it lives in your heart, reminding you of what you've done. And even after you've forgiven yourself, you can't forget it.

We eventually tell Jack everything, including the details of Tommy's letters and what we spent yesterday doing. And while we both agreed there would be no more secrets or lies, we keep one thing to ourselves.

Neither of us mentions the boy that Tommy and Benji watched die in the car after the accident. It's not mine to tell and I understand why Benji keeps it to himself. There comes a time in the telling of all of this that some things can remain unspoken. That the specific details only add to the tragedy rather than end it. This is one of those.

I feel like I've been waiting hours for Jack to say something. We've finished telling him and I can tell he's trying to process it. It's a lot to take in. But my need to gauge a response from him is weighing on me.

"Well, this explains a lot," he eventually says, and again I can't tell what he's thinking. I want to beg him to say something more, but I keep my mouth shut. He runs his hand through his hair, but sits quietly.

My patience is wearing thin and my anxiety is eating at me as I pick my nails, but Benji, again takes my hand and manages to calm me with just his touch.

When Jack starts to speak again, I feel my breathing speed up. It's like I have been holding my breath for the last ten minutes and now my body is trying to catch up.

"I wish you would've told me a long time ago, Campbell," he says. "I'm sorry that you dealt with this alone for all these years."

A deep exhale of air leaves my body and my eyes close. He doesn't hate me. He doesn't think I'm a horrible person. Yet what he says next shocks me. I never expected him to have this reaction.

"I should've tried harder to help you," he says quickly, shaking his head as if he's blaming himself. "Campbell, I let you suffer. I looked the other way even though I knew there was something wrong. What kind of person does that? I'm your brother for fuck's sake and I acted like I didn't care."

"Jack, no," I say immediately, standing and walking over to where he's sitting. "This isn't on you. This was me. I pushed you away. I wouldn't have let you help me."

"But I should've tried."

I can almost feel the guilt he feels. I know it well and I don't want him to think this is somehow his fault.

"That's why we decided to tell you everything. We all have a lot to work through. Not just Benji and me, but you and me too. I want to make things right between us."

"I'm here for you, Campbell," Jack says, and when he stands up, I hug him. All his forgiveness and understanding means more to me than I can ever express.

"Thank you."

It's been a long day and after spending another hour talking with Jack, Benji and him catching up and the three of us returning to a normal conversation, we wish Jack good night. As he leaves, I finally start to feel like my life might one day return to normal. That Benji and I will be happy; that we'll be able to move on.

"You ready for bed?" Benji asks, as I lean against the back of the chair, my body tired.

I nod, my eyes closing with exhaustion and that's when I feel his arms slip around my waist.

"Come on," he says with his mouth against my neck, his words sending shivers up my spine. The sound of his voice is like the warmth of a sunny day, comforting and peaceful as his breath tickles my skin. "Let me put you to bed, my beautiful girl."

I can never say no to him and in this case, why would I.

Chapter Twenty-Seven

I love waking up to Benji. His deliciously warm body is wrapped around mine, and I fit perfectly against his chest. I don't want him to leave, but I know it's inevitable. After we've sorted everything out, we both have to return to our normal lives, at least for the time being.

We haven't had a free moment to talk about what happens after everything. I told him I didn't want to be without him and I know he feels the same, but nothing has been discussed. Prior to him finding Tommy's letter, I was moving there; I was going to live with him and we were going to be happy. I don't doubt that we can have what we want; I just wonder if we're being realistic. How soon can we conceivably put this plan in motion?

I have my job here and while I'm perfectly okay with leaving it, I can't just leave Jack without anyone to take my place. Especially after everything he's done for me. He gave me a job without thinking twice, and while I excelled at it, I would never have had the financial stability I have now if it weren't for Jack. And I realize now that as much as I despise what I do for a living, I love working for Jack. It has been the only stable thing in my life. I actually feel like it's possibly the one thing that saved me all these years.

I snuggle closer to Benji, my nose pressed into the crook of his neck as he sleeps soundlessly next to me. I lie here listening to the sound of his soft, relaxed breaths, his heart beating slowly and calmly under my hand, and I know I have to make this work. I have to figure out how to spend the least amount of time without him. I can't wake up without him next to me every day.

As I wiggle myself closer to him until I'm practically on top of him, he stirs in my arms. If I was trying not to wake him up, I failed. I can't stop touching him.

"Good morning," he murmurs, his hand brushing the underside of my breast softly with the tips of his fingers. "I love this," he adds as he buries his nose in my hair. "You naked and warm in bed with me."

His voice changes and I feel his erection press into my hip. I close my eyes as he rolls his body over onto mine, covering me and placing a series of soft kisses down my neck. He's tender as he makes his way down my body, kissing my neck, my chest, and then gently taking my nipple in his mouth. I whimper at the sensation and murmur his name as I feel him slide inside me.

His touch, the way he feels inside me, all of it is intense; it always has been, a rawness and a need to be together that has only increased with our time apart.

"Campbell," he whispers, and I moan at the sound of my name on his lips. I feel his hands run the length of my body, sending a shiver through me and goose bumps prick my skin. He's warm, but I shudder beneath him. The weight of his body now resting against mine calms the overstimulation I'm feeling.

I wrap my arms around his shoulders as he begins to move, slowly at first, savoring every second.

"God, Benji," I moan as I cling to his shoulders, my fingernails now digging in. He responds to me, moving faster and pulling back so I can see where our bodies are connected. "Please," I beg him, and he reaches between us, his fingers finding me, touching me.

I'm ready and I call out his name again. A loud groan falls from my lips as I come apart under him, my body shaking as I feel him push his hips against mine as he comes undone too. Our bodies sweaty and our breathing heavy as Benji's head falls against my shoulder and I feel his warm breath caress my sensitive skin.

It's perfect.

He's perfect.

"I want to wake up to you like this every single day," Benji says, quiet and sated as we're lying together. I can't believe how much we've changed, how much all of this has changed our lives. Not just the accident, but more than that, how finding each other again has made us both happier than I could've ever imagined. I never thought I deserved this and maybe I still don't.

"I was just thinking about that," I say, but I stop, wondering just how we can possibly make this work. Benji seems so certain and I hate that I doubt it at all. "Benji," I start, but he stops me.

"Campbell, stop. You're stressing over this and I get it. But we deserve to be happy. We've spent too much time apart to question any of it." He lets out a sigh. "I need you, Campbell."

"And I need you too," I answer back and I do, but I can't stop the feeling of uncertainty that continually returns. "But I have a house to sell, a job to leave and what if..." I can't finish my last thought because it's honestly what I'm the most worried about. The one thing that keeps me from just saying fuck it all and moving in with Benji.

"What is it, baby?" he says, running his fingers up and down my back. "Just tell me. No secrets."

I take a deep breath and spit it out because I know if I don't, it'll eat at me, make me worry and stress. "What if it doesn't work? What if you don't want me there?"

Benji laughs out loud and I slap him on the chest. Pushing him away, he laughs again and pulls me back. "Don't make fun of me," I say, feigning insult at his reaction. "I'm serious."

He takes my face in his hands, so I'm looking at him, so I can see all the want and need in his eyes. So I can see that he wants this as much as I do and that there isn't a doubt in his mind that we can make this work.

"Campbell, I'll always want you. I've spent the last nine years of my life missing you and that's not going to change. We were meant to be together and if all of this isn't enough of a sign, then every day I'll show you how much I need you, how much I want you and how this is the way our life is supposed to be."

I melt against him, my head on his chest, knowing I feel everything he feels and that his words can instantly right everything that is fucking with my head.

"Okay," I murmur as I kiss his chest. "I want this. I want everything with you, Benji."

We spend the next hour getting ready and when I emerge from the bathroom, Benji has a cup of coffee waiting for me. He's sitting on the couch, his leg crossed and his ankle resting on the knee of his well-worn jeans, still all scruffy and unshaven, but somehow so gorgeous. His dark hair coupled with his blue eyes makes my heart skip a beat with just a quick glance and I smile at him.

"Thank you," I say, picking up the mug and sitting down next to him.

"So what's the plan for today?" he asks, since last night we both just fell into bed not even taking a moment to discuss what we planned for today. We talked about it briefly since plotting how we were going handle everything, but we never went into detail.

"There's something I haven't told you," I say, but I was never keeping this from him. Our days have been so busy; it slipped my mind and didn't return until we made a basic plan for today.

"Really?" Benji says, his eyebrows going up a little. "What's that?" For once neither of us seems nervous or standoffish, not worried anymore about what secrets live hidden inside us.

"Tommy was married and he has a kid."

"Oh," is all Benji says, and I can see he's trying to process how this affects everything up until this point and after.

"She's the one who delivered my letter. Her name is Samantha and she has no idea what happened, but I think we owe her an explanation too. I think she deserves to know why her husband did what he did. Why he struggled all those years."

Benji nods a little and I get it, it's hard to take in. Knowing that what we did has now affected not just our lives but also all the people surrounding us. That it continued on long after we all separated, leaving many people in the dark.

"She hates me," I say suddenly, trying to smile through the thought, but it still hurts. I don't want her to hate me, but I understand why. I'm not sure I can ever make things right.

"I'm sure she doesn't hate you. She just doesn't know what happened, so I guess we'll add her to our list," he says with a questioning tone to his voice.

"I think we should."

Benji nods again and we both take our coffee with us, heading down to the car prepared to continue with what we started just yesterday. It feels like months, years even that we've been trying to correct everything, yet it's only been one day. The past weighing heavy on both of us, but knowing with each step we take forward, we heal.

As Benji starts my car, he turns to look at me with a cheeky smile on his face. "I think you're gonna need to get rid of this car, too."

"What?" I ask, appalled because I love my little coupe.

"This little thing is just not gonna cut it in those Northern Michigan winters." He shrugs his shoulders as if it's inevitable.

"Fine," I concede immediately, knowing he's right. I barely made it out of his driveway the last time I was there. "But I'll need a cute SUV now."

"Of course," he responds. "This isn't anything about safety. It's all about you looking cute."

We head out for another long day, since we have planned to travel to the cemeteries where Sam, Kelly and Tommy are buried, none of which are in close proximity to each other. Sam and Kelly are buried near the suburb where we grew up, but on opposite ends and Tommy about hour west of it all.

As we drive, I tell Benji about Samantha showing up at my office and how she believes that I'm the reason he killed himself. The guilt pools heavy in my stomach as I say the words, sometimes believing them. I shift in my seat, my hands beginning to shake. I hate that she's hurting over all of this and sees it as my fault.

"She's trying to process it all, Campbell," Benji says reassuringly. "She needs someone to blame. You have to understand that. Even if the only person she has to blame is Tommy. She can't do that. She loved him."

"I know. I just..." I trail off unable to finish my thought because I'm not even sure what to think. I just know I don't want her carrying around all the guilt and hatred and grief I know she's feeling.

He takes my hand and brings it to his lips, kissing it softly. I'm relieved that he's here with me, that I no longer have to go this alone, and that I don't have to hide everything I'm feeling. Release is good.

"I'm not sure she'll even speak to me again," I say, after explaining how I went to Tommy's house trying to find answers.

"She will. Just give her time. I think it's different now. We have answers for her. We can give her a reason. It may never be enough for her, but we can try," Benji says, somehow remaining completely calm throughout this discussion.

"Thank you," I whisper, never more grateful to have him back in my life than I am right now. He seems to understand everything without me ever having to explain it.

The car falls silent, but nothing about it is uncomfortable. There's a lot to be said for silence and sometimes it can be the loudest thing in the room, screaming at you, begging you to break it, but other times it draws people closer together. It says that they can be together, comforted and soothed by the lack of words being spoken.

Quiet is peace. It's tranquility. It's healing.

And as we pull into the parking lot of the cemetery where Sam is buried, silence is the one thing we both need right now.

I can't leave the car and as if Benji can sense my unease, he takes my hand in his, but still says nothing. We sit together and I wonder if his thoughts are the same as mine. I wonder if he's thinking of Sam. For once, I'm not picturing Sam dead, instead I'm picturing him alive. I need to remember him for all the happiness he brought into my life and not the sadness that I was left with.

Benji lets go of my hand, his fingers brushing my cheek, bringing my attention to him. When our eyes connect, his are filled with tears and it's all I need before I start crying.

"You ready, Cam?" he asks, and my heart stops in my chest.

For once, I love the sound of that name.

It makes me remember.

It makes me remember how much I loved Sam.

Chapter Twenty-Eight

We're standing together looking down at Sam's grave and I'm not sure what I expected to feel or what I'm supposed to do. There's no natural reaction to seeing your friend's name on a grave marker; the date there in front of you, so final and definitive. And to know you had a part in why he's here makes it hard to find the feelings to help cope with that.

This obviously isn't the first time we've been here, but the last time, for the funeral, was one of those moments when I was barely functioning. I think there was a point when I tried to shut it all out, thinking he wasn't dead or that I was living a nightmare that wouldn't allow me to wake up. But in the end, it was a nightmare, but it all came true.

I take Benji's hand and look around. We're surrounded by death, yet neither of us speaks of it. It's too painful, too real, too raw and in this case it's far too close. There's really nothing to say and as unnatural and unfair as it is, Sam's death was a part of life.

I do often think about the sequence of events and how just one small change to it all would have left us in a different situation. Had I just stalled when getting into the car or if I had passed out on the beach or gotten sick before getting in the car, we would've left the beach later than we did.

All it takes is one second, one minute, one flash of difference to change everything. And even worse, are the series of events that are created by that one incident. Had Sam not drove that day that family would still be alive, had one of us wasted more time before we left, Sam wouldn't be dead and there wouldn't be all the tragedy that followed it. Kelly and Tommy's suicides, Benji and I living apart, miserable and devastated; it was all caused by one thing, one simple thing that could've been avoided. But it's too late for that now and today isn't about dwelling on the past and what we could've done differently. It's about moving on and finding a way to live with what we did.

We don't come bearing flowers or words to ease our suffering. Sam is dead and nothing we do or say can change that. But as we stand over his grave, our eyes filled with tears, we realize all we can do is let his memory live on. It's time to stop trying to forget; we need to remember. We need to focus on the positive and all the things we have, instead of everything we don't.

I watch Benji mouth a silent goodbye to Sam before both of us brush the grave marker with our hand as we walk away. This will probably be the last time we're here and not because we're insensitive or we don't care anymore, it's because we both know that this is the end for us. While we'll never forget Sam, we need to move on with our lives.

It takes thirty minutes to get to the cemetery where Kelly is buried and Benji jokes about how everywhere in this damn suburb takes thirty minutes. From one end to the other, and while only a short distance, the traffic is ridiculous so it still takes a half an hour.

Benji and I haven't been back to where we grew up in years. Both of us choosing to leave and never really having a reason to return. My parents moved to Florida shortly after I graduated from college and Benji's mom, as far as he knows, no longer lives here either.

It's strange the way the town still looks the same, despite the fact that neither of us have been back here. I feel like I've avoided it all this time, because I worried about the painful memories it might bring with it. The funny thing is, while I'm flooded with memories, none of them are painful. I cry, but it's more about the fact that I'll never be able to share everything I'm thinking with some of the people who helped me create all the things I'm inundated with.

We exit the car much quicker this time, like after the first goodbye, we've found the courage and strength to see this through to the end.

Benji takes my hand in his and using the map we printed before we left, we find Kelly's grave quickly. It's begun to drizzle and the air is cold. Our breath is coming out in small white puffs as we once again stand silently looking down at where Kelly is buried.

This isn't as hard for me as I thought. The first time, I never grieved her loss. I was too lost in a hazy mess of guilt and regret to even think about what she had done. But a part of me always understood what she did and why she did it. As selfish as it was, I knew she couldn't live without Sam. I understood and I often found myself wondering if I would've done the same thing had it been Benji who died instead.

I spent nine brutal years living without him and while it was trying and exhausting and at times I did want to give up, I still had the knowledge that he was alive. I found a small amount of comfort in that. Kelly never had that reassurance. But she did have Tommy and what all of this has shown me is that part of a whole is never enough. It will never be complete.

I wrap my arms around Benji's waist, now shivering from the cold air mixed with the dampness of the rain and he covers me with his body. I feel him kiss the top of my head, his chin resting there as he begins to softly sing *Dear Prudence* and tears flood my eyes. It was Kelly's favorite song and something Benji learned to play on his guitar so she could hear it whenever she wanted.

It's the little things that mean so much. The things that remind me what we all had, a deep, undying love for each other, and nothing will ever change that.

The day carries on pretty much the same way it began. We're in the car together, quiet and sullen as the rain begins to pick up. It's falling hard and fast, reminding me of the day Tommy was laid to rest.

"I went to his funeral," I tell Benji without looking over at him. "And sat alone at his burial," I add, and Benji turns to look at me.

"Oh, Campbell," he says, quietly, almost pitifully. I didn't say it so he'd feel sorry for me. I want him to know, because throughout all of this, I never wanted to be viewed as heartless.

After Samantha came to my office, I felt like I failed Tommy, like I should've tried harder, which is part of the reason I sought Benji out. I couldn't lose someone else I loved.

"It's okay," I respond, feeling his hand brush my arm in sympathy. "I needed to be there, even if I was alone."

"I went to see his grave after I got his letter and before I came to find you," Benji admits, and this time it's me who reaches over and rests my hand on his arm.

"You didn't have to go alone."

"I know, but I did. I needed to grieve on my own." He stops and looks over at me as if he's said something that might have possibly insulted me. But I understand. There are times you just need to be alone. "I guess in a way I needed to see that he was really dead." He shakes his head at the words he's just spoken out loud as if he's questioning himself. "As horrible as that sounds," Benji adds, as if he needs to explain himself.

"That's the same reason I went to the funeral. I felt like it couldn't be real."

"None of it feels real," Benji says dryly. "It's been nine fucking years and it still feels like a dream."

"A nightmare," I add, and Benji nods.

We cry more at Tommy's grave than we did at the others and I wonder why that is. Did we have more time to process the death of Sam and Kelly, more time to live with the regret of what could've been? With Tommy it was unexpected, coming later in the game, like a sucker punch to the stomach. By then, in theory we all should've been fine. But what each of us realized is that the more time that went by, the worse the guilt became. The worse the loss was and the worse each of us felt.

Although we'll never know why Tommy did what he did, we both know he always felt lost without Kelly and as much as it bothered him to share her with Sam, I think he also felt the loss of Sam, too. It had to have begun to weigh on him the way everything began to weigh on Benji and me and after what Benji shared with me about the accident, I imagine it all became too much.

Where or when was his breaking point? When did he finally give up and say 'fuck it all'? I wonder if it was one final thing that made Tommy end his life and I can't help but think about how close I possibly was too. His letter came at a time when I needed it more than anything.

While his death, like Kelly's was completely selfish, in a way it saved me and for that I will always be grateful.

And for the last time today and hopefully for a long time to come, we leave the cemetery. Our goodbyes stuck in our throats, floating around in our heads and left unspoken because we know soon we'll be visiting Samantha and Thomas. Hopefully our goodbye will come in the form of forgiveness and understanding.

We arrive home and Benji slings his arm over my shoulder as we're walking in the house. "Let's get something to eat," he says, and I can hear the exhaustion in his voice. "Something good. Something you love."

"Do you remember what that is?" I ask, raising my eyebrows at him, secretly hoping he remembers but also hoping he doesn't, so I can give him shit for it.

"Portillo's hot dog with ketchup and relish only, cheese fries and a piece of chocolate cake," he says firmly, and then slides his hand down my back and gives me a swat on the butt before saying, "Take that." He's far too impressed with his ability to remember and it makes me laugh.

"Nice job," I congratulate, and now it's him laughing.

"I can't believe I'm about to indulge you like this when I should be shaming you. A ketchup and relish hot dog? Who lives in Chicago and eats that?"

"Me, and you love it."

"I do, because I love you," Benji says, and it doesn't matter how many times he says it, I still feel like I'm melting.

We place the order and as Benji leaves to pick it up, he rolls his eyes dramatically and says, "Traffic is going to be horrendous and all this just for a hot dog."

"But it's for me," I reply sweetly, fluttering my eyelashes as Benji shakes his head.

"I've never been able to say no to you," he responds, and I couldn't agree more. He's the one person in the world I'll never say no to either.

After Benji returns with the food and we're sitting on the couch eating, we begin to talk about what the plan is for tomorrow. It will be the first day we won't be together since he came back, and a part of me is already having a hard time with that.

Jack and I are heading to Florida to talk with our parents about the accident and everything that happened. We'll be gone for two days and when I called my mom to tell her we were coming, she didn't seem too surprised nor did she question me. Her laid back attitude toward everything really coming through, because I think most parents would wonder why their adult children are boarding a plane on a whim to visit them. Yet I was relieved she didn't ask any questions, because I'm not sure how I would've answered them. There is just too much going on to explain in a phone call.

During all of this, we both decided it would be best if we met with our parents separately, and not because we have anything to hide, but because Benji has more than just the accident he needs to address with his mom. I wasn't the only one he stopped talking to after the accident, he left her in the dark too.

I can tell the whole thing worries him, but it's something we need to do. The difference is that I have Jack to go with me. Benji is an only child and I think that's what's bothering him more than anything. He just left his mom, making her wonder about what happened to him, and I'm sure concerned for his safety, too. He didn't have any other connection to his family, maybe if he had, he wouldn't have disappeared the way he did.

Things were harder for him after his parents divorced and even harder after his dad started dating again and pretty much severed ties with Benji. His mom tried her best to make up for it, but I know he was hurt by it all. I can tell he harbors a lot of guilt for leaving her the way his father did and I know he feels like he needs to explain himself.

I've told him multiple times that I'll go with him, but he declines. He tells me it's something he needs to do on his own. I have to respect that.

When we're finally in bed, Benji's arms cradling my body, he says, "I'm going to miss you."

I'm sure most people would find that comment ridiculous. It's only two days, but when you've lived through what we have, you know two days can be an eternity; two days can change your life. Actually all it takes is a few short minutes.

"I'll miss you too," I tell him, pressing my lips to his chest and leaving them there. I take a breath and his smell hits me. He smells like Benji. He smells like safety and home.

And I know not a day will go by that I won't find myself missing him at one point or another. He's the reason I breathe, the reason I can forgive myself, but he's also the reason my heart no longer aches.

We were always meant to be together.

Our bond is as old as we are.

Chapter Twenty-Nine

I'm certain I kissed Benji at least a million times, clinging to him like a teenage girl as he dropped me off at the airport. Jack told me he'd pick me up, but there's just something about a goodbye at the airport that made me say no. Maybe it's the fact that I can say goodbye up until nearly the final moment or maybe it's the selfish part of me that wanted as much time with Benji as possible before I had to leave. All I know is I'm sure I looked ridiculous. But I really don't care. I've spent too much time away from him to worry how stupid I looked saying goodbye to him or what other people thought. I feel like I have to spend the rest of my life making up for our time apart and I figured I might as well start with a goodbye at the airport. Although I'm only going to be gone for two days, actually it's more like only a day and a half, but that doesn't matter to me. It's still time away from Benji.

I thought I would be more nervous as we neared landing, given I'm about to share everything with my parents, but I'm honestly not. I guess the fact that Benji and I finally have everything out in the open has helped, and also the reaction we've gotten since we've finally come clean.

Jack's reaction to the accident, my involvement in it, and my behavior afterward was sympathetic, but not so much that it made me uncomfortable. It's almost like he knew too much would cross the line and I'd have a hard time dealing with my emotions. I'm glad he didn't push it, and I'm also thankful he agreed to come with me. Maybe his presence has played a part in my lack of nerves. It's nice to have him along for support.

I think there comes a point with a situation like this that the relief of sharing it outweighs people's reactions or my own nervousness and guilt. If anything, this is about absolution and forgiveness for myself, and the hope there is an understanding from friends and family. But if there isn't, I know I've done what I can. There is no greater correction than honesty.

The plane lands and as soon as we can switch our phones on, we both do, and find a group text message from our mother.

Mom: Your father is playing golf. Take a cab. I'm not going out in this heat.

We obviously both read it at the same time, because the look on Jack's face has to be a mirror image of mine. I'm not sure why we both have a what-the-fuck face on. This shouldn't come as a surprise to either of us.

"Seriously?" Jack asks, clearly annoyed.

"At least she sent a text. Normally we'd have to call her after waiting outside for an hour."

"Guess you're right," Jack responds, but still lets out a frustrated huff as he grabs our bags from the overhead bin.

Unloading the plane takes longer than usual and Jack is getting more and more pissed off. It seems like he's more stressed about this whole thing than I am. When he practically shoves into the elderly couple in front of us, I put my hand on his shoulder.

"Jack," I whisper-shout, and he turns to look at me. "Relax. We'll get off the plane. And I don't want you running down grandma and grandpa to do it."

"Fine," he says, rolling his eyes at me. I don't get what his problem is. Maybe he decided he didn't want to come after all and this is now just a huge inconvenience for him.

"What's your problem?" I ask, just as annoyed with him as he is with whatever is bothering him. I didn't ask him to come with me; he volunteered.

"Nothing, Campbell," he says, shaking his head as the line finally starts to move. This is the Jack I've known all my life—the crabby, irritable and unpredictable one. The one who is my boss and runs his company like a well-oiled machine, leaving little time for pleasantries. This is the way it's always been and I shouldn't think our relationship would change overnight just because he was understanding and sympathetic after I told him about the accident. I'm sure he's still processing everything, too.

I blow it off. No sense in making a big deal out of something that would've been normal to us in the past.

Jack hails a cab as soon as we're outside, not even bothering to wait in the cab line and when one speeds up to the curb, he barely waits for it to stop before he whips open the door. Tossing in his bag, he doesn't even let me get in first, just climbs in and slides over.

"Okay, seriously, Jack. What the fuck?" I ask, as I slam the cab door and bark out the address to the driver.

He lets out a long exhale before he turns to me and says, "You know how she's going to react, right?"

"What are you talking about?"

"Mom. You know she isn't really going to care." He looks away from me, his head turned and looking out the window now.

"That's okay, Jack. This isn't about her," I tell him, as I now understand why he's been behaving the way he has.

"You're right. This is about you and I don't want you to be hurt by her reaction," Jack says sharply, and again he exhales hard.

"Why are you worrying about this?" I question, wondering why this is suddenly bothering him.

"Because I worry about you, Campbell. I always have, even when you didn't think I cared. I did. I still do and now given everything you've told me, I don't want you to be let down by Mom's reaction to it. She doesn't care."

"Jack," I say, but it comes out sorrowfully. "Mom does care. This is just who she is."

"I'm glad you can just so readily accept that."

His tone is harsh and I understand why he's upset, but this is the way it's been all our lives. He can't expect her to change. She loves us in her own way. The only way she knows how and while it might not be conventional or normal, I've always been okay with it.

We were well cared for and she made us laugh and she read to us at night and made us hot chocolate after we played in the snow. She made our lunches every day and was home when we got off the bus, but she wasn't a hugger and a kisser. She didn't write us notes about having a good day and stuff them in our lunchboxes, she didn't profess her love for her children or brag about our accomplishments. It wasn't in her nature and it still isn't.

I haven't set myself up for anything in my choice to come here. I know what her reaction will be, but she and my dad are another group of people on my list of acceptance and self-preservation. They need to be told what happened, just as I had to tell Jack. It's part of moving on.

I reach over and run my hand down Jack's arm. I'm eternally grateful that he's come to support me and help me see this through, but I can't have him upset over what he thinks our mother's reaction will be.

"It's okay, seriously," I say, trying to reassure him that I'll be fine. "If anything, I'm pretty much geared up for no reaction, so anything beyond that will be a miracle."

Jack looks back over at me, this time a weak smile on his face and I shrug my shoulders casually.

"Sometimes you amaze me, Campbell," he says, but that's as far as we get, because the cab pulls up outside our parents' house.

"Let's do this shit and then get drunk," I say, as Jack opens the door to the cab.

"Hell, yes."

We don't bother to ring the doorbell. Using our key, we let ourselves in, but find the house empty.

"You told them you had something important to talk about, right?" Jack asks, as he walks through the house.

"Yeah. Maybe she thinks we're here to talk about nursing homes so she's avoiding us."

Jack laughs at my lame attempt at a joke. "She gets to live with you," he retorts. "I'll take Dad."

Just as I'm about to argue, the back door slams and we both stop and see our mother walking toward us.

She's ridiculously tan and she smells like coconut and sea salt. Not a bad combination, but paired with her pastel Lily Pulitzer outfit and overly blonde hair, she looks like your typical Floridian. Jack laughs out loud when he sees her and I smack his arm. It has to have been at least three years since we've seen her and six years since she and our father moved down here. I can see she's fitting in nicely.

"Oh good, you're here," she says in the way of a greeting. "Did you put your stuff in the bedrooms?"

"Not yet, Mom," Jack says before adding, "By the way, it's nice to see you too."

"Oh Jack, don't be a crab. Of course it's nice to see you both." She steps over and hugs us both awkwardly, which really only adds to the hilarity of the situation as she says, "Robert should be home any minute."

I chuckle under my breath at her use of our father's name. She's always called him by his first name, like if she called him dad, we'd suddenly have no idea who she was talking about.

"Dad's playing golf?" I ask, as I emphasize his name jokingly.

"Yep. I don't even know how in this heat." She sighs dramatically and both Jack and I laugh this time.

"Ma, it's like seventy-five degrees. That's not hot. Back home it's in the thirties already," Jack says.

"See, that's why I left Chicago. Too damn cold. But here, now it's too hot."

I look at Jack and he nods his head toward the bedrooms and we leave her grumbling about the heat and our father playing too much golf.

"You sure you want to do this?" Jack asks as he shakes his head.

"Yeah. And I know, she's ridiculous, but whatever." I wave a dismissive hand in the direction of where we left our mother as we both retreat to our bedrooms.

A few minutes later our father arrives home and we all meet in the kitchen. He hugs us both and it's entirely less awkward than our mother's useless attempt. Sitting around the table with our mother still sighing dramatically about the weather and golf and something about a bakery being out of her favorite cookies, our father interrupts her.

"So what's going on?" he asks. "You said you needed to talk to us about something?" He's looking at me rather than Jack. I'm the one who called to say we'd be visiting, but gave them little after that.

Jack folds his hands on the table and looks over at me, giving me a soft smile as if to encourage me on, so I decide just to lay it all out there. Parents are supposed to love their children no matter what.

"Remember the car accident when Sam died?" I ask, and even I realize how idiotic that sounds. Of course they fucking remember. My father nods and my mother continues to inspect her no-chip manicure. "I was in the car when it happened. Actually we all were: Benji, Kelly, Tommy and me. And we left the scene after the accident. For the last nine years I've lived with the guilt of what I did and how it affected more than just my own life."

"Oh, Campbell," my father says, my heart breaking at the sound of pity in his voice. "We always knew something was up, but we never wanted to pressure you to talk. I'm so sorry, sweetheart."

I knew my father would respond this way. He was always the more sympathetic of the two, but still reserved.

"Thanks, Dad. I'm dealing with it now and things are getting better," I say, truly appreciating his response. "Benji and I are back together, so that's helping a lot. Having someone who understands it has helped me cope."

My mother looks up from her nails, but her expression hasn't changed. "I wish you would've told us, Campbell. You know I would've found you a great therapist."

And that's that. Her way of solving things is to pawn it off on someone else. Hire a gardener to maintain the lawn, get someone to plow the driveway when it snows, enlist someone to clean the house, find someone to help your kid through a crisis.

I wonder if I should feel hurt or put off by her nonchalant approach, but the more thought I give it, the more I realize this is how she would respond. I'm learning you can't base your feelings on someone else's reaction, because if I did, something like this would definitely hurt. I think her response is actually comforting in a way. People would say she's callous, even cold, but to me, it's normal.

"Yep," Jack lets out on a hard exhale and I laugh out loud. It is what it is and when she starts talking again all I can do is shake my head.

"Did you know they want to build a Perkins here?" She slams her hands down on the table and sighs. "In Marco Island, can you believe it? This is not a chain restaurant kind of town."

"Ma, there's a Little Caesar's here," Jack deadpans, and his ability to challenge her makes me smile.

"You know what I mean, Jack," she replies, annoyed with both of us already.

It is what it is, I think as we all leave the table without any more discussion.

As Jack and I are walking back toward the bedrooms, he throws his arm around my shoulders, but this time there's a smile on his face.

"Went exactly as I expected," I say to him. "Guess that's a good thing."

"Yeah, I guess so. Now let's go get some drinks."

Chapter Thirty

Jack pulls up outside my house, dropping me off from the airport, and just as I'm about to exit, his voice stops me.

"Hey Campbell," he says. "I know you've got a million other things going on..." He stops short and then says, "You're leaving, aren't you?"

I look over at him, his eyes are sad and I hate that I have to tell him yes. I wish there were a way I could make this all work. I feel like I owe Jack so much, and for once since I've started working for him, he isn't concerned about his company or the job I hold there. He's worried about me leaving; for once it's about our relationship and not the one we have professionally.

"I am," I answer, but for some reason I can't look at him when I say it. "I can't ask Benji to give up everything he has worked so hard for." And as I say it, I swear I see a flash of defiance in Jack's eyes, but it fades quickly. It was almost like he wanted to ask what happens to all the time and effort I put into my career, into his company and into both our lives. But it's like he realized that it's futile to argue with me when he knows the only thing I really ever wanted was Benji.

"You don't have to quit," he tells me, and I give him a strange look. Of course I have to quit. I'm moving nine hours away, to the middle of nowhere and there isn't even a possibility of commuting. Jack has also never been a fan of letting people work from home; he says it breeds laziness and unproductivity. Plus he also likes everyone who works for him to have a connection to the clients they deal with, that somehow meeting them in person makes it easier to convince them to give up everything they've worked so hard for. And actually, it probably does. It's a lot easier to say no to someone via an email or over the phone.

"What do you mean?" I ask confused by his comment.

"You can work from there. Most of what you do is internet based and when needed you can come to the office." He shrugs his shoulders as if it's as simple as that. And maybe it is. I've never really liked my job, but it could also be that I was never really happy to begin with. It's hard to find yourself excited about something when the cloud of depression that hangs over you never recedes. Things could be different now that I'm more in control of my life. And I've often thought about what I would do when I move in with Benji. I've never been the kind of girl to not work or to let someone else take care of me. I would like to be able to contribute despite everything Benji has said about it not mattering if I have a job or not.

"Really?" I ask, knowing this could possibly cause a lot of problems for him. "What about the other people in the office? The ones who want to work from home?" I've never wanted Jack to treat me differently from the rest of his employees and by choosing Jack's suggestion; it would definitely make me stand out.

"Who gives a fuck," Jack says flippantly. "I own the company, Campbell, and if that's the call I want to make then I'll make it." He's very firm in his words and it almost makes me laugh. I know no one in the office would challenge his decision even if they think it's solely based on the fact that we're family. "You're my sister and if I want to change things to accommodate my family, then I will."

"Seriously?" I question again, wondering if this could possibly work. "I'm nine hours away. You realize I can't be driving back here once a week, right?" Jack laughs, and it fills the car making me smile. "Stop laughing at me," I tell him and he laughs again.

"I know you're going to be nine hours away and of course I wouldn't demand that you be in the office every week." He rolls his eyes acting like my thought is preposterous. But in all the time I've worked for Jack, he expected everything to go smoothly and perfectly, something like this could really throw a wrench in his plans.

"I know you think I'm demanding, but in actuality it was you who was always demanding of yourself. I've always cut you some slack, but you never took it. Take it now, Campbell. Enjoy your life with Benji and be happy. Don't make this more than it is. It's a job and you'll always have one with me no matter where you're at."

I almost start to cry as I realize it was probably always me that pushed him away. While we never really had anything in common growing up, I used that to become more defiant and closed off after the accident. If he were interested in having a relationship with me, I never would've noticed anyway. And as much as I like to paint him out to be the bad guy, the one who didn't really like me, it was never like that. I notice we have more in common as adults than we ever did before and I know it's now time to move beyond the past and start accepting his help and his friendship.

"Thank you," I whisper, overwhelmed by his kindness. He doesn't have to treat me this way, but I'm grateful he's able to forgive me so quickly. This isn't just about the job. It's about everything he's done for me.

"No problem. We can talk more about it later. Work everything out. Just go and once you're moved and settled up there, we can figure out how it's all going to work. No pressure, though," he adds, and now it's me that's laughing.

"Crazy how things have changed," I say, and Jack nods. Everything in my life used to be high pressure. It's funny because I feel like I can finally breathe again.

I wish Jack goodbye and agree that we'll talk more about the job later on. As I'm getting ready to close the door, I bend down and poke my head back in.

"Thank you. Seriously, Jack. I really appreciate it. Not just the job, but for coming with me, for being so understanding. For everything."

"It's all good, Campbell," he says with a smile on his face, and for once, it is all good.

I walk away from the car giving Jack a quick wave before scampering up the steps to my house. It's only been two days, but I can't wait to see Benji.

He's sitting on the couch when I walk in. I immediately walk over, climb into his lap, and rest my head on his shoulder.

"How'd it go with your mom?" I ask as I press my lips to his neck. I feel his hands run up and down my back and I close my eyes relishing the feel of his body against mine once again.

"You first," he says, and while I love that he always wants to put me first, I need this to be about him. I know his time with his mom was far more difficult than mine was.

"No, baby," I whisper against the curve of his neck, and I feel him shudder in my arms. He lets out a long exhale into my hair, his breath lingering along with the smell of liquor and for a moment I panic. *What happened?*

I push back from him, but as soon as I do, he takes my face in his hands and he shakes his head. Cupping my cheek, he guides my mouth to his in a soft, sweet kiss. His tongue grazes my bottom lip and mine brushes lightly against his as he pulls away. He tastes like scotch and coupled with the way he smells and the warmth of his body, it's intoxicating.

"Everything's fine, baby," he says tiredly. "Just a long day. I needed a drink."

"You taste like scotch," I murmur, my mouth only inches from his. "I like it. Kiss me again."

A loose smile forms on his face as he cradles the back of my neck and kisses me. Guiding me back until I'm lying on the couch, the weight of his body covers mine. I almost forget about our days apart and the reason we were separated, but it comes back quickly.

"Stop trying to distract me, Benjamin Kennedy. Start talking, boy. No secrets, remember?" I say, running my hands up and under his shirt, my fingers trailing slowly down his ribs.

"You're terribly impatient," he says, burying his face in my neck. "I just want to enjoy you for a second. I missed you."

"I missed you like crazy." I wrap my arms around his waist, pulling him closer; I let him find the comfort in me I know he needs.

"There was a lot of crying," Benji says without pulling back to look at me. His words are muffled, but still completely clear to me. "She wasn't as hurt by the fact that I kept the accident from her as she was by the fact that I just disappeared."

"I can understand that," I say, and as much as I understand why Benji did that, I'm now struggling with the reality of it all. At the time both of us thought it was best to hide our feelings and avoid discussing what happened. That somehow this would preserve us and allow us to forgive ourselves. But in actuality all it did was drive the people who could've helped us further away.

I don't think either of us intended to live a life of confinement and solitude, but to surround ourselves with the people we knew and loved was just too tempting. We knew we'd eventually breakdown and tell them everything.

"So how did you leave things with her?"

"Like I'd never even left," Benji says, and although I can't see his face I know he's smiling. I feel it against my neck and it makes my entire body warm. I'm happy he was so easily able to repair years of lost time together. But that's what a family is for. To accept you in spite of the awfulness that surrounds you.

"That's the way it should be."

"I know, but it makes me feel even guiltier for the way I behaved. She was devastated." He pushes up off of me and lifts my legs, resting them on his lap, he sits next to me. "You should've seen her face when she opened the door," he says, and I can tell he's holding back the tears.

"She recognized you?" I ask jokingly, as I run my fingers across his beard. He laughs, and takes my hand in his, pressing a kiss to my palm.

"Yes she did, snarky girl. She started crying the moment she opened the door. I think she hugged me for at least ten minutes before she even said anything."

I start to tear up as he talks. I'm glad things went well for him. He really needed to know someone else cared about what he went through, that someone else missed him.

"She wants to see you, too," he adds, and I give him a strange look. I was always close with Benji's mom growing up. She was more of the mothering, loving person than I ever had in my own mom, but after all this time I figured she would've let that go. "I told her we would stop by before we left to go back home."

It's funny to hear him call Hessel home and that he's already started calling it our home. There's no uncertainty or concern in his voice. He talks about it like it has always been our home. I love it.

"When do you want to leave?" I ask, and I see his face fall slightly. He thinks I'm not coming back with him. But after talking with Jack today and knowing my job is secure, I'm okay with leaving my house and moving in with him as soon as possible.

"I should probably head back soon, in two or three days. I've left things at the store completely unattended. I'm sure my emails are out of control."

I've noticed that Benji hasn't checked his email or done anything with his job since arriving here. It's important that he gets back to take care of things. But I also know we have to find the time to talk to Samantha. Not something I'm looking forward to, but it needs to be done, if only for my own peace of mind.

"I'm going back with you when you leave," I say, completely foregoing the conversation we have to have about going to see Samantha. I can tell I've shocked him, but after that initial surprise wears off, his happiness shines through.

"Seriously, baby?" he asks, pulling me into his arms. He kisses me hard, his lips colliding roughly with mine and I'm smiling as he kisses me.

I love his reaction to this; it shows me that the only place I belong is with him. Not that I've ever doubted it.

"Yes, seriously. I talked with Jack and he's going to let me work from home, so I'm free to go. I just have to figure out what to do with the house."

"Fuck the house!" Benji yells, yanking me off the couch. "Baby, you've made me happier than I've been since you walked back into my life."

He lifts me off the ground, kissing me and squeezing me tightly as I laugh hysterically at his reaction. There are few things that elicit complete excitement and joy and nervousness in me, but Benji can do all that in a second.

When he finally sets me down, his forehead resting against mine, I lean up and kiss the tip of his nose.

With complete sincerity in his voice, he says, "I never thought there would come a day when you'd finally be living in the house with me." His eyes are closed and my face is now in his hands. "I built the house for you, Campbell. I hoped you'd one day come back to me. I built the house for our family."

I don't even know what to say. I'm shocked into silence. He waited for me all this time, never forgetting what we once had, what we now have again. I see him for all he was, all he is and all he will be and I know together, our life can finally begin.

"Thank you," I whisper. "I'm not sure what to say," I add stupidly, and Benji chuckles.

"You don't need to say anything. You already said you're coming with me and that's enough for me. You'll always be enough for me."

In this moment I also realize Benji's business is named after me too. CB, Campbell and Benji. I smile at him, again unsure of what to say and I can tell by the way he's looking at me he realizes I've connected the pieces.

"The store too?" I ask and his smile spreads as he nods his head.

"I thought that if you ever did try to find me, it would be a reminder that I never forgot you. I never could. Everything I did was because of you, Campbell."

As much as I know why I never came looking for Benji until after Tommy's letter, I wonder why he never looked for me.

"Why didn't you ever try to find me?" I ask him, despite knowing I left angry and hurt. I didn't say it then, but my silence made it clear I was done.

"I wanted to, but I also knew you were hurt by my behavior. I wasn't the same person after the accident. I couldn't be who you needed me to be and if I did find you, I would've had to admit everything I saw and everything that happened. I wasn't ready."

"It wouldn't have changed the way I felt about you. I might have been angry, but I still loved you," I reassure him.

"I know that now, but then I didn't."

"All that matters now is that we've found our way back to each other," I tell Benji, kissing him softly.

"You're right."

I've never been happier about the prospect of the future and of what's to come for Benji and me. Now we just have to someway correct this situation with Samantha.

Chapter Thirty-One

There has always been a lot to discuss regarding the accident and the lives we ruined throughout all of this. Tommy's wife, Samantha, being one of them. It's hard to know exactly what to do, but for some reason, setting things right with her seems like a priority. While Benji and I have talked a lot about the accident and the lives it affected, we haven't really discussed how Samantha came to be or the feelings her presence created in me. I've left it alone, focusing on the people most directly involved. In my mind, I've pushed her aside, even though I know she was indirectly traumatized by it all. I haven't wanted to share how she made me feel. The guilt I carry is still stifling, but I know I can't leave her out of all of this.

After much debate, Benji and I decide not to meet up with Sam or Kelly's families right now, but we both agree that Samantha needs an explanation even if she's not interested in hearing the truth. For our own piece of mind, we need to salvage what we can, and possibly purge some of this guilt we have that surrounds Tommy's death. While we were never directly involved, our indirect connection to it all has taken its toll on both of us.

We also have always felt that visiting Sam and Kelly's families would only open a very loosely healed wound. Like ripping off a scab, it's not necessary; it will only create an even bigger scar. Our goal in all of this is not to make someone's life worse, but to help all that are involved heal. There would be no healing for their families should we admit what we've done, especially in Sam's case. There comes a time when we have to be okay with what we've done and know that we can't change it, but we can continue to repair our own lives. I also wonder if there's a part of us that fears their reaction. Maybe someday we'll regret our decision, but until then, we have to learn to deal with it.

We've also given a lot of thought to going to the police in Ann Arbor and confessing. But after Benji's research and his visit to the station many years ago, we've both found that under the law, we would be guilty of nothing.

The passenger of a vehicle, whether they leave the scene or not, cannot be held responsible for what occurs at the hand of the driver. What the law doesn't say is the guilt that will haunt you will always be enough of a punishment.

I often wonder if either of us will ever fully recover from this and the answer is probably not. While we have each other now, and that has healed some of the deepest wounds, I know there isn't a chance any of this will ever magically be erased from our memories. I hope that as we work through this, we find ways to correct what we've done, to somehow make it right.

All of this is the reason I need Samantha to know the truth. I can't have her carrying the burden of hate and guilt that I imagine she feels. I can't have her life ruined by this, or have her think it was somehow her fault. And even if it doesn't work, even if she won't hear me or can't find it in her heart to understand, I will at least have made the attempt.

It's raining when we wake the next morning; relentless and pounding as it hits the windows, the room shrouded in darkness despite it being well after eight o'clock. Benji stirs next to me, his sleep has been utterly soundless and peaceful since we've begun to repair all this damage.

He confessed to me early on that he didn't sleep, sometimes spending countless hours working well into the night just to avoid it. I know the feeling, but now I've found myself falling asleep easily without the use of alcohol and sleeping without waking multiple times. A dreamless sleep, something I never thought I'd find again.

I'm staring up at the ceiling when Benji rolls over and slings his arm across my stomach, letting his fingers run over my skin. Shivering from his touch, he pulls me into his body and I let out a sigh as I feel myself begin to relax against him. But no matter how hard I try, I can't forget what needs to be done today. I shift in his arms, trying to relax completely.

"What's wrong?" Benji asks, pulling back slightly. I don't mean for him to think I'm shying away from him or that his touch has upset me, but that's exactly how it comes across.

"Sorry," I immediately apologize as I move closer to him. "We haven't really talked about Tommy's wife."

"Well, you told me she hates you, which I still don't believe." Benji shakes his head a little and just as I'm about to argue with him, he continues. "I told you before, she needs someone to blame. Maybe she's in a better place now?"

"She showed up at my office," I say, realizing I've told him none of this. The memory of it has me as rattled as the day it happened. I was on the verge of falling apart at that point and her appearance practically pushed me over the edge.

For years I had devoted so much time and energy into keeping up a front, not allowing anyone in to see what I was hiding and one visit from Samantha turned that all to shit. The façade I had in place crumbled, and what I tried to hide was now revealed to everyone.

I remember calling after her in the lobby of the office building where I work, my voice loud, yet still shaky and weak as I practically chased her down. I couldn't remember the last time I cried in public, but that day it was nearly impossible to act like I wasn't.

I take a deep breath. Benji has made this easier on me, but there are still things I'm not proud of. One of them being the fact that I basically stalked Samantha.

"I was so upset already. It was the day after the anniversary of the accident when she showed up and I was trying so hard to hold it together. But as soon as she told me who she was, I fell apart." I feel Benji's arms hold me tighter, encouraging me to go on. "She was so spiteful. She thinks Tommy was in love with me. She thinks that's why he killed himself."

"You can see how she would feel that way," Benji rationalizes, but it only upsets me more.

"It wasn't like that," I immediately defend, even though I know Benji knows that. I can feel angry tears sting my eyes and my throat begins to burn as I try to control myself.

"I feel guilty enough," I say, letting out a small sob with it. "I'm the reason he did this, Benji. I know that. But it's not for the reason Samantha thinks."

"What are you talking about?" Benji says, his voice firm, almost angry. "No, Campbell. You will not blame yourself for this. Tommy made a very selfish choice, something we will probably never understand, but it is not your fault."

I want to move away from him. I hate the feeling of vulnerability that has taken control of my body. I can't hold still and Benji won't let go of me.

"Campbell," he says, and I close my eyes as the tears fall hard and fast. "Look at me," he insists. "I wasn't trying to say this was your fault. I'm sorry I said I could understand why Samantha would feel that way. It was wrong and now I've upset you."

"I went to her house," I admit, letting it all out now. "I needed answers and I wanted to tell her what happened, but I couldn't. She was so angry with me and I didn't even know what to say."

I'm crying and Benji runs his hand down my back trying to calm me. I sit up so I'm now looking at him, and he does the same. He brushes the tears off my cheeks as I watch him take a hard breath.

"I'm sorry," he says again. "But you can't blame yourself for this, Campbell. You can't blame yourself for any of it."

"I think a part of me always will," I whisper. "If I had just found him. If I had tried harder…"

"No…" Benji cuts me off as he shakes his head. "If we're placing blame, Campbell, then we're all to blame. We all made a poor choice. We were just kids and while that's not an excuse, it is what it is. Of course we could've done things differently, but that's why we're doing what we're doing now. We can only go forward from here."

I nod, although the guilt still pools heavy in my stomach and I finally admit to Benji part of the reason I ended up finding him. "I was afraid I was going to lose you too," I blurt out, as I find myself crawling into his lap and burying my face in his neck. "I came to find you because I couldn't bear to lose you, too."

"You never would've lost me, Campbell. I've always been yours and you will always be my light."

Several hours later, we're parked in front of Samantha's house and as much as I know this is something we need to do, I can't make myself get out of the car.

Benji looks over at me, his expression full of sympathy for what I'm feeling at the moment as he says, "I can do the talking. It'll be okay." He runs his thumb along my knuckles, our hands locked together. They've been this way since we left the house. There's an energy I can feel between our connected hands, a nervousness we both share.

"I need to. I can't live with her not knowing the truth," I tell him, but even my words don't sound like my own and nothing about them makes me move forward.

"I know," he says, as he lets go of my hand and exits the car.

I'm not ready, but it doesn't matter and I follow his lead. I feel like my body isn't my own, following Benji up the walk and to the front door as I'm hit with déjà vu. Standing in this very spot just a few weeks ago, I was begging Samantha to talk to me, but unable to give her the answers she needed. I'm hoping today is different.

Benji's hand is shaking as he lifts it to ring the bell. Just that small action shows me he's as nervous as I am. Throughout all this, he's remained calm and steadfast; he's been my rock, but I can see it's all beginning to wear on him. I don't want him to fall apart too, and I know he will if this keeps up. I'm glad to know that after today we can start to figure out what a normal life will look and feel like. We'll be done with all of this and we can finally move on...I hope.

We waited until the late afternoon in hopes that Samantha would be home from work; that is if she even works. I don't know anything about her and Tommy's life together. And before I can give it anymore thought, the door opens.

Samantha's mouth literally drops open like I'm the last person she thought she'd see standing on her porch. Instantly, she's defensive, crossing her arms over her chest, her mouth now set in a firm line.

"I told you not to come back here," she hisses, and Benji takes a step back, but I don't move. I've been here before and while I don't know her well, I do know she's not going to do anything rash. As much as she wants to hate me, she knows I'm the only one who has answers for her.

I saw it when I was here the first time. She wanted to unload everything on me, but something made her hold back. Whether it was fear or hatred or anger or just plain obstinacy, she will eventually give in.

"Samantha, please," I say, remaining as calm as possible. "This is Benji Kennedy." My eyes flicking over to where Benji is standing. "We grew up with Tommy and we'd like just a few minutes to talk to you. Maybe help you understand everything that's happened."

She lets out an irritated sigh, and I can't tell if it's because she's contemplating hearing me out or if she's ready to tell me to fuck off. But before she can respond, the door is pushed open and Thomas is standing next to her.

Without giving it a second thought, she turns to him and in a sweet voice says, "Baby, go upstairs, please."

Thomas looks up at her and then at Benji and me standing on the porch. He smiles at me and waves a little and I can't help but smile back at him, completely enamored with how much he resembles Tommy. His beautiful brown eyes and his shy smile, his eyes so telling of what a wonderful person he will become. I saw it in Tommy and I can see it in Thomas. More than anything, Thomas is why I'm here now. I want him to grow up and not see the mistakes his father made, but see the wonderful man he was.

"I know you," Thomas says, as he points to me and I almost respond in agreement since we met at the funeral, but he then points to Benji too.

I'm certain the look on all our faces says we're shocked and I watch Samantha squat down in front of him, her hands on his arms. "Thomas, you don't know them," she says, softly as if to remind him he's wrong.

"I do, Mommy," he says and wiggles out of her loose hold before scampering upstairs.

Samantha runs a hand through her hair and again lets out a sigh, but this time I can tell she's exhausted, this whole thing is taking a toll on her life, her family and her.

"I'm sorry," she says, but her voice conveys she's anything but sorry. It's just an apology to fill the space. "I really can't do this." She shakes her head and just as she's about to the close the door, Thomas returns and he's holding something.

"Look, Mommy," he says, flashing what appears to be a piece of paper at her. It's clutched in his hand, the paper is wrinkled and tattered and as I look more closely, I notice it's a photograph.

I step forward, but Samantha holds up her hand as if to tell me not to step any closer. She again kneels down in front of Thomas and takes the picture from his hand. Looking at it, she turns it over and reads what's written on the back.

Her eyes fill with tears as she looks up at Benji and me and then back at Thomas. It feels like we stand in silence forever. None of us saying anything, the air between us heavy and any words we'd once spoken are now lost. I can feel the shift, the change in what was once a hopeless relationship, has somehow been altered with just a photograph.

"Thomas," she whispers weakly, and he cocks his head to the side. His little mind wondering why she's crying again, I'm sure. I can't imagine what he's seen over the last few weeks and how much his world has changed. "Daddy gave this to you?" she asks, and he nods.

"He did, but it was a secret. He told me that even if he wasn't here, you and Grandma and Grandpa and these people," he says looking at Benji and me again with that perfect smile on his face, "will always love me."

She pulls Thomas into her embrace as she begins to cry a little bit harder. I don't know what has changed or what about the picture has made her change her mind about us, but something is different.

She lets go of Thomas, but as she does, she whispers something in his ear and he nods his head, leaving the three of us alone as he makes his way up the stairs.

Samantha wipes at her cheeks and swipes under her eyes as she wets her lips and hands the picture to me.

Benji steps closer to me, his hand resting on the small of my back. I can feel the warmth of his touch through my coat and it's enough to relax me. I find myself leaning against him as we both finally look down at the picture.

It's a picture of Benji and me that had to have been taken shortly before the accident, probably only a few weeks before. I remember it well. My head is resting on Benji's shoulder and he's smiling at the camera while I'm looking the other way. I remember Tommy had called my name just before Kelly took the picture, and I looked over at him. He mouthed the word 'smile', but it was too late, Kelly had already taken it.

Before I realize it, my body is flush against Benji's, his arm now wrapped around my waist and that's when I turn the picture over. My hand is shaking; actually my entire body is shaking. Without Benji this close, I don't think I could stand, but as Benji's arm tightens around my waist, I realize he's feeling the same way.

It says, *These people love you and they don't even know you.*

It's written in Tommy's handwriting and what he's written is completely true. I don't even know Thomas, but I love him with everything I have. He's all I have left of Tommy and when I look up and take in Benji's face, there's a love there for Thomas, too.

I hand the picture back to Samantha and she smiles gratefully. It's the first smile I've seen since meeting her and while it's not authentic, it's better than the scowl she's worn. She steps aside, pushing the door open, she gives her head a quick flick as if to tell us to come in and then she says, "I think I'm ready to hear what you have to say."

Chapter Thirty-Two

Samantha leads us into the kitchen and as I walk through the house, I see pictures of Tommy with Samantha and Thomas. Baby pictures and pictures of smiling faces, happiness and joy and all the things that should grace a home. But underneath it all, the happiness is just lying on the surface. While the house is immaculate and beautiful, there is so much tragedy and sadness that fills it. I want to believe that when these pictures were taken and this house was purchased, when Tommy married Samantha, and when Thomas was born, that those days held true happiness; that Tommy's life wasn't always a desperate attempt to escape and forget the past.

I begin to get choked up when I see pictures of Tommy holding Thomas, kissing him and hugging him. It breaks my heart that his child will grow up without a father, that he will never know all the love and kindness that radiated from Tommy. What was left was a broken shell of his former self, wounded and scarred with nothing left to give.

Judging by his house and his wife and the fact that they had a kid together, he tried to recover, tried to carry on, but if anyone knows the difficulty in that, it's me and clearly he wasn't able to do it.

I can hear Thomas playing in his room and I'm overcome with emotion. I feel the tears well up in my eyes, wondering if he has any idea what has happened, what is happening. His life will never be the same. I find myself wondering if Samantha were to remarry quickly, would Thomas even remember his father? I hate myself for thinking it. It's a horrible thought. Tommy was one of my best friends and in the end I should be doing whatever I can to ease some of this stress that has taken over his family.

"Campbell," Benji says, and I realize I've disconnected, lost in my own depressing thoughts.

"Huh?"

"Are you coming?" he asks, as he looks back from where he's standing in the kitchen; Samantha watching me with a sad look on her face. A permanent reminder of what she's going through.

As I take in her face, I'm suddenly reminded of Tommy's funeral and the two women I was seated next to and their discussion of Tommy's suicide and Samantha and Tommy's flawed marriage. "She never would've married him if she hadn't gotten pregnant with Thomas," the one woman had said, and something about the comment hurt. I hated that Tommy wasn't in love with his wife, that he married her out of obligation, but above all, that it ended this way.

But I'm hit with the realization that what was said is probably not the full truth. None of this is, there's still so much hidden and after seeing Samantha, I know we all have a lot to talk about. No one grieves for someone they didn't love, and the way I see Samantha suffering, I know she loved him.

We're now sitting at the kitchen table, although none of us has spoken yet. The silence is hanging heavy in the air and when the first words are spoken, they're loud and I immediately draw my words back to a whisper.

"I'm not sure where to begin," I repeat, but this time I'm quieter. I shake my head; I never imagined meeting with Samantha would be this hard.

Whether Tommy loved Samantha or not, there is now another life involved in all this, a child who never asked for any of this. And while I fight with this thought, I also wonder what would've happened if Kelly hadn't killed herself. Did Tommy love Samantha as much as he loved Kelly? How do you even explain any of it?

I'm now holding the picture of Benji and me that Tommy had given to Thomas, and as I turn it over in my hand, re-reading the words and looking at the picture, I begin to speak.

"I'm really sorry, Samantha," I tell her, but I know those words will do nothing to ease her pain. They've been said to me more times than I can count and quite honestly, all they did was add to my hatred of the situation. What are they even sorry for? And those words will never bring back what was lost.

"Thank you," she replies, giving the obligatory response, and already this conversation is off to a bad start, fake and contrived.

I look over at Benji who has been pretty much silent since all this began and I realize up until this moment, this is the first time we're meeting with someone who has a connection to what occurred. She was more directly involved than I ever realized.

He takes a few seconds and begins the conversation I should have started.

"So, Tommy, Campbell," he says motioning to me, " and I all grew up together. I don't know how much he's told you, but there were actually five of us."

As he speaks Samantha shakes her head as if to say she knows nothing, which I know is true. She admitted it to me when we first met and all she's known up until this point is speculation and ideas that have been created by her mind; bits and pieces of information she gathered from Tommy while he was still alive. Yet none of it is whole and none of it is the truth.

Benji keeps talking, "There was Sam and Kelly, too. We were inseparable. But when we were nineteen, it all ended."

I reach over with my hand and cover Benji's hand that is resting on the table. My touch stops him and I immediately pick up where he left off. I don't want him to do this alone, especially since it's me that Samantha blames.

"We were in a car accident that killed Sam and instead of staying, we left. We left Sam and the family in the other car dead. Tommy was the one who witnessed most of it."

I'm not sure how much more to say. There are secrets that Benji and I keep still between us for a reason, but I don't know if they're necessary for Samantha to understand the turmoil that plagued Tommy's life.

I look over at Benji and with a small shake of his head I know to leave off the fact that the two of them watched that young boy die in the car.

"At the time, Tommy and Kelly had been together for about four years," Benji adds, but he pauses as he tries to figure out exactly how to explain Tommy's relationship with Kelly. "A week after the accident, Kelly killed herself. It devastated Tommy and that's when things slowly started to unravel."

Samantha has yet to say anything and I'm not certain how much further we should take it. It still doesn't give her an accurate description of the trouble and horribleness that we would all come to face at the hand of our decision. I can only hope it's enough to allow Samantha to forgive me and forgive Tommy for what he's done.

"This explains a lot," Samantha finally says. "I always thought it was you he was hung up on," she states, looking over at me. "But it wasn't. It was the other girl. It makes more sense now. Her death and the accident, his drug use and the response he had to his parents death."

"What?" Benji practically shouts, and if he hadn't beaten me to it, I would've said the same thing. "Tommy's parents are dead?"

"I'm sorry, I guess I have a lot to share with you too," Samantha says, as she takes a deep breath. "I always thought this was something that was between Tommy and me, that our relationship was just shit because of how we got back together," she says, as she adds quietly, "Not like we were ever really apart."

I give her a confused look, not understanding exactly what she's saying. Like Samantha, Benji and I know nothing about Tommy's life after the accident.

"We met after he transferred to the University of Wisconsin, but I never really knew much about his life before that. He told me he needed a change and I never questioned it." She runs her hand through her hair and lets out a sigh as she continues. "We were young and I guess I never realized how out of hand his drug problem was. It was college. We all drank and did drugs, but as the years went by, Tommy didn't stop like most people did. We graduated, got jobs, moved in together, but as much as I loved him, I'm not sure we were ever happy."

I often find myself wondering what our lives would've been like had the accident not happened. Would I have ended up with Benji? Would Sam, Kelly and Tommy have stayed together or would they eventually have realized their arrangement just wasn't possible? Each of them realizing one loves the other more; Kelly loving Sam more than Tommy and Tommy loving Kelly more than anyone. Would Tommy have eventually asked her to choose?

I feel sorry for Samantha because I know Tommy didn't love her like he loved Kelly. It just wasn't in him to replace her and not that that's what I think he was trying to do, but I do think he was trying to numb the pain.

I give Samantha a weak smile, hoping she sees we understand what she's going through, how difficult it must have been for her to live all these years without an explanation of why Tommy behaved the way he did. And even after now knowing what he dealt with, I'm not sure it eases any of her years of trying to help him and the suffering she still feels.

"I wanted to save him," Samantha says, laughing a little but there's no humor to her tone. "You know, like the love of a good woman can save anyone. But even I knew it was a lie." She shakes her head at her comment, but I understand. She wanted to see the good in Tommy and at some point she must have or she wouldn't have stayed. He was an amazing person, kind and generous, his personality was infectious.

Benji and I say very little as she keeps talking. I imagine most of this she has kept hidden from her family and friends, because the more she talks the more that comes out. Like she's wanted to say it for years. There's a comfort factor with us that she hasn't found with anyone else. We understand what she's been dealt and we would never judge her choice to stay with him. Had things between the three of us not ended badly, I know Benji and I would've stood by Tommy, too.

"I finally tried to give him an ultimatum. I tried to tell him it was drugs or me, but there was a part of me that just couldn't leave him. I had moved back in with my parents, but I still couldn't cut him out of my life. I worried about him constantly and spent just as much time with him as I always had. Then I found out I was pregnant."

"What changed?" Benji asks, and I already know. I've had this talk with Samantha and while I know it wasn't something she wanted to share at the time, she still did. But as she tells it now, I can see she's more comfortable talking about it than she was before.

A simple smile crosses her lips as if she remembers the moment and discussing it has brought back all those feelings and emotions. "He stopped everything as soon as I told him. No more drugs. It was unreal how easily it all ended." She stops, and I see the tears form in her eyes. "We were normal for like five minutes." Samantha looks away and mumbles, "I'll never know normal again."

I want to tell her that we all make our own normal and not to live with what people expect you to be and do. One day her life will be normal again, normal to her. It might not be the mom and dad with the two kids living in the perfect house with the perfect marriage. Her and Thomas' life will always be flawed, but what happens in the future is up to them. And as

I sit here and listen to her talk, I know I want to be part of that future. I want to be part of Thomas' normal.

"I thought it was all over," Samantha starts before I can even begin to console her. I want to, I want to tell her how both Benji and I understand what she's going through. The loss can be debilitating. "But then..." she begins, looking at Benji and me. "What you've told me explains his reaction to his parents' death. I just wish he would've told me," she whispers, the tears now falling down her cheeks. "They were killed by a drunk driver."

Samantha buries her face in her hands. It's hard to make out her words, muffled and through the sobs. Benji squeezes my hand tightly, both of struggling to get through another loss. Another loss that hits far too close to home.

"It was about six months ago," Samantha mutters. "It tore him apart." She wipes at her tear-streaked cheeks with her hands as she looks at us. "I think all those memories from the past returned. He was haunted and restless. He became distant and withdrew from everything. I thought he was using again, but he began to obsess over finding Campbell."

Again Samantha looks at me, her eyes sympathetic. She stops speaking as if she's trying to choose her words wisely.

"I hated you and I'm sorry for that," she says, her eyes never leaving mine.

"No apology necessary. I can imagine how all of this looked to you. I have so many regrets, Samantha, and I never expected you to apologize to me. It should be me apologizing to you for all the stress this caused you."

"I realize now that his need to find you had nothing to do with being in love with you, but everything to do with coping with the death of his parents. He needed to find both of you. You two were the only people who understood what he was going through."

"Why didn't he find us?" Benji asks. "He was able to get the letters to us. Why didn't he just reach out to us?"

"I don't know. I found the letters with his body. I guess it became too much." And again Samantha is crying. I want to hug her, tell her it's going to be okay, but I'm sure those words will be pointless. "How do I ever explain this to Thomas?" Samantha asks, almost begging someone for an answer. "How do we ever move on?"

"You will," I tell her and when she looks at me the anger and hatred toward me is gone. "It might not be what you expected, but you will. Do you think I expected to lose my best friends, that I'd drink myself to sleep every night and stop talking to the person I fell in love with when I was five?" I ask, shaking my head, answering my own questions. "As much as it hurts now and will probably always hurt, you need to find something that brings you joy. You have to repair what you can."

Samantha rises from the table and in response, I follow her. She stops in front of me and in that instant, I don't think about it. I hug her and I feel her stiffen slightly, before she wraps her arms around me and sobs into my shoulder.

I can't control myself and I'm sobbing along with her as Benji stands next to me, leaning in, he presses a quick kiss to the top of my head. I never thought when we showed up here unannounced that it would end up like this. Samantha's forgiveness means more than I can ever put into words. And while none of us will ever know the exact reason Tommy took his own life, we can be there for each other.

I pull back from Samantha, both of us still crying, her hands shaking as I take them in mine. "I know you don't know us, but we want to be here for you and Thomas." I look over at Benji and he nods in agreement. I can only hope that she'll allow this, because we need to set things right and this relationship might be our only hope.

"You're all Thomas has left of his father," she says clutching my hands. While she doesn't come right out and say it, I take her response as a yes. I don't even know where we'll begin, but at least it's a starting point.

I didn't come here to find forgiveness; more to take a step forward in healing. The fact that I found it makes moving on so much easier. I'm not sure where we'll go from here with Samantha and Thomas, but I'm grateful to her for sharing their story and for allowing us to be a part of Thomas' life.

We wish Samantha goodbye and leave without saying goodbye to Thomas at her request. She had asked us not to because she wants an opportunity to talk to him about who we are and attempt to explain a few things to him about his father. We have to respect that. We left our contact information and an invitation to visit Benji's house when the weather gets better. And from here, we can only hope that Samantha allows us to be part of their lives. It's all we can do.

Chapter Thirty-Three

Benji left this morning and even though I said I would go with him, I stayed behind to pack and also to catch up on all the work I've missed. I'm sitting at my desk in my office thinking about how this will probably be the last time I'll be here. I have plans to finish packing up everything I need and head out in the next day or two for Benji's. The two of us spent the better part of last night packing so that everything is ready, only leaving a few of the things I need. I have movers coming over the weekend and I'll be leaving some things behind for the renters I hope to have soon.

Jack has taken care of placing an ad for me and has told me he'll handle any issues that should arise with renting my house. While I'm sad to leave, I know it's time to start my life with Benji. Up until now I've just been going through the motions, not really living. I'm excited to see where all of this will lead.

"Hey," Jack says as he comes into my office. "Didn't think I'd see you today."

"Yeah, I know. I figured I should get ahead of things before I move. Not sure when I'll have my office," I use my fingers to quote the word *office,* "up and running." Now that I'll be working from home, I need to get everything squared away before I can even think about starting work. Even though most of my job is done through email, phone calls and internet research, I'd like to have an office set up in Benji's house so that I don't have everything scattered all about. There's usually a lot of paperwork that goes along with my job.

"I'd really like it if you'd just take some time off," Jack says firmly, like he's my father or something. Demanding, but still concerned and it makes me laugh. He's standing with his hands on his hips, trying to look intimidating, yet failing. He doesn't scare me.

"Whatever you say, boss," I tell him, rolling my eyes as I flick my hand in the direction of the door, shooing him away.

"Just take it easy," he says back. "You've been through a lot and just because things seem to be settling down doesn't mean this move and these changes are going to be easy."

I love that Jack is voicing his concern for me. This is something that in the past both of us would've ignored and right now it makes this move a little more difficult.

"I know. Things are different now, though. I won't be bottling anything up anymore. I think we both know how that turned out."

Jack nods with a small smile on his face, but I can tell behind his eyes there's sadness. Now that we've finally started to form a relationship, I'm about to leave. But I don't intend to forget Jack or everything he has done for me.

I stand up and walk to where he's standing, reaching up, I wrap my arms around his shoulders as I pull him in for a hug.

"Thanks, Jack."

"Of course, but I don't need you going soft on me now. I still need the hard ass bitch who helps run this company. If that goes away, I'm firing your ass."

I'm laughing now because I know that has been my go-to method for dealing with this job and I often wonder if I'll be as successful without it.

"No worries, Jack. I can turn it off and on like water from a tap."

"I'm not so sure about that," Jack says, rolling his eyes. "You and Benji are all, 'baby this and baby that,' you're quite nauseating."

"Get out, you asshole," I say, winking at Jack as I shove him out the door.

I spend the entire day at the office catching up so I don't have the extra work hanging over my head. My phone chimes just as I'm walking out the door and when I pull it from my purse, I see a text from Benji.

Benji: I'm home and I miss you terribly already. When are you coming home?

I laugh at his text. Jack is right we are nauseating, but I love it.

Me: I miss you too and I'm glad you're home safe. I'll be at our house tomorrow night. I promise.

I've debated about when I should leave since I will have to come back in three days to deal with the movers, but I don't want to be away from Benji any longer than I need to. As I'm trying to figure out whether I should contact Jack about being here to help the movers instead, another text comes through.

Benji: I love that you called it our house and I love you.

Without giving it a second thought, I call Jack and ask him if he can take care of getting the movers sorted at the house over the weekend. In the past I never would've considered relying on someone else for help, let alone my own brother, but a lot has changed and the fact that he agrees to help me without questioning it, makes me smile.

I finish the night out by tagging everything that will be moved to make it easier on Jack and the movers. Anything that will remain is left on a list on the counter in the kitchen.

And when I finally make it to bed, I'm exhausted but feeling like the weight of everything I've carried over the last nine years is gone. It's like I'm a different person.

I wake early the next morning, my car packed and with Jack seeing me off. I wave goodbye, and as bittersweet as it is to leave my house, my job, and my brother, it's been a long time coming. I have very few reservations about leaving everything I've ever come to know, to start over again. But in a way it isn't starting over, it's picking up where I left off. This is the way my life was always supposed to be. It just took me nine years and far too much bullshit to get here.

My car is sliding all over the road the farther I drive north and the slicker the roads get. I don't dare tell Benji. One, because he'll worry and two, he'll definitely make me get a new car immediately. I laugh as I think about how insistent he'll be about it all, but I also know he worries. After what we've been through, the last thing either of us needs is a car accident to scare the shit out of the other one.

When I finally pull in the driveway nine hours later, due to my extra cautious driving, Benji's truck isn't here. I knew I should've stopped at the shop instead of going straight to the house, but I'm tired of driving and I'm ready to get things settled.

I send Benji a text to let him know I've arrived and that I'll start making dinner. I hear back from him quickly telling me he's finishing up and should be home within an hour.

Making it easy on myself since I know I have a lot of unpacking to do, I pull out a pot, some noodles, and grab a jar of spaghetti sauce from the pantry. Leaving everything on the counter, I head to the bedroom to begin unpacking and find myself immediately distracted, forgetting all about starting dinner. The boxes are stacked all over the room and some of them have already been unpacked. Benji has made room in the closet and cleared out the dresser for me. He had started putting away some of the stuff I sent him with when he left, but there's still plenty to do.

The hour passes quickly and before I know it Benji is walking in the door and happily calls out, "Baby, I'm home!"

A ridiculous smile is plastered on my face as I yell back, "I'm in the bedroom!"

I hear Benji take the stairs two at a time, practically running up them and I'm laughing when he walks into the bedroom.

I'm sitting on the floor looking up at him, his hair disheveled, his flannel shirt unbuttoned revealing the white t-shirt underneath, a huge smile across his face. He smells of freshly cut wood and I close my eyes as he leans down to kiss me.

"Welcome home," he murmurs close to my mouth, his lips softly brushing against mine.

I fall back, laying down on the rug as Benji crawls up my body, the weight of him pressing into me. His face is in the curve of my neck as his lips press tiny kisses against my skin. I wrap my arms around him pulling him closer and enjoying how relaxed and comforted he makes me feel.

"My shoulders are killing me," I say, as the pain of being slumped over boxes for the last hour hits me. "Will you rub them for me?" I ask.

With his mouth next to my ear, his warm breath against my skin, tickling me and making me smile, he says, "Funny, because my dick is killing me. Will you rub it?"

I burst out laughing, pushing him off me as I sit up. With Benji sitting in front of me, a sly grin on his face, I can't help but find him completely adorable. "Cheeky boy," I say, as I kiss the tip of his nose. "How about we have dinner and then you can seduce me with your terrible attempts to lure me into having sex with you."

"Terrible?" he questions, his hand over his heart as he fakes like I've insulted him.

"Yes, baby, terrible. You can do better than that. Actually, you don't need to. I'm pretty easy. It wouldn't take much to get me in your bed."

"Oh, believe me, I know. This coming from the girl who lost her virginity to me in a tent when we were fifteen."

Benji puts out his hand and I take it as he helps me up off the floor. His beautiful blue eyes are locked on mine as if he's recalling the memory of that night. He was perfect then and he's still perfect now.

"Do you ever wonder why our parents still allowed us to sleep in a tent together when they obviously knew we were fooling around?"

"Nope. Never. I didn't care. I was just happy to get you alone and naked." He shrugs his shoulders as if that's seriously the only thing that crossed his mind.

"You're hopeless."

And suddenly I find myself locked in his arms as he walks me backward toward the bed. Benji's hands already under my sweatshirt as he runs them along my spine, his fingers leaving my skin burning everywhere they've touched.

"I might be hopeless, but you love me and you love what I do to your body; the way I make you feel." His voice is deep and throaty and sexy as hell, and if we were planning to eat dinner, it's definitely been postponed.

"Aren't you hungry?" I ask, and Benji chuckles, his mouth next to my ear as he begins nipping and sucking on my earlobe.

"Oh, I'll have something to eat," he responds, as he lays me down on the bed and his hands immediately move to the waist of the yoga pants I'm wearing. Within seconds he has my pants and my underwear off. Tossing them to the side, he whispers, "You need to wear these pants every single day. Easy access."

I laugh, my head falling back against the bed as Benji pushes my shirt up exposing my bare stomach. His mouth begins to kiss a path of warm kisses, his teeth grazing as he goes and he stops at my hipbone, biting lightly.

"Benji..." I moan and he settles himself between my legs. My body is aching with anticipation with what he's about to do. I'm desperate for him.

But he's teasing me, taking his time. I feel him grip my thighs as his mouth continues kissing and biting as he goes. I'm squirming in his grasp, waiting for that moment when his mouth is finally on me.

"Please," I beg out loud in frustration, and when his mouth finally touches me, I bury my hands in his hair and call his name again. The word echoing in the silence of the large bedroom.

He's slow and deliberate, taking his time, making me beg him, and teasing me with his tongue. My hands are pulling at his hair, forcing him closer to my body as my legs begin to shake. I'm close and he knows it and desperately I want more, but he pulls his mouth away from me. His hands leave my body as he slips out of his jeans and begins to kiss his way back up to my mouth.

Before I know it, he's inside me and we softly moan in unison at the feeling.

"I love the way you feel inside me," I murmur, my eyes closed. The weight of Benji's body is pressing against me and there's nothing like it. I want to be surrounded by him; I want him to cover me. I wrap my arms around him, pulling him closer, and he begins to move slowly.

I feel like I'm on fire and his skin is warm to my touch. I can feel the light sheen of sweat on his back as I dig my nails in, urging him to move faster.

"Faster, harder," I plead and Benji grins against my mouth as I wrap my legs around his hips.

"Baby, you feel so fucking good. Let me enjoy it," he murmurs back, his hips pushing against mine.

The tension builds in both of us despite his slow movements and Benji pushes up on his hands. When I open my eyes, I see where our bodies are connected, I see him watching and that's when I come undone. Calling out his name, I feel him push into me one more time and that's when he falls apart too. Groaning out his release as his body collapses on top of mine.

Hot and sweaty, both of us exhausted, but sated. We lie together, neither of us moving as I run my hands up and down Benji's back, feeling the lines of his muscles and the softness of his skin. The perfection of this moment, of this day, and of the last few weeks hits me and reminds me how lucky I am.

I can't believe this is my life. That after everything we've been through, we still have each other, we will still have a life together.

"Are you hungry now?" I ask, as Benji rolls off of me and lets out a low groan. He's lying on his side, his hand resting on my stomach.

"I am," he says smiling as he traces a circle around my bellybutton. "But I have something to talk to you about."

His smile has dropped from his face and his brow is furrowed. I can feel my heart rate increase instantly and now I'm worried about what he has to say. I thought most of our problems were past us, but clearly something has been left out. I look away from him; scared my face will give away everything I'm feeling.

"Okay," I answer, as he places his hand on my cheek, his finger brushing lightly.

"Look at me," Benji says, drawing me back to him. "I need to tell Alex and Annie what happened."

I can feel my body stiffen almost immediately at his words and I adamantly shake my head.

"No," I respond without giving it any thought. "We agreed that it was on a need to know basis. Our families and Samantha being the only people fully involved in this. No, Benji. No."

"Campbell, you have to understand, they've been with me basically since the accident. My behavior, your behavior, none of it makes sense to them if we don't tell them what happened."

I roll away from him and climb out of the bed. Gathering my clothes from the floor, I enter the bathroom and close the door. I can hear the sheets rustling and Benji sighs loudly before he knocks on the door.

"Campbell, please hear me out. I don't want this to be an argument especially on our first night together." I hear his head fall against the bathroom door. I know I'm being childish, but he doesn't understand.

"These are your friends, not mine," I say through the closed door.

There is judgment and ridicule that comes with telling people. They're not always as forgiving and as understanding as the people in our life have been so far. What if this ruins Benji's friendship with them? What if they hate me for running away from him all those years ago? Worse, what if it gets out and people find out what Benji has done? It could ruin his reputation in this town, his business could suffer, and the repercussions could be more than either of us are willing to deal with. It isn't just about clearing the air and helping Alex and Annie understand, it's about our lives, which are finally returning to normal. I'd hate to think what could happen.

"It scares me," I add quietly as I reach for the doorknob, finally admitting what this is really about. It isn't about keeping the secret from them, it's about what could happen if we tell them, and not just with Alex and Annie, but with everyone we've told.

"They're your friends now too. Please open the door," Benji asks again, and I open it to his sad, pleading eyes. Without stopping to think about it at all, he takes me in his arms, hugging me fiercely as he buries his face in my hair. "I don't want to argue with you, but we need to tell them. Please understand that. I know you're worried, but they're our friends, they'll understand. We owe them an explanation."

I nod my head. I do understand, but the worry consumes me. "Not now. Can you give it some time, please?" I ask. It all seems so sudden and overwhelming. I was finally starting to calm down and I really don't want to start over again.

"Whatever you need," Benji says, and now I feel selfish for even asking.

Maybe he's right.

Chapter Thirty-Four

Benji is gone when I wake up. That boy wakes up far earlier than I'm used to. I was still burrowed in the duvet when he kissed me goodbye and told me he was heading to the shop to get an early start.

It's not late by any means and I'm hoping when he gets used to me living here, he'll start sleeping in or at least sticking around for a morning quickie.

I head downstairs just as the sun is beginning to rise, casting its glow through the floor to ceiling windows and illuminating the beautiful craftsmanship of the house. I grab a cup of coffee and take it up to what will now be my office.

It's a beautiful room overlooking the small pond on the property. I have a feeling the scenery will prove to be a huge distraction. In Chicago my office looked out onto the building next door, a steel and glass building with little appeal. Actually I was quite lucky I even had a window, so this is a huge change.

Before I arrived, Benji had outfitted the room with the most amazing furniture and not just because it was designed and built by him, but because it somehow fits me perfectly. I couldn't have picked better furniture and I sometimes wonder if he'd made it specifically for me.

The desk is an a-frame made from reclaimed wood that's worn and distressed giving it a beautiful aged look. Next to it stands a matching bookshelf and armoire, both are mostly empty, but Benji did attempt to unpack some things in my absence.

I laugh as I think about it. I got a text from him with pictures of books and files asking where I wanted him to put them and after the third text, I told him to just leave it. I know he was just trying to be helpful, but I could tell he was annoyed with my responses, which were too specific.

I flop down into the desk chair, spinning it around as I take it all in. The beautiful view, the custom made furniture, all in this perfect house, in the perfect room with everything I ever dreamed about all sitting right in front of me.

I thought my dreams were lost right along with Sam, Kelly and Tommy. Ripped out from under me and shattered. I never thought I'd be happy again, that I'd find Benji and we'd be living the life we talked about all those years we spent together.

But here I am, smiling and laughing, waking up to a life that has become mine. Up until this moment, my life hasn't felt complete; it hasn't felt whole. I will always miss the people I've lost, my heart will always ache just a little, but when I found Benji again, it all began to heal.

I've been at it for several hours when I hear Benji come in through the front door. He's not done working. He'd have parked in the garage and come in through the door that connects to the house if he were. It's still too early in the day and I wonder if he'll keep the same hours he did before I moved in with him.

"I'm upstairs!" I yell. "In my beautiful office." I giggle, still in shock that this is all mine. Even the beautiful boy downstairs.

"You hungry?" Benji asks. "I brought food."

"I'm always hungry."

Benji is sitting at the bar top on the island with a few slices of pizza on a plate in front of him.

"Pizza?" I question. I know I've only been here for a day, but when I spent those few days here with him before there wasn't a pizza place in sight.

"The gas station recently started selling pizza," Benji answers, shrugging his shoulders as if he didn't just buy our lunch from a gas station.

"You bought pizza...from a gas station?"

"I did. Beggars can't be choosers. Just eat it. Even bad pizza is good. It's pizza."

"Baby," I say, laying on the sympathy. "How did you survive this long without me?"

"I ate a lot of frozen pizza."

"What am I going to do with you?"

"Love me?" he suggests, and I laugh. I've loved him for as long as I can remember.

As we eat, we chat mindlessly about what I've gotten done so far and what Benji's been working on. He's been playing catch-up since spending so much time with me in Chicago. A lot of orders came in while he was gone and he has a few custom orders to work on. Despite the fact that I'll still be working, I know it means a lot to Benji to be able to take care of me, so I'm glad his business has been extremely successful.

"I have to ship today," he says, actually sounding annoyed by the fact that he has to drive into Canada. "I have this huge dining table that was supposed to go out a few days ago. I had the UPS pick up scheduled and had to cancel it." He looks over at me and gives me a shy smile. "I had to cancel it to apologize to my girl."

"Sorry," I answer back, still feeling bad about keeping Tommy's death a secret from him. We both owed each other apologies and even though it's past us, I still struggle with the way it all went down.

"No more," Benji says, shaking his head as he leans over and kisses me. "We're over this, remember?" I nod, attempting to convince myself as I slide over and rest my head against Benji's shoulder. He kisses my hair softly before he adds, "It'll take time, baby, but please know I'm not angry with you about what happened between us after the accident. I never was."

"I know, thank you. I hope you know I feel the same way."

"Of course I know," he responds, his fingers under my chin as he lifts my head and kisses me again. Smiling now, he asks, "You wanna come with me?"

"Up to Canada?" I ask, and Benji nods as he takes another bite of his pizza. "You know I'd love to, but I really should stay here and get things situated."

"You're breaking my heart," Benji complains jokingly, and I giggle.

"Silly boy, I have a job, remember? Without an office, I can't work."

By now Benji has finished eating and is cleaning up; each time he walks by me, he brushes against me or stops to kiss my neck. He's making it incredibly difficult to say no to him. He's always been my biggest weakness, my most wonderful flaw, the best thing in my life and nothing has changed. I want to go with him, honestly. I want to be near him always, but that's unrealistic.

"You never have to work," Benji replies, a seriousness to his tone.

"I know that, but I want to work."

Maybe there will come a time when I'm okay with relying on Benji for financial support; after we get married or have kids, but until then, I'd like to contribute.

Benji smiles at me and I know he understands my need to work. He's never been one to demand things of me and I find it calming that nothing has changed.

I finish eating as Benji sticks the leftover pizza in the refrigerator and readies himself to go back to work.

I watch him pull on his boots, every muscle in his body flexing with his movements. He's beautiful and perfect and there's nothing about him that I don't love. Just watching him makes me question my decision to stay home and unpack.

"Don't think I don't see you checking me out," he says, winking at me from across the room.

I roll my eyes at him as I walk over and swat him on the ass. "Get back to work. You're far too distracting," I chide dramatically, and suddenly I find myself pinned against the front door, Benji's hips pressing against mine, my arms above my head, and his hand locked around my wrist.

When his free hand slides up my shirt and cups my breast, my head falls back and my eyes close. I can feel him trail his warm mouth along my jaw and across my neck, his hot breath igniting my skin until I want to beg him to kiss me, touch me, take me, and then he whispers, "I'll show you how distracting I can be."

My body is flush against his and the heat between us feels like hot sparks touching every part of me and just when I think I can't bear to be this close to him without my hands on his body, he lets go of my wrists.

I immediately slide my hands under his shirt, letting them trail down his firm chest until they reach the waistband of his jeans. I slip my fingers under, but never going any farther as he takes my face in his hands and kisses me fiercely. It makes me weak, my knees practically shaking with an overwhelming need for him.

I moan into Benji's mouth and I feel him smile as he pulls away. His forehead now resting against mine, a cheeky grin on his face as he says, "I have to get back to work, but we'll be finishing this later."

"God, I fucking hope so," I mutter back, still disoriented from his blatant attempt to distract me but not follow through.

Benji kisses me again, but this time it's soft and sweet. My body responds and I sink into his arms, once again finding it difficult not to go with him.

"I'll see you in a few hours," Benji says, stepping away from me as he puts on his coat and a flash of guilt forces itself in. I want to go with him, but I can't. We can't spend every second of our lives together. But before I know it, the guilt is replaced with worry and panic about him driving up to Canada alone.

It's snowy and the roads are not always clear. They can be slick and at times unsafe for driving. Yet for some reason I can't make myself voice my concerns. Like if I don't say it out loud, if I don't talk about it, nothing bad can possibly happen.

I turn away from Benji, I can't let him see the worry that has taken over. He'll recognize it straightaway and the last thing I want is him stressing over all my insecurities. Nothing is going to happen to us.

I thought the same thing nine years ago.

My stomach churns and my chest tightens. I take a deep breath. It's nothing.

"I'll see you later," I tell Benji, a fake smile on my face as I turn to look at him. "I'll just be here unpacking and bored." The more I talk, the more natural it feels. That's exactly what I'll be doing. This is normal.

We're normal.

"Baby," Benji says, and just when I think he's going to ask me if everything's okay, if I'm okay, he says, "Can you take some time and think about what we talked about last night? About telling Alex and Annie?"

I nod my head in response. It's still something I'm not fully comfortable with, but I don't want it to lead to an argument again and it's not like I completely disagree with his reasoning for telling them, I just have my reservations. "I will," I finally respond, and Benji smiles at me.

"I love you, Campbell."

"I love you too."

As boring as it is to unpack all these boxes, I'm finding it keeps me busy. I know the movers are coming this weekend with the rest of my things, so it'll be nice to have all of this sorted before they arrive.

My office is now set up. All my files stored and labeled, along with my desk ready. I could actually start working now if I wanted, but I'd rather knock out the rest of the unpacking and have the evening to relax with Benji.

I move on to the closet and by the time I'm finished I realize I've been at this for several hours. Night has taken over, the sky dark, and when I look at the clock, it's well after seven. Benji has been gone far longer than I would've thought.

I look for my phone, realizing it must still be in my office, so I go hunting for it. Finding it on my desk, I see I have a missed text from Benji.

Benji: Running a little behind. Should be home in an hour.

I breathe a sigh of relief until I notice the text is time stamped at a quarter after four. It's well beyond an hour late.

I can feel myself begin to panic. My heart is racing, my palms growing sweaty as I grip my phone in my hand. I can't jump to conclusions; I can't let my irrational side take over, so I call Benji before this gets out of hand.

Straight to voicemail.

By the third call, each one with the same response, I'm well past the panic stage and I don't even know what to do.

I feel sick to my stomach, yet I'm angry. I want to cry, but then I want to tell myself I'm being stupid.

It can't happen again.

It won't happen again.

But even my own words are lost.

I'm standing in the kitchen with my car keys in my hand, not certain about what I'm thinking or what I plan on doing, but knowing I can't stand here and wait.

The front door opens and just the sound has me running toward it, I don't even notice it isn't Benji that comes through it.

It's Annie.

"Where's Benji?" I almost scream at her, my words unusually loud in the quiet of the house.

"Campbell," she says, sensing my panic, not that it's hard to miss, but her soothing tone does nothing to calm me. "Benji's truck slid off the road…"

I don't hear anything else as I shove past her, nearly knocking her over. If she were still talking I wouldn't know it, because I'm already outside. My keys in my hand, but my feet only covered in socks as I run across the icy and snowy driveway to my car.

This is my worst nightmare come true. It's happening all over again and all I can think is, *I'm going to lose him too.* After all this time and everything we've been through, this can't be fucking happening.

But it is.

I'm not thinking about anything else other than finding Benji. I have no idea where he could be or if he's okay or what I even plan on doing. My only thought is to find him, so I'll drive until I do.

Chapter Thirty-Five

The road is black, the sky dark, and without streetlights, it's nearly impossible to see. Right now I hate these fucking country roads. I'm in the goddamn middle of nowhere; a black abyss of nothingness, like the whole town is covered in ink.

I'm not even sure what I've set out to do. I left the house in such a frenzy, my thoughts in a jumbled mess of panic and fear, completely propelled by finding Benji. My only thought is to drive the route he would've have taken from the shop to the shipping warehouse just over the border. After that I've got nothing.

What if I come across his truck, destroyed and mangled on the side of the road? I'm certain I'll fall apart. Up until this moment I didn't realize I'm a loose cannon. All it will take is one small event to push me over the edge, especially since I've finally become comfortable with the thought of having a normal life. Will I always live with the fear that something horrible is going to happen? That fate will intervene and ruin things for a second time?

My car fishtails as I take a turn too fast and I curse out loud at my stupid car and my inability to drive it in the snow. I slow down despite the fact that my need to find Benji is coursing through me like fire.

My eyes are scanning the road as I drive, but coming up with nothing but emptiness. The roads are deserted and the town is completely shut down. In this vast wasteland of fields and forests, everything looks the same as I leave town and find myself surrounded by absolutely nothing.

I keep looking at the clock, my mind silently pleading to anyone or anything to stop punishing me. Is this my final punishment for what I did all those years ago? Find happiness again, believe it will last, and then watch it get ripped out from under me?

Twenty minutes have passed and there is still no sign of Benji or his truck. If I was panicked before, it has now hit epic proportions. My entire body is shaking under the weight of the stress and I'm pretty sure I'm going to vomit.

I take a deep breath in through my nose and exhale slowly out through my mouth in an attempt to control myself and possibly stop myself from losing whatever I ate today all over my car.

I'm on my third breath when I see the road dully illuminated about a mile ahead of me, and suddenly I'm thankful for the obscene dark of these country roads. I hit the gas petal, causing my car to once again slide along the road, but I don't care. The faster I reach the lights ahead the sooner I'll know if it's Benji.

The closer I get, the more the lights come into focus and I can make out two distinct sets of headlights. Slowing down as I approach, I recognize Benji's truck and in front of it is Alex's.

Without thinking about it, I slam my car in park, barely making it off to the shoulder, but I couldn't give a shit. I pay attention to nothing as I run across the road. I can hear Benji calling my name and while it should ease my fears, I find myself breaking down at just the sound.

By the time I reach him, I'm sobbing. Deep wailing cries as I throw myself into his arms, my entire body shaking uncontrollably. I can't even speak as I wrap my arms around his neck, holding on so tightly I'm sure he's struggling to breathe.

"Campbell, baby, settle down," Benji whispers in my ear, but I hardly hear it over my sobs. His hand is now rubbing circles on my back, trying to soothe me, but right now, I'm inconsolable.

As if he realizes this isn't going to be solved with a few simple words, he stops talking and just holds me. My feet are burning, cold and soaked as I stand in the snow with no shoes on. But I don't care.

Benji's okay.

We're okay.

A few minutes pass and my hold on him finally loosens. I'm settling down as I come to grips with the fact that on the surface everything is alright. But obviously underneath it all, I'm still a shit ass mess. My rational side realizes I can't have this reaction to every minor incident that occurs in our life; yet moving beyond it is proving far more difficult than I thought.

"I'm okay," Benji says, before I can say anything. My face is in his hands and he kisses my forehead as I nod my head. My hands are gripping his coat as the cold finally catches up with me and my body begins to shake again.

Benji slips off his coat, putting it around my shoulders as he kisses me again. His hands running up and down my arms, warming me as much as he can with the winter wind blowing relentlessly across the openness of the road.

"I know you don't want to hear this," Benji eventually says, breaking the silence. "But this kind of thing happens a lot out here. That's why I called Alex. He'll pull my truck out and I'll be on my way."

I hate the casualness to his statement. Like we haven't watched a car accident destroy us in the past. To me, this incident could have easily turned ugly.

"It doesn't happen to us!" I yell, and out of the corner of my eye I see Alex step out of his truck.

"This is why I wanted to tell Alex and Annie," Benji says, letting out a deep sigh as he steps back from me slightly. "Campbell, you're standing in the middle of the road in your socks in the winter, crying."

"You make me sound unstable," I quip, feeling myself grow angry at his lack of empathy for my feelings. He's lived this nightmare right along with me. If anyone should understand, it's him.

"I know you're not, but imagine how this looks to an outside observer." Benji glances over at Alex as he stands waiting patiently for me to get my shit together. Alex gives us both a sympathetic smile and I feel my face heat up, reminding me that he's seen all of this.

Embarrassed by my behavior and by how totally ridiculous I must look, I quietly apologize to Benji. "I'm sorry. I overreacted," I admit, not sure what more I can say. At this point there's no sense in defending my behavior.

"You didn't really, though," Benji states. "Given what we've been through, this is a natural reaction to hearing I may have been hurt in a car accident. I'm certain I would've responded the same way."

Leading me back across the street to where my car is parked, he opens the door and waits for me to climb in.

"Go home," Benji says firmly, but I can hear a kindness behind it still. "Alex is going to pull my truck out and when I get home, we're going to sit down and explain all of this to them." And even though his words are definite, I can't help but resolve myself to agree with him. He's right. They need to know what happened.

"Okay," I say, smiling up at him as his perfect blue eyes look down at me. "I love you."

"I love you more than you'll ever know, Campbell," he says back, the words echoing his own all those years ago, yet in this moment, they're exactly what I need to hear.

I make it back home in about thirty minutes, but the ride is slow and I keep questioning my reaction to Annie telling me Benji's truck slid off the road. I can't live like this, in a perpetual state of paranoia that something horrible is going to happen to us. It's unrealistic and eventually it will drive me crazy.

I really thought that just getting it all out in the open would allow me to move on, but clearly there's more to all of this than I ever realized. Jack was right. Just because I think it's over doesn't mean it just disappears. I have a lot more to work on.

I'm still freezing when I walk in the door. I know Annie has left; her car is no longer in the driveway, so I strip off my clothes, leaving them as I walk upstairs and into the shower.

The water is so scalding hot against my freezing cold skin that my body goes numb almost instantly. My feet and hands are tingling as they finally catch up and begin to sense the temperature of the water. I adjust the water, but I still don't move out from under the stream. I let the hot water fall over my body, washing away the awfulness of the day as I try to clear my thoughts.

I spend far longer in the shower than I intend to, but there's something about the silence and being alone combined with the hot water that allows me to relax. I'm wrapped in a towel and when I walk out of the bathroom I find Benji sitting on the bed waiting for me.

He looks tired, exhausted actually, but he still gives me a smile and calls me over to where he's sitting using just one finger. His shirt is unbuttoned and untucked, the bottoms of his jeans soaked and he's already taken off his boots and socks, but he still looks amazing. There is something about his face, the dishevelledness of his appearance, his dark brown hair and his full beard matched with his beautiful blue eyes that will always be a comfort to me. There's home in his eyes, a love that has been there since we were kids.

Stepping between his legs, he pulls me closer to him as his hands grip my hips. I can feel the chill of them through the towel and it makes me shudder. Benji leans forward and presses his lips to the bare skin of my arm, his mouth resting there for a long second.

"You okay?" he finally asks.

"I'm sorry," I whisper, looking down at him.

Sometimes we give the appearance of normality, which is easy to do. I've been doing it for nine years, or at least trying. But each attempt brings failure. Along with it comes my inability to fully understand my reactions, my feelings and my response to events or words. Even something as simple as a song on the radio, a time on a clock, can remind me of everything. This will always be a part of my life, a part of our lives, and we both need to learn to cope with it in ways that won't outwardly affect everyone around us, including each other.

Benji has always been the more reserved of the two of us, even before the accident, while I tended to internalize everything and allow the stress to consume me. But as much as he likes to give off this casual aura, he's shaken by this moment too.

"I don't want you to be sorry," he says, taking me onto his lap. "I want you to be okay. I want us to be okay and I know it's going to take time, but tonight is exactly why we need to get everything out. We can't live here with Alex and Annie not knowing."

He takes a deep breath and runs his fingers through my wet hair, my body cradled against his.

"When I saw you..." Benji starts, but stops, his hold on me tightening. "It was too..." He stalls out again and sighs hard. "Fuck, Campbell," he mutters. "Your face looked exactly like it did on the night of the accident and it scared the shit out of me."

"I was terrified," I admit. "It's the first time since we've been back together that we've had to deal with something similar and I didn't handle it well."

"Honestly, neither did I," Benji also admits. "I should've called you first."

"Why didn't you?" I ask, curious about it. It was something I wondered the entire time I was driving to find him, when I did find him and even now. I guess I assumed he knew how I'd react so he kept it from me.

"My first instinct, because it happens somewhat frequently in the winter here, was to call Alex. My truck slides off the road and if it's not damaged and I'm not hurt, I call Alex."

My eyes widen slightly at his words and Benji leans back so he can look at my face.

"Baby, I know what you're thinking, and no, I've never been hurt in an accident out here. Not since…" he starts to say but doesn't complete his thought. He wets his lips and waits another second before adding, "Not since the accident with you."

"Were you scared to call me?" I ask. "Why did you send Annie over?"

"I called Alex as soon as it happened. It's just what I naturally would've done." He shrugs his shoulders and I understand that his initial reaction wouldn't have been to call me, but I still don't understand why he didn't after the fact. "It wasn't like I didn't think about you. I just knew you wouldn't be able to help me and by the time I got off the phone with Alex my battery was nearly dead. I tried to call you, but my phone died."

His story is plausible. Living out in the middle of nowhere, the phone will constantly search for service, draining the battery, and I can fully understand why Alex would have been his first point of contact. He's spent nine years without me, without anyone really, and for him to suddenly decide to call me would've been out of the ordinary for him.

"I understand and I guess this is something we both need to work on, huh? Me not reacting like a crazy person every time something goes slightly wrong and you not keeping me in the dark."

"Yeah," Benji says, smiling at me now. "Guess we'll always be hesitant to upset or worry the other, but you're right, we still have a lot to work on."

He pulls me in and I lean down to meet him, his mouth connecting with mine in a kiss that's soft and slow. It says everything we haven't said, how much we need each other, how much we both want this, and how our lives will never be the same again. We're heading toward happiness.

"Alex and Annie will be here in an hour. I'm going to take a shower."

I stand up and Benji begins to remove his clothes and I once again notice his tattoo.

"It's true, you know," I say, gesturing at the contrasting black ink against his skin.

"It always has been."

An hour later Benji is showered and we're standing in the kitchen. Benji's opening a beer while I'm straightening up when a small knock comes at the door and it opens just a second later.

"Hi," I say, greeting both of them with a smile and a quick wave. I head over to where they're standing as they take off their wet boots and hang their coats on the rack by the door.

With Benji following behind me, he hands Alex a beer and we all move over to sit down on the couch.

"So, I'm guessing there's more to this story than 'we just broke up'," Annie says, breaking the tension that has filled the room. She looks over at Benji and gives him a quick smile. Up until this point, not much has been said about Benji's relationship with me. Why it ended or what led up to it ending. I think both of us tried to forget it ever happened and by not talking about it or at least not the details of it, we felt we could brush it off.

"Full disclosure," Benji says, giving me a look that says forgive me. "I filled Alex in after you left and I'm sure, because he can't keep anything from Annie, he told her too."

Alex laughs out loud and it makes me smile. Benji knows Alex well enough to know he'd have told Annie and in a way I'm grateful. It takes some of the pressure off of both of us. He was able to tell Alex in an environment that was natural to them, when they were alone and things were settled.

Annie shakes her head, rolling her eyes a little. "They're hopeless," she says, looking over at me as if I should know exactly what she means and I do. When you're in love with someone, you keep nothing from them. Benji and I watched it ruin our relationship, but it's funny that the truth is what ultimately brought us back together.

We spend the next hour filling Alex and Annie in on what happened. But this time there are no tears. I don't know if it's because we've told this same story so many times, or if we've finally come to terms with what we've done or possibly the fact that Alex and Annie have no direct connection to the accident. Maybe it's a combination of all these things, either way; this time is easier.

Annie asks a few questions, but nothing prying or uncomfortable and when all is done, we sit around sharing stories and laughing. It's still funny to me every time they call him Ben, but I figure eventually I'll get used to it. But I do know there will never come a time that I call him that. He'll always be Benji to me.

I hated that I doubted Benji's judgment about telling them, but that fear will always remain. One day there will come a time when someone doesn't respond this favorably, not that I imagine there will be many more instances where we'll need to discuss any of this. For our sake I hope this is the end.

When we climb into bed, I slide over until I'm pressed against Benji's bare chest. I can smell him and feel him, warm and comforting.

"You ready for this?" he asks, as he kisses the top of my head and I can feel the smile on his face.

"I've been ready my whole life."

Epilogue

We've had a hard year, but we've also had some of the best times we've ever had in our lives. It's funny because while Benji and I still struggle with the weight of it all, it hits each of us at different times. We have different triggers, different times of the year when it's harder, and moments when one of us falls apart, but the other doesn't. Maybe that's a good thing, because one of us is always there to pick up the pieces.

We found ourselves in therapy shortly after telling Alex and Annie, because we realized that although we've shared everything with our family and friends, there were internal battles that kept us from moving forward. It's helped tremendously.

But I also think we've been able to see the light at the end of the tunnel now, and with each day that passes, we find ourselves falling into patterns of normalcy; almost a correction of all the things that have gone wrong. Sometimes I think it was fate that created the accident and now fate is righting what was made wrong. Or at least correcting it.

While Samantha and I will never have the kind of relationship that would ever be considered close, she doesn't keep Thomas from Benji or me. She doesn't have to allow us to be a part of his life, but she does, and I've never been more grateful to someone in my life. Having Thomas be involved in the things we do and being involved in his life has allowed me to forgive myself for giving up on Tommy. Maybe that's what Tommy always wanted; Benji and me to be a stable figure in Thomas' life.

We spent his fifth birthday with him, a party thrown by Samantha that she invited us to. Later on, Samantha and Thomas came to visit. It isn't that she doesn't like me; I still get the sense that she blames me for Tommy's death and maybe I am partially to blame. I could've done more, I know that, but that's the reason I'm making a conscious effort to be in Thomas' life.

We have Thomas, and I hope it's something that lasts. He's fate's replacement for losing Tommy.

My relationship with Jack changed far more than I could've ever imagined and since moving in with Benji, we talk on a regular basis and not just about work. It's funny to think that I had to move nine hours away for us to form a friendship when we spent so much time together before. I actually enjoy him now. Shortly after I left he met a girl who he has fallen madly in love with. I just adore her. She's sassy and sarcastic and she keeps Jack in line. She's perfect for him. I often wonder if my happiness has something to do with his. Either way, I'm glad we've both found what we needed.

It was only a few weeks after I moved in with Benji that I found out I was pregnant. It didn't really come as a surprise, but what did was the fact that I was pregnant with twins. Finding out around the twenty-week mark when I had my first ultrasound, both of us sat there staring at the screen, utterly silent.

I was the first to cry, and it was after the ultrasound tech told us we were having a boy and a girl. It wasn't the fact that the babies were twins; it was that they were a boy and a girl.

While fraternal twins are the most common, especially a boy and girl, to me, it felt like fate once again set things right. Like it was replacing what we lost all those years ago. What was once five was now whole again with Thomas and now our babies.

The day they were born was bittersweet. With Benji by my side, we both held them and cried, naming them Kaya and Andre, meaning forgiveness and strength. But never forgetting how we got here, their middle names hold far more significance and sentimental attachment.

Kelly and Samuel.

This is our life now and it may never be perfect, but it's our life.

And sometimes out of a tragedy comes something beautiful.

Acknowledgments

First and foremost, I need to thank my readers. My sincerest thank you goes out to everyone who purchases my books and reads them. Whether you love them or not, all your reviews, comments and messages are deeply appreciated. They make this all worthwhile.

To my amazingly talented cover designer Sarah Hansen of Okay Creations. (www.okaycreations.com) Your time, effort, and work will never go unnoticed by me, as will your insane amount of talent. This cover is absolutely perfect and I can't tell you enough how much I love it. Thank you!

And then there are my betas, the girls who have been with me from the beginning. I adore each of you and not just for being willing to read my books without question, but also because of your friendship. Kelly, thank you for being my grammar queen. Your knowledge of commas, semi-colons and other random punctuation will always be unmatched by anyone. Not to mention your hilarious comments regarding my characters and your response to being killed off. Julie, this time around you have a job, you're going to school and maintaining a social life, all while still living with your parents, but you always have time to read my books. Thank you for staying up till three in the morning to read my book and then texting me while driving to tell me how much you enjoyed it. There might be ten plus years between us, but that never mattered. Love you, cuz! Kristen, thank you for always standing by me and asking me how my writing was going even if it was in secret. Your note taking is ridiculous and so are your nonsensical ramblings and overthinking, but regardless, they made my book better. Natalie, there are many times I wish there wasn't (or is it weren't??) an ocean between us, it kinda sucks, but it never stopped you from helping me. Thank you for reading this one chapter by chapter. Your comments and messages are insanely useful and hilariously funny all at the same time. I will always owe you for all your help.

And he's always last, but certainly not least, my wonderful husband, BJ. Thank you for everything. The list is endless and I'll never be able to fit it all, but you know what I'm talking about. You've made your way into every book I've written in one way or another and I hope you don't cringe when you come across those parts. Thanks for being cheeky so I always have writing material. I love you more than Zingers.

Made in the USA
San Bernardino, CA
06 March 2015